Elizabeth Gill was born in Newcastle upon Tyne and as a child lived in Tow Law, a small mining town on the Durham fells. She has been a published author for more than thirty years and has written more than forty books. She lives in Durham City, likes the awful weather in the north east and writes best when rain is lashing the windows.

Praise for Elizabeth Gill

'Elizabeth Gill writes with a masterful grasp of conflicts and passions hidden among men and women of the wild North Country'
Leah Fleming

'Original and evocative – a born storyteller'
Trisha Ashley

'Wonderful . . . full of passion, pain, sweetness, twists and turns'
Sheila Newberry

'Enthralling and satisfying'
Catherine King

'An enchanting read for all true romantics'
Lancashire Evening Post

'Drama and intrigue worthy of *Call the Midwife*'
Big Issue

Available in paperback and ebook

The Foundling School for Girls
Orphan Boy
The Coal Miner's Wife
The Quarryman's Wife
Miss Appleby's Academy
The Fall and Rise of Lucy Charlton
Far From My Father's House
Doctor of the High Fells
Nobody's Child
Snow Angels
The Guardian Angel

Available in ebook only

Shelter from the Storm
The Pit Girl
The Foundryman's Daughter
A Wartime Wish
A Daughter's Wish
Snow Hall
The Landlord's Daughter

. . . and many more!

Elizabeth Gill

A Widow's Hope

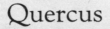

Quercus

First published as *The Road to Berry Edge* in Great Britain in 1997
by Hodder and Stoughton
This paperback edition published in Great Britain in 2020 by

Quercus Editions Ltd
Carmelite House
50 Victoria Embankment
London EC4Y 0DZ

An Hachette UK company

A CIP catalogue record for this book is available
from the British Library

PB ISBN 978 1 52940 071 7
EBOOK ISBN 978 1 78206 176 2

10 9 8 7 6 5 4 3 2 1

Typeset by CC Book Production
Printed and bound in Great Britain by Clays Ltd, Elcograf S.p.A.

Papers used by Quercus are from well-managed forests and other responsible sources.

For Judith, who loves books

One

That October Sunday was the first time in ten years that Faith had put off going to John's grave. It was mid-afternoon before she got round to it, and even then she hesitated. She could have excused herself with the knowledge that Sunday was such a busy day for her with chapel in the morning and Sunday school, and again in the evening, a big meal with her parents in the middle of the day and then sometimes visiting, but her reluctance had nothing to do with any of this. John's brother, Robert Berkeley, was coming home and the news had shocked her because it brought back many memories she would much rather have forgotten, memories that had for such a long time not mattered to her even in the churchyard, but she had known that coming here would make the memories more vivid and it did.

It had been one of those perfect autumn days, completely still, the birch trees half-clothed with lemon and lime coloured leaves, and where the wind and rain had done their work the sycamores had shed their bright orange covering. In the churchyard brown dead leaves were caught in tufts of grass behind the gravestones.

The sky was almost cloudless blue with tiny high wisps of white like thin trailing scarves. It would be bitterly cold later, she thought; already the air was turning sharp. On these days least of all could she bear to leave John's grave. Each turning away was like a fresh betrayal. Each Sunday that passed was another Sunday without him, and yet it had been so long now. She stared in wonder at the dates on the stone – *1870–1893*. It was nineteen hundred and three now, a new century, ten years since he had died, ten Christmases without him. How could it be that long?

There was no one else in the churchyard but the grass was thick and damp and she heard the swish of skirts behind her. When she turned slightly from placing precious peach coloured roses, the last from her mother's garden, on the grave, Nancy McFadden stood behind her, smiling.

She had little to smile about, Faith thought, a baby in her arms and a small boy at her side. It was common knowledge in the town that Sean McFadden knocked his wife about and kept her short of money. Nancy was pretty. She was younger than Faith, in her early twenties; Faith was almost thirty. Nancy had bright yellow hair and deep blue eyes. Faith met Nancy often in the churchyard because Nancy came to see to her father's grave and Faith came to John's.

Faith always felt plain when she saw Nancy. They were

both too thin, she thought, but her own hair was an ordinary brown and her eyes were a nondescript colour between brown and green. Nancy was ill fed and ill kept, but Faith couldn't help envying her because of her looks and beautiful children. They were both exactly like Nancy. The little boy had golden curls and the baby had skin like the roses Faith had held in her hands. She also felt lucky when she met Nancy because Nancy had no money and no comfort, whereas she had a home with her parents halfway up the hill opposite the park, plenty to eat and her work in the town and at the chapel. Her father had made some money in railways and was a gentleman now.

Faith kept sweets in her pocket. William knew that she did and had his gaze fixed in her direction but he hung on to his mother's skirt. Faith adored children and went to him, getting down to his level, talking softly, magicking the different coloured sweets from her pocket until she had him giggling.

'I hear Mr Berkeley's due home,' Nancy said.

Faith got to her feet.

'Apparently,' she said.

'Do you think it'll make any difference, Miss Norman?'

'I don't know.'

'How's his dad?'

'Not good.'

'He's been bad a long time. I don't remember Mr Berkeley very well. Things are in a bad way,' Nancy said.

Faith didn't need Nancy to tell her this. Josiah Berkeley,

John and Robert's father, owned the steelworks which provided most of the work in the town. He also owned the pits. The Berkeleys had owned all this since the pits and the old ironworks had started back in eighteen fifty. Josiah had been ill for almost a year now. He had collapsed in his office and had to be taken home. Even before then, Faith thought bitterly, since John had died, Josiah had not been the same man, people said.

Gradually in Berry Edge things had become more difficult after John had died and Robert had left. The demand for steel was not so great, or so she heard, and when the orders went down the men were put on short time. So were the pitmen, and it affected the other small industries in the town, the shopkeepers, the milliners, the bootmenders, the tailors, the builders, everybody.

Faith didn't know what to say, whether to be reassuring. Nancy was ready to believe, possibly the only person in Berry Edge, that a man she did not remember, a man who had been uneducated, a man who had caused his brother's death, shamed his family, left Berry Edge in disgrace and not returned, could save them because of his name.

Faith could never think of Robert Berkeley without anger. She had hated him for ten years.

'I'm not very hopeful, Nancy,' she said.

'People say he was a good workman.'

Faith smiled. 'It was the only positive thing anybody ever did say about him. John is dead because his brother was jealous and stupid, and his parents haven't been the same since. The works has gone down and dragged us all with it and now . . . If he doesn't come home soon there'll be nothing left.'

'You would have thought he would have come back before now,' Nancy said. 'Surely he knows how bad things are.'

'I doubt his parents could stand the sight of him. They wouldn't have sent for him now if things weren't so difficult. He's living in Nottingham.'

'What do people do there?'

'He's probably got a job in some foundry, married with two or three children, quite happy, caring nothing for anybody else. Rob was like that, feckless, selfish.'

'Somebody'll have to do something,' Nancy said.

'I doubt it'll be Rob. The only things he was ever capable of were drinking and . . . you know the kind of things, Nancy.'

Nancy sighed.

'Yes, I know. The kind of things my Sean's good at,' she said.

They began to walk back across the churchyard. William kicked at a pile of leaves close beside the wall and Faith thought of how she had loved this time of year when she was a child, how excited she had always been with the anticipation of Hallowe'en, Bonfire Night and Christmas.

At the gates they parted, Nancy to go down to the bottom of the bank, Faith to carry on climbing up past various houses, terraced at first on either side and then more prosperous, detached. Her parents' house stood alone in its grounds with big gates, one of several nearby, but she reached Rob's parents' house first just below it on the left side of the road.

Faith let herself think about Robert Berkeley. He had been twenty-one when he left Berry Edge. She wondered whether he had changed. John had been two years older, the kindest, gentlest man that she had ever met. John and Robert had hated one another. John had been the son that every man wanted, intelligent, good without seeming pious. He had graduated brilliantly from university and was set to take over from his father later and turn the steel foundry into something even bigger and better; whereas Rob had disliked school, had left as soon as he could in spite of his parents' protests, gone into the foundry at fourteen and made his way up. The men liked him. The girls had liked him too, Faith thought, remembering, because both brothers were attractive. They differed in that John had blue eyes and Rob had grey, but Rob was loud and careless and John was quiet and thoughtful. She and John had been four weeks away from their wedding when his brother had got him drunk and argued with him. John had fallen into the Wear at Durham and drowned. Rob had gone in after him, tried to save him but it had been no good. His brother was dead.

Faith wished that she and Rob never had to meet again. Having him there in Berry Edge without John would be hard for her. Not that Rob would care for that, he had never cared for anything.

She called in at his parents' house. She never stepped inside without thinking how happy she could have been there if she and John had been married, going for Sunday tea with John and their children. It was no longer a happy house and hadn't been those past ten years.

It was shabby, neglected, as though the people who lived there didn't notice. It was cold and dusty and Faith could not help but compare it with her own home. They were not rich but there was enough for good food, decent clothes, a carriage, servants. There was none of that here, nor had there been for a long time. The house had about it an air of hopelessness. Every day John's mother went to his grave and the rest of the day she spent upstairs sitting with her husband. He had for a time lost the use of speech and one leg and was still unable to leave his bed, though he was getting better.

Constant letters to Robert Berkeley had not brought him back, but now at last it seemed that his mother had persuaded him. Faith thought that only desperation would have done so. Their lives had been ruined by what Rob had done, and although as far as Faith knew they had never said he was to blame, they had not stopped grieving for John all that time. They had called it an accident, but that was not what the people of the area had called it, and Rob had gone. Their lives and Faith's life had been ruined. She made sure that there were always fresh flowers on John's grave rather as though his mother was in fact her mother-in-law and the attention was another form of housekeeping.

Faith sat by the fire with Margaret Berkeley and asked after Josiah. Margaret always said that he was a little better, and it was true; but he needed to be a lot better, and he was not. She gave Faith tea and they sat in the living room. From the window as they talked Faith could see the garden and she could imagine herself a child again, when only the present had mattered.

She had grown up with John Berkeley, she thought that she had always loved him. He had carried her over muddy patches in fields, sent her love letters when she was twelve, been big enough to make her feel small, and he had had the brightest, bluest eyes that she had ever seen.

In the autumn she thought of herself and their friends sitting around the bonfire after the first blaze had subsided, poking potatoes with a stick, wishing they were ready before they could be while Rob and his friends shouted and laughed and leaped over the bonfire. She remembered playing hide and seek in the darkness of the railway and the first warm kisses from John's cold lips, the two of them hidden away while the others searched. She thought of the scary games at Hallowe'en, but of never being scared because he was always there, and Christmas . . . She could barely manage to think of Christmas, years and years of mysterious presents, the fear that there would be no snow, the parties, the music, the holly gathering, the carols and the village chapel and John there with her.

It seemed to her that Rob had always been breaking in or spoiling something, getting in the way, sneaking off so that he didn't have to go to chapel or to school, untidy and late for meals and doing dreadful things. As a child he flooded the back kitchen, set the carriage house on fire, broke into the parish church and drank the communion wine. He had the kind of restless energy which tired everybody and he would never do anything that anybody else wanted to do. He always had different ideas. He wouldn't go to school. They sent him to boarding school and he ran away three times, back to Berry Edge.

No matter what anybody did Rob went his own way and no amount of beatings, endless days of bread and water and bedroom, had made any difference.

In the end, as he got older and more difficult, his parents had given up, Faith thought. They had one son who was a credit to them. They let Rob go to work in the foundry and they concentrated on John. Rob had acted like a workman, Faith thought, he would go out with the other young men at the foundry, get drunk, run after women and spend his money freely. He never went to chapel, he stayed out all night, he had fights in Durham with his friends against rival workmen.

The past ten years had been an enormous vacuum, a time when Faith could not be happy because you couldn't be when you had to try, and she was always trying to be. Other young men didn't belong to her, couldn't. She had watched her friends marry and have children, she had seen the joy on their faces and the disappointment on her parents' when she had refused every opportunity. She was too old now, nobody asked her. There were no parties to meet people, everybody her age was married. There was no future, nothing but the past, so clear in her mind, the memories which could not be touched or spoiled. She had wiped Robert Berkeley from those memories until now because every time she thought of him it hurt her. She needed her hatred of him to fill up the space in her head which reminded her of the things that she and John would have had: a home, a marriage, a family, all of those had been denied her because of Rob. She had comforted his parents, she had done a lot of good work, she had helped people in ways she would not have done if she had married and had children. Through the chapel she had helped out with babies, with food, with comfort, with the sick and dying. His mother poured more tea and Faith tried not to look out at the garden where they had had a swing and picnics and played games. She listened to what Margaret was talking about. It was the Christmas arrangements at the chapel. Did Faith know anything about them? Faith knew all about them and proceeded to explain.

'Robert will be home well before then, at least we hope so,' Margaret said.

Christmas was only a few weeks away. Faith wished it was over and done with.

Nancy went slowly down the hill towards her house in the rows at the bottom. She was reluctant to go back and there was no need to hurry. Sean had been drunk at dinnertime, come home, eaten his meal and spent the afternoon in bed. It had been his routine on Sundays for almost as long as they had been married. He would not be awake until teatime and after he had eaten his tea without a word or a backward glance he would be off to the pub for the evening session, to come rolling home at some advanced hour of the night when respectable people, and certainly Nancy and the children, were long gone to bed.

Nancy and Sean had been married for nearly five years now; it felt to Nancy like a lifetime. She could remember quite clearly what her life had been like before, living with her father, looking after him and the house because her mother had died when Nancy was a little girl. It had been peaceful and quiet at home with her father. It was the worst day of her life when she met Sean at her friend Vera's wedding. She could remember how she had felt, the excitement.

She had thought he was the most impressive looking man she had ever seen. She remembered the McFaddens from church when they had all been children, two sons and four daughters; but only the mother, Alice, went now. Her family were grown and her husband was dead. Sean and his older brother, Michael, lived at home and neither of the two was ever seen inside St Mary's Catholic Church at Berry Edge.

By all accounts Sean could fight and drink with the best of them, but Nancy had seen his black Irish eyes shining with merriment, and his white even teeth, his handsome face and thick dark curls. He was a catch, a steel melter, he made good money. Vera had introduced them and Nancy thought that Sean McFadden had the warmest wickedest eyes she had ever seen.

He had asked her to go for a walk with him the following day, which was Sunday, and then he took her back for tea to his mother's house. Nancy wasn't expecting that. Their house was immaculate and the sandwiches were small and cut into diamond shapes. The teacups had roses on them. Nancy had been very afraid that she would spill her tea.

Michael was there. He looked so much like his brother that Nancy was taken aback at the resemblance. He had fine dark straight hair, but apart from that he could have been Sean. In the front room, wanting something to say, Nancy admired a carved wooden horse on the mantelpiece, one of several carved animals in the room. Sean said grudgingly, 'Our Michael made it. They don't give him enough to do down the Diamond pit, he has time for such foolishness at home.'

'It's lovely, Michael,' Nancy said, wanting to touch but not doing so under Mrs McFadden's hawklike gaze.

That summer when Sean was free they went out together. They spent time walking when it was fine, having picnics on the riverbanks in Durham or going around the shops where he bought her small presents which Nancy tried to refuse.

One day in September, when she was alone and her father was at work, there was a knock on the back door. When she opened it, Michael stood there.

'I brought you a present,' he said, offering the package in his hands.

'A present for me? You'd better come in,' Nancy said.

He followed her into the kitchen. Nancy glanced hastily around, wondering if it was nearly as clean as his mother's kitchen would be. She took the package and thanked him, and asked him to sit down. She unwrapped the package. It was a wooden horse, beautifully carved and polished.

'Oh, Michael, it's lovely. You did this for me?'

'You liked them, nobody ever said anything before.'

Nancy made tea.

'Are you thinking of marrying our Sean, Nancy?' he asked after they had talked generally.

'He hasn't asked me but I hope he will. Why?'

'Nothing, I just wondered.'

'You don't like each other, do you?' Nancy said, realising the truth.

'No.'

'Why not?'

He looked directly at her. His eyes were not wicked like Sean's; they were hard and dark and clear.

'I'm not going to call our Sean to you, Nancy. We're brothers, we fight.'

'I know that. I know he has bad points, he goes to the pub too often and he – he swears. But I care about him.'

Nancy saw Sean that Sunday. He lay on the rug in her front room and went to sleep, but when she came back in from washing up he opened his eyes and said, 'Where did you get that carved horse?'

'Your Michael gave it to me.'

Sean opened his eyes wide.

'Our Michael did? I thought . . . When?'

'Tuesday, he came over.'

'Nobody told me. So that's it.' Sean sat up. 'It's our Michael you want really, not me,' and he laughed and pulled her into his arms. 'I think he fancies you, I really do think so.'

'Don't you like him, Sean?'

'He's always trying to tell me what to do, ever since my dad died. He's only a year older than me and he's got no right to come round here making up to you.'

'He wasn't making up to me.'

'What else do you call it when he gives you presents? If it was anybody else, that's what you would call it, the dirty sod,' and Sean got up and took the wooden horse from the dresser and threw it into the fire.

Nancy was horrified. She tried to save it but Sean wouldn't

let her near, and when she fought with him he just laughed and pulled her down on to the sofa. Her father was out and Nancy was immediately conscious of being alone in the house with Sean. He held her there and kissed her. When she wouldn't let him have her mouth, he kissed her all over her face and neck and throat and put his hands on her. The touch of his fingers was a sweet shock.

The fire burned even more brightly with the aid of the wooden horse and Sean held Nancy in his arms and his hands and mouth did disgraceful, magical things inside her clothing. Only later when the evening drew in, when she and Sean were sitting demurely on the sofa and her father came home, did she become aware of how far the fire had gone down, how dark the shadows were in the corners without its brightness. The wooden horse had burned away completely and was lost among the ashes under the grate.

Nancy and Sean had been married the following spring. They lived with Nancy's father and she looked after both men. At first it was easy but a few months later Nancy's father died and after that Sean showed Nancy no love or respect. Things weren't so bad until Nancy became pregnant, but she realised soon after William was born that Sean hated children, hated her getting fat, hated any kind of responsibility. It was all just a burden to him which he pushed from him with drink. Sean, Nancy thought savagely, was like a lot of the men she saw around her. He didn't want a wife. He wanted a whore, a cook and a cleaner, not somebody to share time and children with, not somebody to be beside him. He wanted her to be dirt under his feet, and like one of those statues of the Holy Mother in the church, very far above him and well beneath him; but not a real woman, not a real person.

The odd time that Nancy saw Michael in the street she was horrified and astonished to see how much like his brother he was. Michael was so big and goodlooking that the lasses threw themselves at him. Nancy heard the talk. Alice came to her sometimes crying because he might have got this lass or that lass into trouble. He became a union man and upset the bosses, and he drank and fought and swore. But he was never like that with Nancy. When they met he was polite and smiling, and he liked the bairns, she could tell that he did. He spoke softly to them and always gave William a shiny penny. He would have done more, much more, Nancy knew, if she had said but one word to him. But she didn't, she couldn't. She remembered when she had been a little lass and her father had been fond of saying, 'You've made your bed Nancy, and now you must lie on it.' That was what her marriage was like. Marriage was for life, it was for good, it was forever, it stretched out before her like one of those Roman roads they had built around here so long since. There was no turning from it, there was nowhere to hide, no corners, no way out. She could not tell anyone that she had made a mistake, she could not complain because no one wanted to hear. She was married to Sean McFadden for always now, she could not leave because there was nowhere to go and she had no money. She could not be rescued in a town like this where a man's word was law in his home. She had to endure the neglect, the beatings, the poverty, the pregnancies, the abuse and the humiliation of knowing that the money he made he spent on drink and other women. All Nancy had were her bairns, her house, her friend Vera, and the odd meal at Alice's when Alice would have them there, she worried so much about them upsetting her tidy house. There were no longer carved wooden animals in Alice's front room, and when she enquired about this Alice told her that Michael had stopped doing his carvings, that one night when drunk, out of temper he had thrown them all on the fire. It seemed the worst thing of all somehow to Nancy.

'They were only to dust,' Alice said.

Two

'I can't spare you,' Vincent Shaw said.

Harry glanced across to where Rob was standing by the fire. He didn't blame him for standing there, the night was bitterly cold and a harsh wind blew across the Nottinghamshire countryside. The house was well protected by many acres of woodland but tonight it seemed that the wind howled under the doors. His father, he knew, would not be talked into letting him go to Durham with Rob, and he had already decided that he was going, so he tried to be tactful.

'You have to,' he said, 'you can't let him go back there among the barbarian hordes alone.'

'I see no reason why either of you should go,' Vincent said, looking to where his son-in-law stood, turned slightly away, towards the fire. They had had several arguments before now about this and Rob gave no indication that he was listening.

They were in the library, a wood-panelled room which

Vincent was very fond of, Harry knew, not because he ever did any work in there nor because he ever read any of the books, simply because he had always wanted a large library. It was one of the many reasons he had wanted to buy this house five years earlier. The original part was a twelfth century abbey, the gardens were huge, the drive was long and lined with lime trees, the rooms were big and wide and many. It was the most magnificent house that he had ever seen.

'You'd love it if you were ill and we ignored you,' Harry said, 'the man is his father.'

'What has his father done for him these past ten years, that's what I'd like to know? Bugger all, I've had to do it.' When this produced no reaction from Rob, Vincent added, 'We all come to death and failure in the end. What are you going to do, save him?' Still nothing happened. 'Are you taking part in this conversation, Robert, or are you merely providing decoration for the otherwise boring room? And where did you get that suit?'

Rob turned, finally looked up, his eyes just a fraction darker than the grey suit that he wore. He regarded Vincent's yellow checked clothes with slight amusement.

'I went to a tailor,' he said.

'Your clothes must cost you a bloody fortune,' Vincent said.

'It's more than could be said of you,' Harry put in.

'London,' Vincent said, 'all the way to bloody Savile Row for clothes.'

'Why go all that way when you could go to the corner shop like Father does?' Harry said, and won a grin from Rob.

'You're not going to Durham, either of you,' Vincent said. 'I can't manage without you.'

'I'll go alone, then you'll have Harry,' Rob said.

'You call that help?'

'Vince—' Harry protested.

'And don't call me "Vince", you arrogant young bastard, I'm your father. I'll flay you to within an inch of your life.'

'I wish I had ten shillings for every time you've said that to me over the past fifteen years,' Harry said. 'You're not really going to let him go alone?'

'A lot of use you'd be up there in the wilds,' his father said, and left the room.

Harry sighed.

'You could have told him you wanted me to go with you.'

'I don't.'

'If you don't, you know, you'll only wish you had.'

'When I do I'll let you know.'

'Did you tell my mother?'

'She went off to see about packing my thick underwear. If the world was to end tomorrow it would be her first concern.'

'There you are,' Ida Shaw announced as she came in. His mother, Harry reflected, was in a way as odd as his father. He was tall and thin and wore brightly coloured clothes and long flowing coats, and she was short and fat and rather untidy. She did a lot of gardening in the summer, and even though at this time of year there was little to do outside she always looked as though she had been outdoors, her hair slightly ruffled and her cheeks tinged pink. Their daughter, Sarah, Harry's sister, had been beautiful. Harry couldn't think where Sarah's beauty had come from; neither of their parents was physically beautiful.

Ida always looked at them as though she thought they could be doing something illicit, drinking to excess, playing billiards for money or even making free with one of the maids. They never did but she always looked as though she expected them to. She tried to look severely at Harry and it was a huge effort for her. Sarah had died two years ago and Harry was now her only child.

'Do you have to make your father swear?' she said.

'Nobody makes him swear, Mother, he was born foul-mouthed.'

'You could hardly have expected him to let you go to Durham. He thinks it's bad enough that Rob should go.'

'Yes, we know. Half a dozen times we've had the same lecture.'

Ida went to Rob and smoothed her fingers down the lapels of his jacket. It was almost, Harry thought, as though she was gaining and giving comfort to both Rob and herself for the loss of Sarah. She touched Rob and Harry a lot, as though to reassure herself that they were both still there, and Harry knew very well that his parents were upset about

Rob leaving. He hadn't yet told his mother that he was going too. His father was blustering about the business, but it was their actual leaving that he minded.

'You have to go,' Ida was saying now to Rob as she gently caressed the soft material of his jacket. 'Your mother has written again and again, so I know that you must, and she wouldn't have asked if they hadn't needed you badly.'

'They've managed without him for ten years,' Harry said.

His mother threw him a look that would have iced ponds.

'Kindly leave the room, young man,' she said.

Harry went. He was thirty, but for the past twenty years as far as his mother was concerned he had not aged at all. His valet was just passing in the hall.

'Pack my things, will you, I'm going with him,' Harry said.

Three

It wasn't until they got back from the funeral that the thought occurred to Nancy. They wouldn't have to put up with the bastard any more. She couldn't think why it had taken her so long to realise, but then of course there were set ways to see these things. People expected you to be shocked and you were, people expected you to cry and you did that too. What people didn't expect was that you were relieved and she was. She was so relieved that her husband, Sean, was dead that she couldn't think beyond that.

It wasn't until Alice and Michael and all the other people had gone that she sat down by her kitchen fire and smiled into it, and thought that she would never again have to put up with the way that he behaved. Nobody would ever come drunk and singing through that door. Nobody would complain about the meals or how she looked or what she did. He would not call her fat and ugly. She would not have to put up with his table manners, his belching and breaking wind and the fact that he had so little respect for her that, however tired she was, or however dirty he was, he would force himself on her in the darkness. He was dead.

Nancy leaned forward into the warmth of the fire and thanked God for her freedom, for her stupid feckless husband who had been killed by a spillage of molten steel from a huge ladle lifted by a crane. Sean, everybody knew, was often drunk at work and had increasingly been sent home for being a danger to other people's lives. He was not supposed to be anywhere near. He had been laughing and singing and carrying on. Even his friends had not been able to defend his behaviour to the manager so that Nancy would be due any money for the accident. In fact the foreman had given her money and the men had each given some and she would be allowed to keep her house, but Nancy doubted whether there would be any more. The manager had told her gravely that both Sean and one of his friends should not have been there. They had behaved stupidly. The other man had been dismissed and Sean was dead. It was, Nancy thought, another instance of the works not being as it should, but she was not going to argue. She couldn't help being glad about Sean, she would manage somehow.

Later she went upstairs and tiptoed into the bedroom. William and the baby, Clarrie, only a few months old, were both asleep. The funeral had taken almost everything she had. She didn't know what she would do now. She tried not to worry. She climbed into bed and thought again of the luxury of having all that room to herself. He was not snoring there beside her, or worse still pinning her down. You would have thought, Nancy decided, that men would get tired of doing something which women took no pleasure in and which was always the same, but he didn't. That and drink were all he had ever thought about. Nancy fell asleep thinking that she would talk to Vera about it. Vera did cleaning at the top end of the town where the terraced houses stood beside the park. She might be able to help with some work.

The next day people dropped in to see that she was all right. Nancy was just glad there was enough baking left to provide a bit of something for each of them to have with the endless tea she provided.

At last in the evening there was only Vera and herself sitting by the fire. Nancy couldn't get used to the peace. She didn't have to keep listening for his footsteps in the yard, because if he had found her sitting over the fire like that, Vera would have scuttled out and Nancy would have kept well out of the way of his hands. It was worse when he was not drunk, for some reason, but then he was nearly always drunk. She had come to be glad of that. Now there was no longer any reason to listen, she and Vera could sit there as long as they liked because Vera's husband, Shane, was the kind of man who didn't mind what his wife did as long as he got his meals and a clean shirt.

'I need some work, Vera.'

'I know, but what, with bairns that small? Will his mother take them?'

'She didn't offer and I didn't ask. How did you get your work?'

'I just went to the door. Mind you, if you could think of something better you'd be as well off. Scrubbing other folks' steps is less entertaining than scrubbing your own and that's not saying much.'

'Work's hard to find.'

'It is that,' Vera said, 'but I could take the bairns sometimes and at least he won't be coming in drunk no more.'

Nancy couldn't help but smile.

'Do you know, Vera,' she said, 'I never thought I'd live to see the day when I was glad to watch anybody put underground, but I did.'

'He was a bugger,' Vera agreed.

Nancy couldn't think how she would make money but she knew that she would have to do something soon. The neighbours were kind. Over the next few days they brought food. One brought a stew and another a cake and some bread, and Nancy, having paid for the funeral, was glad of what little she could get. She didn't quite know what she was going to do now.

In the evening two days later Michael turned up. It was quite frightening. Nancy had just put the children to bed when she heard the sound of his boots in the yard. He knocked on the door, but even so Nancy jumped up from

Sean's chair because it made her tremble. She clutched on to the chairback and then she went to the door and opened it. Her experience told her that Michael was not drunk, but Sean sober had still been a person to watch carefully. Michael waited in the doorway.

'I just wondered if you were all right,' he said.

Nancy let go of her breath.

'I'm fine, thank you.'

He pulled his cap off his head and became himself, the black silky straight hair and hard dark eyes.

'I just wondered,' he said.

Nancy invited him in even though inwardly she cursed herself for doing it, offered him Sean's chair, but although he looked at it he took the hard chair that she usually sat on. Nancy gave him tea.

'I didn't mean to put you to a lot of trouble,' he said and Nancy cursed herself again for offering. He was nobody in her house, he was not his brother. 'I hope you won't be offended, Nancy, but I've got some money and I want you to have it.'

It should have been easy, she should have been able to take it. Like Sean, Michael made good money, hewing coal, even on short time he made enough. He put the money down on the table and a big pile it was, all winking and blinking in the lamplight. Nancy shook her head.

'I couldn't,' she said.

'I know what you think. I know you don't want to be

beholden to any of us after the way our Sean treated you, but you've got two bairns to think about. Take it, Nancy, it would make me feel better.'

'What have you got to feel bad about?' Nancy retorted. 'You're not my husband. You're not bouncing me off the walls, keeping me short for drink, never coming home sober but once every blue moon. You're not bad tempered and going with other women and . . .' Nancy ran out of breath and got up and turned her back on him. 'Keep your money, Mick, I don't want it.'

'If my Mam hears you calling me "Mick" you'll get trouble,' was all he said as Nancy recovered her breath, and her temper, and was ashamed at having gone on like that at him when it was nothing to do with him.

His mother was like that, she knew, they all had great long names except for Sean and his mother insisted there was no shortening of them. 'I'm sorry, Michael, I know it's nothing to do with you but I don't want anything from you.'

'Pride's all right when you can afford it, Nancy.'

'It isn't pride. I don't want to give you or anybody else the right to walk into my house.'

'Half the time when he came back here black and blue it was me,' he said. 'If I could have done more I would have. I miss how things might have been, you know.'

Nancy did know. It ate your guts did what might have been, not just the big times when you could have changed the world, not just the middle sized times when you might have had the sense to keep your gob shut and think, but the little times, the fleeting chances that were lost, the kiss that was almost sweet, the picnic where it nearly didn't rain, the few times that she and Sean had begun to laugh at exactly the same moment. It was not just the past that was gone, it was somehow the future as well, the trying harder to make things right, the mellow way that older married people grew together, the corners rubbed off, the summers that were to come. It was the husband she had not had that she missed.

Michael didn't stay, and when he got up and didn't take the money he had put down on the oilclothed table, though Nancy didn't want to accept it, she made herself say nothing but thank you. When he had gone she sat back down in the easy chair and thought. Was that how Sean had been? Was that what had attracted her, that big, dark, capable look? Was he like Michael when they met, and had it only been the idea of having to keep her and the children that had made him want to go to drink and men's conversation and other women?

Two days later Vera came back with some information.

'I think I might have found you a job,' she said. 'Mrs Berkeley wants somebody to clean for when their Robert gets back. What sort of a lad wouldn't have come back well before now considering how things have been all this while, Mr Berkeley so poorly and the works in such a state?'

'He likely wouldn't want to, would he, after killing his brother and they wouldn't want him to, would they?'

'You could go and ask, Nancy, there's nowt lost. Just make sure she pays you, that's all.'

Nancy unwillingly left the children with Sean's mother two rows away at the bottom of Berry Edge bank. Vera said that she would be glad to take them when she wasn't at work, but she was that day. The Berkeleys lived halfway up the bank, it wasn't far.

'I'm going to go out and look for work,' she told Alice.

'I can't take the bairns every day, Nancy, I've got a lot to do.'

Alice turned out her house every day. It wouldn't have surprised Nancy to discover that their Michael had to live in the yard. He was the only one at home now, the four daughters had married and gone.

'I hear our Michael came to see you the other night?' her mother-in-law said.

'He popped in to see how the bairns were.'

'He's all the wage I've got, Nancy.'

'I have to be going,' Nancy said.

She hated leaving the bairns there. How was she to work? If she didn't leave them with his mother or Vera she would have to pay, and if she had to pay she would be working for very little. Nancy trudged up the hill towards the Berkeley house. If Mrs Berkeley didn't take her on she didn't know what she would do.

*

When Faith got back from a chapel meeting one day soon after her talk with Nancy in the churchyard, she found her mother engaged on a strange task. She was looking in Faith's wardrobe. As Faith came on to the upstairs landing she could see her mother through the open door, pondering.

'Mother, what are you doing?' she said.

'I'm looking for jumble, dear.'

'You won't find any there.'

'You're like your father, Faith, you never throw anything away.'

'Not when there's use left in them.'

'Somebody else could use this, I think,' her mother said, extracting an old blue dress from the far reaches of the wardrobe. 'How many times has this been mended?'

'I wear it all the time.'

'I know you do.' Her mother eyed her. 'I think a trip to Durham might be a good idea, something new perhaps.'

And then Faith understood. She took the dress from her mother and put it back into the wardrobe.

'I don't need new dresses, Mother, I'm not going anywhere,' she said.

Her mother said nothing more as though she had accepted the decision, but Faith knew that it was not so. Her mother left the room, went downstairs and when Faith followed her was busy pouring tea by the sitting room fire.

'I know that I've disappointed you and I'm sorry,' Faith said, 'but nothing will change because Robert Berkeley is coming home, and I'm certainly not going to buy a new dress for the occasion.'

'I hope you're wrong,' her mother said. 'I went to see them this morning and Margaret says he's bringing another man with him. I don't think they're very pleased about it.'

'That's just what Berry Edge needs, another workman,' Faith said.

'We don't know what kind of a man he might be,' her mother said, sipping tea.

'And is this the reason for clearing out my wardrobe? Really, Mother.'

Her mother picked up half a buttered scone but didn't eat it.

'It's difficult not to think of how things might have been,' she said. 'We could have had three or four grandchildren by now.'

'I know that.'

'Do you? You never talk about it. After you were born and they told me I couldn't have any more children because I had been so ill, you have no idea how I longed for a family like other women had. It's strange how you can miss people who weren't born. I often think what our son would have been like, maybe two, another daughter. I don't mean to blame you, Faith, I understand how you felt about John, it's just that our lives are so very empty now, filled with detail but without joy. Children bring that as nothing else ever could. And it's – it's interesting. Families are what people talk about. When

I meet other women and hear about their grandchildren it hurts me. I feel as though our lives stopped completely when John died.' Her mother looked at her straighter, Faith thought, than she had done in years. 'There was nothing wrong with Robert, Faith, he was a fine young man.'

'How can you say that?'

'Because it's true. He was headstrong, yes, he was a touch wild but dear me, it's no more than many other young men. He only looked so bad in John's light. A man's the better for a fault or two, it makes us easier to live with ourselves.'

'John had no faults,' Faith declared.

'You're an embittered woman, Faith.'

'A dried up old spinster,' Faith said. 'So I am, and Robert Berkeley is to blame.'

Four

Harry had thought County Durham was a lot further away than it actually was. He had never been that far north before and had been under the mistaken impression that after Yorkshire there was Scotland. Harry had heard that the north east was a grimy collection of tiny, ugly houses with dirty foundries and pits. He had heard that the women wore aprons and headscarves, the men were black from work, with thick guttural voices, that there was no culture, that there was no beauty, that there was nothing of any significance in Durham. So as he drew further northwards he gazed out of the train window surprised at the pretty farms and small neat fields, and when the train pulled into the station at Durham it was quite a shock.

Any dirt, any disfigurement that might have spoiled Harry's impression was hidden under a cloak of snow and the view from there was a full picture of the small city. The little houses were transformed into the kind of thing which you read about in children's stories, with thick white window ledges and gleaming silver roofs. There were church spires and best of all the Norman cathedral set square with its four towers and the castle close beside, grey against the snow, bright in the sunshine. Rob barely glanced at it but for Harry it was like a homecoming, small enough to be cosy. He felt as though it was welcoming him like he was a son as the train slowed and then stopped high on a hill above the city. He stayed quite still to try to keep those moments of first seeing the place fresh in his mind.

'It's beautiful,' he said.

'You've seen Venice, Rome and Paris,' Rob said roughly, 'let's get out of here.'

Harry persuaded him to linger a little. The streets had magical names such as Silver Street on a tiny twisting bank which led down to Framwellgate Bridge. He hung over the bridge because the view from there was of the River Wear, and the cathedral and castle rose up sharply amidst bare, black, winter trees. The river had a pale grey sheen on that sunny winter's day. On either side there were houses, some of them with gardens which went straight down to the tow-path and the river. Saddler Street was through the market place on another bank and wended its way up to Palace Green where the castle and the cathedral stood with pretty stone buildings around a square. It was all tiny banks and hidden lanes and bends so that everything was a surprise.

*

It was early evening by the time they got off the train at Berry Edge. This was more like Harry's idea of what a north east industrial town would be. It sat high up on the edge of the moors, and there were pit wheels and pit heaps, and all the grime and muddle and smell of coal and coke and steelworks with tiny houses built right beside the pits and the works.

An old man with a horse and trap was there to meet them. Rob recognised him, greeted him, was rewarded with nothing more than a grunt and didn't speak again until they reached the front door of what looked to Harry like a very small house, and then Rob thanked the man and lifted the luggage down himself. The horse and trap went away without another word from anyone and Harry glanced around him.

There was no drive to speak of, just a short distance between the house and the gate posts; there were other houses around and some of them did not appear to be prosperous.

Rob opened the front door and went inside. Harry followed him, and for the first time realised that his brother-in-law had come from a very moderate kind of background. A tiny fire burned in the hall. A skinny woman came towards them. She wore an extremely dowdy dress. Ida would have died first, his mother was a fashionable woman when she had company or went out and loved the latest styles of hats and dresses.

'Hello, Robert.'

'Mother.'

There was no kissing, there was no embrace. Harry was introduced, she said little and then there was a trek upstairs to icy rooms, carrying his own luggage. Harry began to wish that he had stayed at home, and when he saw his bedroom he wished it doubly. It was shabby and dark and there was no servant to do the unpacking. He was not used to being without his valet and wasn't sure what to do. The room was small and the furniture in it hideously large. The bed was uncomfortable. Harry left his bags on the floor and went across the landing where Rob was calmly putting clothes into a chest of drawers.

'You wanted to come,' he said without looking up.

'I didn't say anything.'

Harry wandered around. It was dark so he couldn't see anything from the window and this room was no better than his own, overpowered by an enormous wardrobe that you could have stored dead people in and a grate that Harry would have sworn had never seen warmth.

'There are no fires in the bedrooms, Rob,' Harry said, obvious in his misery.

'Welcome to Berry Edge,' Rob said.

Later, when Harry was contriving for the first time in his life to do his own unpacking, a pretty, golden-haired girl came into the room, struggling with a bucket of coal. Mrs Berkeley had spoken of her in front of them. Her name was Nancy McFadden. Harry rushed over and took the bucket from her. At his home men did such things.

'Eh, sir, no,' she said, 'you'll get all mucky.'

'You ought not to carry that.'

'What for?'

'What?'

She smiled shyly. Harry grinned. She was very pretty with big blue eyes.

'I'm sorry to come in when you're busy, sir,' she said, 'but Mrs Berkeley is bothered about these fires. You must be frozen.'

'I am,' Harry agreed.

'Don't worry, sir, I'll fettle it,' she said, and so she did. Much to his astonishment, she began busily twisting newspaper into neat rolls and then fastening them in a kind of bow. She put sticks on top and a touch of coal, and to his delight the fire soon began to burn. 'There now, it'll be lovely shortly. Oh, and Mrs Berkeley says if there's anything you want just tell me, sir.'

There were several things Harry thought of that he would very much like her to do for him, but since all of them were less than respectable he merely shook his head and thanked her.

Rob had dreaded more than anything seeing his father again. They had never got on. John had been such an easy child, so when he wasn't, his parents were surprised and displeased. Rob kept them busy during his childhood when he ran away both from home and from school, got drunk, and went around with girls his mother didn't like. Really, Rob reflected, he was fairly normal, but they didn't see it like that because of John, and the more they tried to alter him the worse it became.

Even now it was difficult to think of John with equanimity. Rob hesitated on the landing outside his parents' bedroom door, and then went softly inside.

His father was sitting up, propped on pillows and was a shock. He seemed to Rob an old man, ill but not defenceless, and all the greeting he gave Rob was, 'So you finally came back.'

Rob had imagined this, had rehearsed what he was going to say, had thought how it might be, but years of Vincent Shaw as a father figure had altered his perception of these things and he knew immediately why it was. Northern men like his father showed their children no affection for fear it would make them dependent but Vincent, wonderfully strange to Rob, believed in showing love, and Rob knew that Vincent had liked him almost as soon as they met. Vincent admired him, had told Rob many times over the years how brilliant he thought he was and, although Vincent had at various times treated Rob badly in different ways, there had always been somehow a generosity of spirit about it. Rob had never been afraid of Vincent but he was afraid of his father. In his presence Rob knew now that he would always be a child of ten or eleven, sick with fear, unable to speak while his father rolled around him a blinding sarcasm. He was ten, stupid, worthless, evil perhaps and his father was about to put him down across some convenient piece of furniture and thrash him into helpless misery.

He backed away and banged into the door. The doorknob seemed so sharp it brought him into the present again. He had rarely been in here, his parents' room was out of bounds. Rob was used to Ida Shaw's idea of bedrooms and her ideas were very different. There was little privacy in the Shaw house, strangely he thought. For one thing there were servants. Maids went in and out with bedding and towels and cleaning equipment, the male servants brought buckets of coal and Ida waffled about making sure that everybody had every creature comfort. You could be almost sure of not being alone in your bedroom except when you were asleep, and even then if you left your door open you could awake in the night and find a cat curled up against your stomach. Animals were meant to be banished from the house, but if a window was left open or the door ajar it was surprising what happened.

Parts of the house were old but she would have nothing to do with these except in summer when you needed all the draughts you could get. In the winter Ida believed in fires in every room and hot meals three times a day. Everybody was well fed and well kept. Servants rarely left. Ida treated her maids almost as well as she treated her children; she fussed over their welfare, became concerned about their love affairs, was unhappy when they were ill, made sure they ate properly. On their birthdays and at Christmas she gave them the kind of presents which any girl would have been pleased with.

The bedrooms were big and airy with windows to let in the light and thick curtains to keep out the draughts. The furniture was modern and the walls were bright. There were dense carpets and pretty bedcoverings.

This room was small and dark. The furniture seemed huge and ugly and made the room look even smaller and darker.

'I hope you're feeling better,' he ventured.

'I've been ill for most of the past year. Your mother did write several times asking you to come home.'

'Yes, I . . . I know.'

'You must have been doing something very important in Nottingham.'

They had. Vincent had been excited about the expansion of the bicycle factory and the way that sales were soaring. That spring and summer Ida had designed and built a Japanese garden. Rob had tried to pretend that his parents were not demanding he should come back to Durham.

'Who is this young man you've brought with you?'

'Harry is very clever. I thought he might be able to help.'

'Really, and what is his particular field?'

'He's an engineer, but he's good at most things.'

He had to be, living with Vincent. If you weren't good at things you soon learned to be, because Vincent wouldn't tolerate incompetence of any kind, especially from his son. If Harry had not been as good as he was he would never have survived. But Rob knew also that privately Vincent was very proud of his son, so perhaps had Harry not been precociously clever, Vincent might have behaved differently towards him. Harry was strong and bright and totally capable, and it was just as well. Since Sarah had died his parents' love might have suffocated him otherwise, even though they pretended it was not so. One of the reasons Rob had allowed Harry to come with him was that Harry needed to get away for his own sake.

'An engineer? Really? And what kind of work are you doing to bring you into the company of an engineer?'

Rob had long imagined what it would be like if and when he ever did come home and told his parents how well he had done, that he, Vincent and Harry had bought a house with rolling acres, gardens which had fountains and waterfalls, rooms with paintings and books, and good furniture, crystal and silver, everything of the best. A house built of honeyed stone, filled with music and books and, until Sarah had died, laughter and good conversation and many friends. The place where he had spent the happiest times of his life. He had thought he would be able to tell them that he had prospered beyond anything they could imagine, that his ideas and designs were respected and sought after by people not just here but in other countries. He had imagined bringing Sarah here and letting his parents see the kind of woman who had agreed to become his wife, so that they would see how beautiful and educated she was and how much she loved him, that he was worth someone like Sarah loving him. He wanted to show them what he had done, the huge achievements, the monumental successes so that finally they would know he was no longer the stupid, disgusting, small boy of ten who had to be beaten into submission. Only he couldn't say any of it.

'I work in a bicycle factory,' he said.

Mr Berkeley did not come out of his bedroom so Harry didn't meet him. Another shock awaited him at dinner. There was no wine, nothing but water on the table, and it was the plainest dinner that he had ever seen with stark-looking vegetables unrelieved by even a teaspoon of butter. Nancy served it. There seemed to be no other servants. After dinner Harry cornered Rob in the hall.

'I need a drink.'

'So do I. Let's go.'

Harry thanked Mrs Berkeley for the dinner and they went out. It was a cold dark night and the wind swept through the small town. The first pub they came to was the Station Hotel.

'We can't go in there,' Rob said, 'the men drink there.'

'Does it matter? This is a small place. Won't some of the workmen be in every pub?'

'How keen are you?'

'Keen enough,' Harry said and opened the door.

He instantly regretted it. As they walked in the hum of voices ceased. Silence fell. At least he had enough sense to let Rob order the drinks but as he listened to the sound of Rob's voice he realised something else. Rob no longer spoke as the people of Berry Edge did. His accent was flawless, he spoke like the Shaws. Harry stood close beside him at the bar. There was a very big man near them; Harry nodded towards him and then said in a low voice, 'Christ, I hope he's on our side.'

Rob took one look at the man and was instantly transported into his childhood.

'Mickey?' he said. The man turned to him, and Rob could see and feel and touch all those long golden wonderful times playing games and making fires and running across the moors, hiding in the darkness on the railways and lying in the long grass being anybody but himself, being powerful and free. This man had been a boy then, had been his best friend.

He regarded Rob from cold black eyes and the illusion fell away.

'Mr Berkeley?' he said.

Rob had never felt so foolish or unwanted because they knew who he was now. Somebody spat on the floor, cursing. Rob held the big man's gaze. Michael McFadden. They had had so much in common as children, both had brothers whom they hated and fathers whom they hated more. Michael rarely went home. His father drank and had an evil temper. There was barely enough to eat in their house because of his father's drinking. Rob remembered laughing and saying that the food had stunted Michael's growth.

And his own childhood had been hard in other ways. Rising at four, prayers at five, being made to sit still and study all the time, trying to get out like butterflies that banged against the windows, being beaten after each escape. But his memories of Michael McFadden were caught up in summer days and winding streams and laughter. Rob could not extricate himself from those precious memories. He could not help almost smiling still, and he realised then that he had held on in his mind to everything that was most important to him about Berry Edge, all those years. He thought also of the beautiful, golden-haired woman in his mother's kitchen. She was called McFadden. How lucky Michael was if he was married to the delightful Nancy.

'Is Nancy your wife?' he said, ready to be admiring, and that was when he knew he was really back in Berry Edge. Michael McFadden smiled. He was even colder when he smiled. Rob's heart dropped and all the golden memories crumbled. He had learned over the years not to back off but his instincts shrieked at him to run. In that one sentence he had wrecked something important.

'My wife? Do you hear that?' Michael said to the pub. 'He wants to know if Nancy is my wife.'

'Christ,' Harry said softly.

'Don't you speak to her then, Mr Berkeley?' He drew out the last two words, lingered over them and Rob remembered his first name on Michael's childish lips. He was already sorry that they had come into this pub and he could feel the temper from way down inside, the temper which he had thought he had so well controlled until Sarah died. He had thought it well schooled over those years, almost buried, it had had so little cause to stir. He had seen himself calm, he had seen himself as his friends and colleagues did, he knew that his abilities brought him respect and that through the love he had received from Sarah Shaw he knew himself accepted; but since Sarah had died the peace had fallen away and now the slow burn of temper began to edge its way up from his stomach.

'Of course I speak to her, Michael, why shouldn't I?'

The first name was insult now and Michael knew it, Rob could see.

'Oh my God,' Harry said

'Well you should know then that my brother, Nancy's husband, Sean, died in your bloody works.'

'I didn't know. I'm sorry. I only just got here—'

'That makes you one of the lucky ones,' Michael said and there were murmurs of agreement. 'We've been living in this bloody hole on part pay from your stinking pit because there's nowt to do.'

'Enough for beer, though?' Rob said.

'For God's sake,' Harry said just above a whisper. 'He'll kill you.'

'I'm surprised you came back, the works have finished us all off while you've been running away, Mr Bloody Berkeley.'

Rob hit him. Harry closed his eyes over it.

Rob had forgotten how good it felt to plant your fist in the middle of somebody's face. The rage in him felt like a volcano running over the top, and it wasn't just the insults or the way that the men had shown their disrespect, it was the whole of Berry Edge somehow against him all that time. He didn't see himself, he didn't really see Michael, it was white heat just like the furnace, like the steel pouring, pure and high and liquid, all that it should be, just himself and that.

The men were well backed, shocked. When he had gone in, the murmur of pub voices had felt like a caress. He could have been at home here, had thought for seconds together that he was and then he remembered. Berry Edge was always like this, it was the foundry that had belonged to him. The people didn't care what he felt like or what he thought, here it was only what they could see; and they had seen him as a coward, as weak, and in Berry Edge there was no place for the weak except on the bottom being trodden into the ground.

Michael came back at him. The pub was suddenly a great big space in the middle with only himself and Michael, the odd chair breaking like sticks, clattering across the floor, and the smell of beer and tobacco became to Rob the most wonderful memory, the smell of the steelworks, the men's clothes warm and sweated, sand and boots and all those things which he had forgotten for so long. Berry Edge smelled like nowhere else, even though he had been in factories and foundries all his life. He was a boy again with a boy's dreams, standing at the doorway of the works knowing where he belonged, the heat of the steel pouring, the cold of the snow outside, the men pausing and smiling and talking. He had loved that foundry like nothing else, it had been his like it would never ever belong to John, it was his because of the men, their company, their friendship, their skills. They would work with him and the results were clean and solid and important. He had belonged here on the high fells where men had built the iron works because of the raw materials. He had thought it would always be his home, that he could shape and mould it like the steel, that he could create something important here but it was gone, it was all long gone and he knew it now. These men were not his friends any more, they were not his workmates. They hated him just like everybody else. They would have liked Michael McFadden to kill him, they would at least have liked Michael McFadden to leave him senseless on the floor. But Rob was clearheaded, never more so than now. Michael had been drinking.

By the time Rob could see beyond the rage, Michael McFadden was down on the floor and not about to get up. In the silence there were moments of distilled satisfaction while Rob took in the assembled men with one sweeping look.

'Anybody else?' he offered.

The men shifted but nothing happened, and then Harry touched him on the shoulder.

'Come on,' he said. He talked softly, persuaded Rob outside into the bitter air and then the world crashed around Rob. He stopped, leaned back against the house next to the pub.

He thought, everything he touched he spoiled, everything he went near he lost. It was Berry Edge after John died. It was his nightmare. He had sworn never to come back. Guilt swamped him, took over, sweated its way through his body in spite of the cold night. He could never belong here again and he hated it because it had spoiled his life. It got him awake in the crawling hours of the night with its knives and whisperings, gnawing away until he could see a white image in his head of the person that he had tried to be, the person inside, that he was so sure he was meant to be, injured and bloody and on the ground; and it was because of this place.

Harry waited for a few moments and then asked anxiously, 'You hurt?'

'No.'

'You sure?'

'Yes.' He looked at Harry and was glad for the first time that Harry had come with him. 'Do you think he'll be all right?'

'I don't think you did him any permanent damage. Of course he'd had a few drinks, otherwise he would have been more of a problem. Pity it couldn't have been outside on a nice sunny day with the whole town watching. You have to show them.'

'I don't want to have to show them, at least not that way. He was my friend.'

'Hell, Rob, you don't have any friends here except me.'

'I'm glad you're here.'

'I knew you would be.'

They walked slowly down the bank to the house and into the kitchen. Nancy clicked her tongue in the manner of one well versed in Berry Edge ways and said, 'Fighting? Well, really, Mr Berkeley. You haven't been back two minutes.'

She sat Rob down and bathed his face and knuckles.

'Who did this?'

'Your brother-in-law.'

'What, Michael?' Nancy stopped, stared. 'He's bigger than you.'

'I noticed,' Rob said, backing from her fingers.

'Keep still. Drinking, was he?'

'Yes, thank God. I didn't know about your husband, Nancy, I'm sorry.'

'You'll be the only one then. He was a . . . he was the worst man I ever met and it was his own fault, he was drunk at work. They kept sending him home. Something was bound to happen. Where did you go for a drink?'

'The Station Hotel.'

'You should know better,' Nancy said. 'You can't go drinking in there. Did you win?'

'You're very interested about this, aren't you, Nancy?' Rob said.

'Where can we go drinking?' Harry asked her.

'Nowhere here. You'll have to go to Durham.'

'Should you be here at this time of night?' Rob asked.

'You don't live in?' Harry asked.

'Me, sir? I've got two bairns.'

'Are you all the help there is?' Rob said. 'We'll have to do something about that so that you can go home to your children at a proper time.'

'Shall I walk you?' Harry offered.

'I'm safe on the streets here, it's my home,' Nancy said.

Nancy bandaged Rob's hands and after that she went. Mrs Berkeley stayed upstairs with her husband. Rob and Harry sat by the fire.

'How does your father seem?'

'He's dying.'

Harry looked into the fire for a little while and then he said, 'You gave me the impression that the works here was little more than a smithy, but it seems to me quite a big affair?'

'It is.'

'Then why do your parents live like this?'

'I don't think they have any money.'

'But they must have made money out of it, Rob. We live lavishly compared to this.'

'They're modest people, unlike your parents.'

'Why be modest when you can live well?'

'They live among the people who work for them. Perhaps it was just tact in the beginning. Now I think it's necessity.'

'What did you hope to achieve by coming back?'

'I don't know.'

'Your mother didn't even kiss you, after ten years. Ida kisses me every time I go out the door or come back.'

'You didn't kill your brother.'

'I don't think you're going to better that one here, Robbo.'

'I don't think so either,' Rob said.

Five

Michael pushed aside all offers of help as he left the Station Hotel. His whole body ached, his face especially, but it was his heart that bothered him most. He could feel his hate for the Berkeleys stir and light. How could Rob come back now after all this time, and looking like a dog's dinner, all neat and talking like a southerner, as though he had never belonged here?

He thought back to that night ten years ago when Rob had left, several weeks after the death of his brother, when all Berry Edge was against him. He had come to the house they had remained friends for years after they were children even though they didn't work together. Michael had been in the pub with Rob when John drowned so he knew for certain that Rob had had nothing directly to do with it, though he also knew how fiercely the brothers had quarrelled. He was tired by then of saying to people that Rob had not pushed his brother over the bridge. It was what they wanted to believe, so they believed it.

He knew that life had become intolerable for Rob during those weeks, that his parents had blamed him, that his friends at work had talked about him, that many people had stopped speaking to him, that Faith Norman had been left as good as widowed four weeks away from her wedding. She had almost collapsed. John Berkeley's death hung over Berry Edge like a pall.

He remembered standing outside the house in the bitter cold wind.

'I'm going away, Mickey.'

'Away? Away where?'

'Anywhere that isn't here.'

'But you can't.'

'What else can I do? My parents are heartbroken, people hold me responsible, I hold myself responsible—'

'You shouldn't. I fight as bad as that with our Sean twice a week at least.'

'Your Sean's used to drink.'

'It was an accident, Rob.'

'That's not how it seems. I have to get out of here. Come with me.'

For a moment it seemed to Michael a possibility, a light. Getting away. And then reality clutched him. His father was dead, he had four sisters and his mother to support.

'There's your Sean, you don't have to stay.'

'Our Sean drinks his pay, you know that. I have my mam to keep and the girls to look after. I can't go anywhere.'

He remembered Rob's despair. He remembered Rob walking away, remembered how he had felt watching Rob leave the rows, wondering how long it would be before he came back. He remembered missing him and how from the beginning things had gone downhill, like the guts had been taken from Josiah Berkeley. He no longer treated the people of Berry Edge as his extended family, he no longer provided seaside trips in the summer for the children or parties in the winter for his men and their families. Margaret Berkeley had sat on councils and committees, helped those who needed her. Even the lowest, most feckless families in Berry Edge had known that the Berkeley family was there for them, Josiah to keep the work coming in and the money going out: Margaret to smooth the problems, Rob in the works alongside the men and John, his father's best helpmate, backing him always, clearsighted with new ideas and new ways.

The structure had collapsed, the support was gone. Margaret went daily to her son's grave, Josiah often took to his bed with small ailments that he would once have shrugged off. The works suffered, the people saw that the heart had gone from Berry Edge. Houses were not maintained, work was no longer well done. Berry Edge lost its reputation for turning out fine steel. It was as though the self-respect and motivation had left when John died.

Michael had heard that Rob was coming back. He had expected the same cowed young man who had left, but

Rob had walked into that pub and there was everything about him that exuded success and prosperity. His hands had seen no work for many a long day, Michael thought, he was nothing to do with Berry Edge, his neat shiny hair and his perfect suit. It was as though Rob hadn't aged at all, but the men in the pub were ill dressed, ill housed, older and tired. They had lost their self-respect. They were living in this dirty, worn, down at heel place on short time without comfort of any kind while Rob was tall, slender and sleek, good looking and rich. All Michael had wanted to do was push a big fist into his face. Rob had done well, Michael could see by his clear grey eyes. He did not belong here any more and he had no right to come back here and flaunt the satisfaction of his existence in other people's faces. The worst thing was that he seemed to think he had a place here, a right.

If Michael's own face hadn't hurt so much he would have smiled. He had forgotten the basics, of how much courage, how much guts it took to achieve that apparently artless perfection. Rob had had ability. Nobody had seen that ability, his parents had been too busy attending to their obedient, pious son to notice, but Michael knew it. The works had been Rob's whole world, even as a child. He had had such plans for it and would bore Michael for hours about how he would alter things when he ran the works, how he would make conditions better for the men. There would be baths and showers and a proper dining room that served good food, sold as cheaply as possible. He would build new houses beside the moor for good clean air and they would have three bedrooms, a bathroom and electricity. There would be better schools and places of leisure and the men would be able to buy their own houses by paying monthly into a building society. He would expand the works with new machinery so that it would all be more efficient and turn out better products. On and on he would talk while Michael lay back in the heather on the moor with his eyes closed. He had tried to point out to Rob that he would never run the works, that John would be given the steelworks at Berry Edge but Rob couldn't see that, he thought that his love for the place would remove all obstacles.

Between then and now, Michael thought Rob had achieved whatever, and more, he had set out to achieve. Michael had never seen a rich man before now. He had seen two tonight and not newly rich, not that kind of flashy rich that some men use to show their achievements; it was way beyond that with a modesty, a sureness, an acceptance of their wealth.

And Michael had underestimated Rob. He could call himself names for that. Twenty years of Berry Edge had put the kind of steel into Rob that no amount of success or prosperity could ever remove. He had knocked Michael across that room with more authority than Michael had ever seen in a man. There was a small part of Michael that was glad, pleased he had come home, warm at his success; but most of him just hated Rob for having loved it all so little in the end that he did not come back sooner. He had let it all rust and decay and fall apart until the people had ceased to complain about the Berkeleys. No one spoke Josiah's name. They did not care that he was dying, that his wife had turned into a shabby shadow who neglected her home and her responsibilities. Many people had left, shops were closed, businesses had shut down. Children went hungry and barefoot in Berry Edge. The back streets were dirty and tumbling down. Men propped the walls outside the houses so often there were dark patches where they would stand, and the women fought a perpetual battle to keep their children clothed and fed on permanent short money.

Robert Berkeley owed a debt to Berry Edge which he could never repay, Michael thought, and his coming back now was just the final insult.

Michael didn't go home, he didn't want to. He was the only one left there now, the girls were up and married and Sean was dead. There was only his mother. Michael hated her. She never sat down. From dawn to dark she scrubbed and polished and cleaned. There was no comfort, there was no sympathy. There was nothing for a man coming back from the pit. She didn't cook because she didn't want to dirty the pans, the fire was never lit in the front room for fear somebody might move a cushion. They lived on small, neat sandwiches with the crusts cut off, and weak tea.

He wanted to leave, often he almost left but she had no one. Her daughters had moved away and didn't visit. She had no friends, only Nancy came to see her. His mother hated Nancy, lovely kind Nancy with the golden hair whom his brother had abused in every possible way. Michael's love for Nancy was the only thing that kept him going and he knew now that she would never love him. She thought he was Sean.

He made his way helplessly to Nancy's house and waited outside for her. He liked her damp, shoddy house. There was always a good fire, there was always hot food, there was always Nancy singing and cuddling her bairns and even though she didn't trust him she would smile and fuss and make tea. He stood back in the shadows and waited for her to come home. It would not be long, the children were to collect and put to bed.

When Nancy got home Michael was standing outside waiting for her.

'I heard all about it,' she said, looking him over for damage. She opened the door, the house was cool, the fire had been banked down all day. She opened it up and lit the lamp, then she looked carefully at him. Bruises were darkening on his face and there was blood.

'Mr Berkeley made a good job of you, didn't he?' she said.

'I was drinking.'

'He came back here to try and help—'

'Help? The place doesn't need help, Nancy, all it needs is a bloody undertaker. He knew when he left what would happen, and now look. Ten bloody years. There was nobody but him to do anything about it. That brother of his, for all his fancy ideas he didn't know half what Rob knew, what the men were called, how the place worked. He could do almost everything. Now look at it, and most of these houses aren't fit for pigs. How could he do it, Nancy, how could he make such a mess of things and then leave and not come back? He's gutless.'

'Are you going to sit down?' Nancy said, and when he did she bathed his face like she had done Rob's, only there was a lot more damage.

'I can't go home like this,' he said roughly when she had finished. 'Can I stay here? I'll sleep on the couch, I won't get in the way or be here in the morning.'

'You aren't fit to go anywhere,' Nancy said. 'He made a mess of your face. Do you hurt anywhere else?'

'Just bruises, nothing serious.'

'Right. I'll go and get the bairns from Vera. Put the kettle on, will you?'

They sat down to eat when Nancy had reheated the stew from the day before. Michael took one mouthful and stopped.

'Something the matter with it?' Nancy said. Sean had been

in the habit of throwing his plate across the room when he didn't care for his dinner. Even William was looking anxiously at Michael.

'It's the nearest thing to heaven, Nancy,' Michael said.

Nancy smiled in relief and William went back to concentrating on his plate.

'Mr Berkeley doubled my wages. We'll have meat every day,' Nancy said.

'Did he now? When was this?'

'Tonight. And there's to be more help.'

'He's probably thinking that you should have had compensation for what happened to Sean.'

'Sean was drunk, Michael, and well you know it, and so were others.'

'They should never have been allowed in the works.'

'He'd already been sent home twice that week for being drunk. What are they supposed to do, smell everybody's breath as they go in?'

'I can see he's made an impression with you already. Who's the other one?'

'That's Mr Shaw. They both talk lovely.'

'What does he do?'

'I don't know. He's rich,' Nancy concluded.

'How do you make that out?'

'Well, when people are just sort of respectable, you know, I mean like those who live in the terraced houses up near the park, they're not like that. The people Vera works for, they treat her awful. Now Mrs Berkeley she treats me nice, but Mr Berkeley and Mr Shaw, they treat me like I'm special.'

'That's just because you're young and bonny.'

'I don't think it is. I think it's because they're real gentlemen. I never saw a real gentleman before. Mr Shaw took the coal bucket off me, he didn't know how a fire lights. You should've seen him trying to do his unpacking. He's never done that, and their clothes . . . I never saw anything like them.'

'Their suits,' Michael said.

'Ooh, yes, lovely. And their shirts. Somebody packed them properly, somebody who knows about things like that. Mr Shaw said the maids live in at his house. He offered to walk me back.'

'I'm glad he didn't,' Michael said.

Nancy gave Michael the back room. It was no hardship, the children slept with her. He stayed the following night too. Nancy panicked during the day. Not that he had been any bother, he had asked for nothing, would have gone off to work without eating. Nancy despised herself for taking Michael in and feeding him, but when he came back that night and asked if he could stay again Nancy wanted to say no and couldn't.

'Just for tonight. I don't want my mother going on at me about this.'

'You should leave home,' Nancy said.

'I can't. I'm going out now. I'll come back not too late and just sleep and I'll be gone in the morning before you get up.'

'Indeed you won't,' Nancy said roundly. 'I promised William you'd read him a story when he goes to bed. And you can get your clothes off and get washed properly, I'm not having any mucky pitmen in my house.'

'Nancy—'

'I've got all Sean's clothes. God knows they fit you,' she said.

Michael might not have been Harry Shaw but he cleaned up a treat, Nancy thought, looking critically at him later. He was thin because the only times he ate much were when he went out and that was probably rubbishy pies and the like, but he really was nice looking. She fed him a big dinner. He didn't criticise anything. He put the bairns to bed while she washed up, and when they sat down afterwards she said, 'You can have Sean's chair, if you like.'

'No, you have it Nancy. You think I'm too much like him already.'

Nancy sat down.

'When I saw you standing outside my door last night my heart nearly stopped,' she said. 'Drunk and fighting. Sean was nice like you are until we got married. After I fell pregnant with our William he never spoke another kind word to me.'

'He was always like that, you just couldn't see it,' Michael said.

'I only had my dad to go on. I didn't know much about men.'

'Your dad was the exception.'

'I didn't know that. I didn't realise your Sean was a good looking nowt or I would never have married him. And there's no good you saying you're nothing like him. I've had your mother around here half a dozen times crying, thinking you've got some lass into trouble.'

'That's just for your benefit. Wait 'til she finds out I slept here, it'll be all over Berry Edge by Thursday.'

'I don't care what your mam says.'

'I know, otherwise I wouldn't have asked to stay.'

'I think I can hear Clarrie crying,' Nancy said, starting to get up.

'Stay there, I'll go,' he said and went.

When Nancy got back from work the following day his mother arrived just as Nancy was sitting the children down for their tea.

'You've got a nice job at Mrs Berkeley's, eh? That lad was a nogood,' Alice said. 'Drove his mother to despair and his father nearly to death after he killed their John. I wouldn't have him back in my house.'

Nancy concentrated on cutting bread for William and said

nothing. It wasn't Rob she was thinking about, it was Michael. She hoped that he wouldn't come back again that night; she was obviously incapable of saying 'no' to a McFadden, and he was so easy. He would eat anything and was complimentary so that she wanted to plan meals. He hadn't gone out the night before for a drink, they had sat by the fire and talked – Nancy didn't remember the last time she had done that with a man – he had brought Clarrie downstairs and rocked her back to sleep.

That morning he had left before she was awake, everything spotless as though he had not been there. The loaf of bread had been smaller but he had cleared up after himself.

As for Rob, he had been a complete surprise to her. She remembered him vaguely as a boisterous young man who worked hard, but he was so genuinely polite, so well spoken, so careful of her and caring, asking her about her wages and her hours and her family circumstances. Rob was obviously the kind of man who could sort things out, Nancy thought, and it was a rare quality. On top of that he was a picture, with enquiring grey eyes and cool elegant manners.

Harry was more open than Rob, he chatted and smiled and his eyes were rather warmer on her than Nancy felt comfortable with, but, since his actual behaviour was very proper, she felt safe to meet his gaze and enjoy his teasing.

Another maid was to be started so that Nancy could go home at Friday teatime and not be there on Saturdays or Sundays. She would have liked to argue with Rob about this because she was convinced the Sunday dinner could not happen without her, but she could tell that he wouldn't tolerate argument from anyone, so she had said nothing and been grateful for his help.

'I understand my Michael spent the last two nights here, Nancy,' Alice said now. 'I thought you called yourself respectable.'

Nancy, to her own annoyance, began to blush under her mother-in-law's harsh gaze.

'You took my Sean and look what happened,' Alice said. 'Michael's all I've got left.'

'It's nothing like that,' Nancy said quickly.

'What is it like then? My son in your bed.'

'He wasn't in my bed!'

'He's a good-looking man, Nancy. There's plenty after him and you know what people will think.'

'I don't care what people think. He got knocked about in a fight, he didn't want you worrying.'

'I worry more when he doesn't come home. I wonder which slut has him in her bed. One of these days he'll get it wrong and have to marry some lass I wouldn't even want in my house. Then what will I do?'

'If Michael had wanted to get married he wouldn't have

waited until now, Alice. He's just a wage packet to you, isn't he?'

'I know about widows,' Alice said, 'young lasses like you who are used to a man in their bed. He's a good wage packet, I don't want you pinching him.'

'Don't worry, I won't be,' Nancy said.

Six

The steelworks at Berry Edge was a shock to Harry. He had never seen such a big business in such a bad way. He and Rob walked slowly around it, to the various shops and mills where the different goods were made for mines, ships and railways. They went into offices where nothing seemed up to date and there were few orders. Rob took Harry around the yards and the different processes, and in all the buildings and grounds, over the railways where the ore came from Spain and the coke came from the various pits around Berry Edge, which the works owned and where the coal was made into coke. Harry found from the beginning that he loved the way the different processes were carried on and how it all meshed together: the ores from different parts of the world blended red, the coke being brought in from the mines, the melting troughs, the openhearth processes, the way that it took so many hours to produce the steel. He liked to watch it being tapped out into ladles and into ingot moulds and seeing it cool and solidify. He liked the care that was taken to make sure that it was the right temperature and the right consistency. He liked to watch the steel running white, orange, red and blinding. He liked the sparks which flew in all directions when the men were making the steel. It was almost like the day he had stolen into the kitchen as a child and watched the cook making cakes, the various ingredients added and mixed to change texture and colour and consistency, finally poured out into tins and put into the oven; except that no cake had ever been so white and so perfect and so exciting to him as when the steel poured in a sleek white stream into the moulds.

There was an air of defeat hanging over the place; there were not enough orders, there was not sufficient work. Michael McFadden had been right, Harry thought. It was almost a graveyard. The men had lost heart. They were often absent or careless about their work. They took no pride in it because there were no management skills here, there was nobody to make it cohesive. Harry was glad that his father was not there, he hated more than anything in the world to see incompetence.

Rob was quiet as they walked, watched and studied, and Harry wondered what he was thinking. There was between himself and the men a huge gap of time and respect which could possibly never be bridged, and the fact was that it should have been taken care of all along by a series of skilled and educated men who would have brought the foundry on and even propped it, while the old man was ill and probably before that. The workforce had been let down like a country estate that Harry had once seen, where the son had been killed in a riding accident and the old man had drunk himself to death. It was a kind of monument to heartbreak and despair, as though it was a fist shaken in God's face, a giving up of the worst kind.

If Josiah Berkeley had run the place efficiently, Harry thought, there would have been no need for Rob to come home. Perhaps the old man had done it on purpose, perhaps he had even run it down because he had known how much love Rob had had for this place. Perhaps he had even hated his second son sufficiently to destroy it so that he would come back and see the ruins, which the tragedy he had brought on them had made.

Rob retreated into a silence so complete over those first few days that Harry was afraid of a gulf between the two of them, such as had not been there since they first met.

At first Rob wouldn't talk, but Harry persisted. Finally, within the big scruffy office put aside for the foundry manager, Rob sat in the chair behind the desk and Harry sat on the empty desk, since there was nowhere else to sit. As Rob brooded, Harry said, 'It needs an awful lot of money, my father was right, don't you think? Too much money. What are you going to do, bankrupt yourself over it?'

'Probably.' Rob looked up. It was the first time he had

looked straight at Harry for days. 'You don't have to stay. Go back to Nottingham.'

'You need financial help. A lot of your money is tied up—'

'I'm going to untie it.'

Harry shook his head.

'I have to do this,' Rob said.

'You don't have to, Robbo. You can take loyalty too far. Why don't we just go home?'

'I can't. You go.'

'I'm not going anywhere. I've only just got away. Besides, I have money—'

'No! I won't let you do that.'

'I want to do it.'

'No.'

'You can't ask Awkward Features for any. He'll just tell you to bugger off, and if you go down he'll laugh in your face. It's worse than you thought it was, isn't it?'

'Yes, and I don't want you mixed up in this. Times are hard in this industry. You'd be much better off in Nottingham building bridges and making bicycles. They're sure markets.'

'Well, at least you didn't tell me to go back and make lace. Am I meant to be grateful?'

'You don't like it here. If you put your money into it you'd be stuck.'

'If I don't put my money into it you're going to be stuck.'

'I'll manage.'

'You should let it go, speaking professionally.'

'I would if I could.'

'You're as bad as Vincent,' Harry said.

It was Saturday. If he had been at home Harry would have been getting ready to go out, but nobody said anything. He prowled the house. It was early evening, they had just come back from work. Rob had taken to using his bedroom like an office, since his parents sat in the living room during the late evening now that Mr Berkeley had begun to venture downstairs a little. He had yet to speak to Harry, even though Rob had introduced them, and it was difficult for Harry not to wish that the old man was ill enough to stay upstairs where nobody but his wife could see his scowls and put up with his rudeness.

There seemed nowhere to be. Harry felt he could hardly go downstairs. Reluctantly he opened Rob's bedroom door. Rob was sitting at a table by the window, even though there was no light from it. The day had been dark since one o'clock, cold and damp. The fire burned merrily enough and Rob was going through some papers he had brought back from the office. He didn't look up or acknowledge Harry in any way.

'Let's go into Durham,' Harry said.

Rob stopped then and looked up briefly.

'Why?'

'It's Saturday. I haven't had a drink in a fortnight and even you must be tired of working by now, we've done nothing else. Let's go out.'

Rob looked up again and this time suspiciously. They knew each other too well, Harry thought with a sigh.

'You've made some kind of arrangement, haven't you?'

'No.'

'What then?'

'Nothing, I just want to go out.'

'For a drink?'

'Are you getting hard of hearing? I said so, didn't I?'

'You can't have met a woman already. You haven't been here long enough.'

'No.'

'So?'

'So . . . when I went to that meeting in London with Hardisty last month he said that he comes up here on business occasionally and that there is a woman living in Durham called Susannah Seaton. She is very beautiful and she sells her favours very, very expensively. She doesn't work on Saturdays.'

'You've saved your time by not going then, haven't you?'

'I thought she might make an exception.'

'Go then.'

'I can't go on my own.'

'You can hardly expect me to come with you.'

'I doubt she works alone. Come on, Rob.'

'Certainly not.'

'Why not?'

'I don't buy women.'

'It isn't a sale, it's just a kind of loan. You can borrow her for the evening.'

'I don't want to borrow her, thank you.'

'Are you sure?'

'Certain.'

'How long is it since you had a woman?' Rob glared at him so much that Harry almost retreated. 'Don't go all northern on me. You haven't spoken a civil word in a week. I know it's difficult—'

'You don't know anything!'

'I know one thing. If you don't stop acting like you've gone into a monastery you'll end up marrying some stupid money-grabbing little bitch just because you can no longer resist putting your hands up her skirt.'

Rob said nothing and for so long that Harry held up both hands in appeal.

'I can't go into Durham on my own, can I?'

'I am not going to bed with some woman I don't care about who doesn't care about me, who goes to bed with men for money. It's disgusting.'

'Christ, Rob, there's a halo forming over your head.'

'Shut up!'

'You've never done that, have you?'

'No, I haven't.'

'That's because you never needed to. You talk about your

brother, about how he never did anything but work, about how dull and religious he was. You're going just like him. We used to have fun—'

'Sarah's dead!'

'Two years, Rob. Two bloody years. How much longer are you going to pretend that she's coming back?'

Rob grabbed Harry and slammed him up against the nearest wall.

'You devious bastard!'

'Go on then, hit me. You blame everybody. You enjoy knocking people on to the floor. It's the only thing that makes you happy.' And Harry wrenched free and walked out.

He went to his own room. The fire was burning in there too. Every time he thought about his sister a coldness pervaded his heart, sickness hit his stomach, emptiness flooded his brain. He could no longer think that she was there or that she had just gone away and would come back to them as Rob did. He had tried to pretend that there was nothing the matter, that things would go on as they had, but now that he was not in Nottingham it was obvious to him that things would never be normal again. There was a noise at the door. He didn't even turn around. Rob shut the door and then he said, 'I'm sorry.'

'No, you're right. I am a devious bastard.'

'Let's go out,' Rob said. 'We'll have a drink.'

*

It was bitterly cold in Durham and Harry soon regretted having insisted on coming here. Rob didn't seem to want a drink, he had nothing to say, he had let himself be talked into it because he felt the debt of bringing Harry north to this place, making him feel obliged to invest time and money. He even felt guilty over his house and family and their inhospitality, Harry knew. After one drink at the pub in the market place Harry suggested moving on. They walked down Silver Street and on to Framwellgate Bridge and there Rob stopped. It was too cold for standing around, Harry thought, but he didn't say anything.

'Don't you want another drink?' he said after a minute or two.

'This was where John fell in,' Rob said.

'How do you know?'

'What?'

'How do you know? You were in the pub over there.'

'About here, people said.'

'We don't have to have another drink, Rob,' Harry said, regretting the whole thing entirely by now. 'We can go.'

'I don't want to go to Berry Edge. I wish I'd never come back here. You have no idea how much I hate it. I want to be back in Nottingham with Sarah.'

He spoke so softly that Harry could only just hear him.

'I miss her every minute, every second. I still can't believe that she's dead. I feel as though nothing in my life is worth having, nothing at all and it's not just . . . it's not just that I miss her. I want her. I want her so much I think I'm going to die of it sometimes. I can hardly remember what she feels like or tastes like. It's like being locked up and left to starve to death. Nothing can fill it up, food doesn't or drink, or work or friendship, or anything.'

Harry leaned back against the bridge, partly so that he couldn't see the murky depths when John Berkeley had drowned.

'Can I say something?'

'What?'

'Why don't you go to bed with somebody else?'

'You think that's the answer to everything.'

'No, I don't. You can't betray her by doing it and as for betraying a memory, I think that's not possible. You're alive. Don't you sometimes think that it's just another woman's arms around you that you might want?'

'No.'

'Are you sure?'

'No.'

'Did you think you might find somebody else?'

'Straight away. I thought I had to, I thought I couldn't bear not to but I didn't. Every woman I meet is just a big disappointment. I can't see them properly any more for want.'

'But you wouldn't go to a whore?'

'No.'

'Not even once.'

'Harry—'

'All right. Pretend I didn't suggest it. You nearly broke my head earlier on. I do know when people have had enough.'

'Do you?'

'We can go back to Nottingham, any time you like.'

'Warm bedrooms, good food, wine that makes you think of Paris.'

'Oh, don't. The beer's good here. Let's go and have another pint.'

Rob hesitated.

'Where did you say she lives?'

'What?'

'This woman.'

'Just over the river,' Harry said, nodding in the direction of the houses whose lights burned across from the cathedral and castle.

'Maybe we could go and see. Could we just go and see?'

When the doorbell rang Claire was downstairs making some tea.

'Claire!' Susannah shouted. 'Answer that, will you?' and she went back to her book. It was a cold, wet, late November evening and she was glad to be sitting by the fire. She heard the door opening, she heard voices and then Claire's footsteps on the stairs. She came in with an envelope in her hand.

'Got two men in the hall and this,' she said, proffering the envelope.

'Two men? What is this, a railway station? You didn't invite strangers into the house?'

'One of them had this letter. He wanted you to read it.'

'They're not stealing the silver while you're up here, are they?'

She opened the letter and read it. It was from a wealthy London businessman. She rarely saw him, but two or three times a year he wrote very politely asking if he could call. He paid well, he brought her expensive presents and he had written now to ask if she would be kind enough . . . and so on. Susannah sighed.

'What are they like?'

Claire pulled an approving face.

'Real class,' she said.

'Well, I suppose. Old?'

Claire laughed.

'Fairly decrepit,' she said. 'One of them's more friendly than the other.'

'Oh Lord. All right, send me the awkward bastard.'

Claire went off downstairs. Susannah discarded her book and sat by the fire. She listened to his footsteps on the stairs, listened for the slow plodding sound of age and was mystified. She heard him walk into the room, and let him close the door before she looked up. Men always stared and Susannah knew without any immodesty how beautiful she was, so she deliberately didn't look up until they were in front of her. She knew what to expect because they were all alike basically:

greedy-eyed, fifty, fleshy, self-important because they were rich successful men who could afford her. They were boring, married and needed nothing from her other than the gratification which her beautiful body could give them. Sometimes they didn't even need that, sometimes they couldn't manage that. Mostly it was pure vanity that sent them to her. They even thought that she liked them and what they did to her.

He said, 'How do you do?' in a flat, polite voice and Susannah looked up, ready to be whatever he wanted, and then she couldn't remember what she was supposed to say or do. If he was thirty he didn't look it, tall and slender, and she knew immediately that he was very rich because only the very rich would have dared to dress that plainly. He wore no ornament of any kind, not a ring, not a watch, nothing but a very dark suit so expensive that it made Susannah's fingers want to touch it; and a white shirt. Men's eyes gave them away and Susannah had seen greed and lust and want and excitement in them, but his eyes were as cool and grey as the river beyond the window and told her nothing.

She was on her feet now, though she hadn't been conscious of getting up. He was taller than Susannah and she was quite tall for a woman.

'Good evening. I'm Susannah Seaton.' She held out her hand and he took it and smiled.

'Robert Berkeley. I hope I'm not intruding.'

His voice didn't betray his origins. Susannah knew how to treat men, they were usually so eager, clumsy, nervous or over-confident, revealing themselves for what they were, ignorant about women, their needs overwhelming their intelligence. She despised them all, though she had learned not to hate them. She made them pay dearly for what they had. With their money she had rented this big house which overlooked the Wear and furnished it sparingly with beautiful things. She bought clothes and books and wine, the best food, telling herself that she and Claire deserved all those things.

The men she took now she had selected very carefully indeed. She was half inclined to tell this one that he couldn't stay because she had never taken a man her own age into her bed – it worried her – but then Hardisty would be offended and Hardisty was too valuable to lose. She tried to think what young men might be like and couldn't, and then she had a sudden desire to find out what he was like, whether he was just as selfish and uneducated as the others. He would have to be to get so far so young, he would have to be ruthless and dangerous and ready to cut the ground from under other people's feet, and he didn't look anything like that.

'Come near the fire,' she said. 'Isn't it a shocking night. Too cold to be outside.'

He drew nearer and Susannah didn't know what to say.

'Would you like some wine?' she said, escaping across the room.

'Yes, please.'

Susannah decided to be bold. She gave him the wine,

looked straight at him and said, 'Is it something special that you want?'

'Special?'

'Yes.'

'Yes, you,' he said.

Susannah was rather pleased about that. She led him into the other room, the bedroom which had a huge bay window and looked across the river, and by firelight she lit candles. It was a plain room with a big bed and good but not heavy oak furniture. She drew the curtains around the windows, reflecting that although she was wearing ordinary everyday clothes, no make up, no perfume, she was wearing the kind of silk and lace frothy underwear which men liked.

Susannah went to him, touched him, just put her fingertips on the front of his shirt to see what he would do and he gathered her into his arms and kissed her very gently on the mouth. Susannah was astonished. Men never did that and she never let them. They came to her to slake their hungers, often without any thought or any preliminaries. They did not come to her to kiss her sweetly on the mouth like that. He sensed her reluctance and stopped.

'I've got it wrong already,' he said ruefully.

Susannah was completely disarmed. She didn't know what to say.

'You'd better tell me right now if there are other things I'm not allowed to do. I don't want to be thrown out, it's too cold.'

'It isn't that, it's just that people don't.'

'Don't they? And I was so sure that it was the place to start. Forgive me, I'm a beginner.'

There was a carefully controlled hunger in him, but even when she gave herself to him freely and pressed against him it didn't alter anything in the way that she would have imagined. Part of Susannah waited for him to lose control so that she could dislike him. When he didn't she tried to make him do so. The embrace became a battleground to her. Her underclothing was one of Susannah's weapons but although he caught his breath at the sight of her body it still didn't make him grab at her. She began to realise that this was not a battleground to him and never had been. He didn't understand such a thing. She would have bet anything that he had never bedded a woman he didn't love and therefore didn't know how to. He treated her as though they were lovers. Susannah had not been treated in such a way in her life. It was a kind of respect she had not met. This man knew nothing of whores, he knew nothing of use and rejection. He made love to her. Worse still her body responded to the kisses and caresses of his mouth and hands. Susannah's body went completely out of control as it had never done before. She was horri-fied. Words formed in her mind which had never been there, soft encouraging lovers' words escaped her lips, and the kind of cries which she silenced for shame. Mindless pleasure was something Susannah had not experienced;

her whole being was totally concentrated on what they were doing.

Susannah had been a shock to Rob. He had had visions of prostitutes in dirty little side streets, and he had seen others on the streets of various cities. None of them had ever looked anything like Susannah Seaton. To begin with she was beautiful. She was, Rob thought honestly, more beautiful than any woman he had ever seen. Also, she was his type physically, she was like Sarah had been, tall, dark with a neatly rounded figure and intelligent brown eyes. She had worn an expensive white dress, very little jewellery. She looked a woman of taste and breeding. She looked like a lady. He could not believe it.

He had tried to be natural and not to stare, but the idea that she might actually take off her clothes and let him have her seemed totally unreal until she led him into the bedroom which overlooked the river. A fire had burned cosily. She had smiled and talked softly, and as she had done so Rob began to want her as he thought he had never before in his life wanted anybody. He realised then that Harry was right. He was young and needed a woman in his arms. Part of him was sorry to admit it, ashamed to indulge a weakness but she undressed for him, encouraged him, gave herself to him, and even afterwards Rob couldn't be sorry. He had made himself be aware that she was not

Sarah, that would have been something he could not have forgiven himself, but he found that he didn't need to. He even felt happy briefly, not the kind of happiness he had ever known when he was married, just like a pale ray of sunshine on a long rainy day to remind him that there was still something to be gained from life. He had watched her. She had taken down her hair. The bedlinen was white and her hair was black. Her skin was like milk. She had smiled at him and he had known again that feeling of joy: in spite of what had happened he was still alive. He didn't have to feel guilty that he was happy here just for a few moments when she smiled at him, held out her arms to him. Even more important than having her was the way that she put her arms around him. In many wild moments after Sarah had died he thought that nobody would do that again, and that he would never want them to.

There was not enough room in the bed for Susannah to scorn herself openly. She knew that she couldn't turn away from him or let her face show anything. He was too intelligent, he would see. He was silent. Usually men wanted to know how brilliant they had been and Susannah always told them. Sometimes they wanted to talk or sleep or have a glass of wine, even do it again straight away or at least try, as though it was a matter of mathematics and the score was important. Susannah lay with her arms around him for a few minutes, and then he moved away, glanced at her and said, 'What was the book you were reading when I came in?'

That was new, Susannah thought, conversation about books in bed.

'It's a novel by Dickens called *Great Expectations.*'

He began to laugh. Susannah was astonished. She propped herself up on one elbow and watched him. There was never laughter in her bedroom, not that kind anyway, not genuine amusement.

'Is that what you have, Susannah, great expectations of the men who come here?'

'Heavens, no, never,' she said. He seemed to think that was even funnier, and she knew immediately that laughter was the most important thing she had given him that evening.

He stayed. Susannah went to sleep in his arms, something else she had not done before. It was so comfortable. When the daylight came she opened her eyes and he was dressed and standing by the window, looking out over the river at the castle and the cathedral. Winter sunlight was pouring into the room in the late morning. She didn't move, but he sensed that she was awake and said without turning around, 'I'd forgotten how beautiful the view was.'

'Most men prefer the view inside the room,' she said, smiling, and he turned around at that.

'I didn't say that I preferred it,' he said, and went back to her. She held out bare arms which she fastened around his neck and when he put both arms around her she clung on.

'Don't leave.'

'I have to.'

'Come back to bed.'

'I have to go.'

Rob kissed her on the forehead and then her face and all the way down the front of her neck.

'Next Saturday?' he asked.

'Saturday, yes.'

'Go back to sleep,' and he kissed her again and left.

Harry had woken in his favourite position, warm against a young woman's soft breasts. From somewhere he could hear church bells calling the people to Sunday service. He remembered that he was in Durham and that all he had to look forward to was Rob's dark, gloomy house, his ugly mother and another of the plainest dinners in the world. He wouldn't get a drink with his dinner and at the end of the day all there was was a lumpy bed.

He drew back and looked at her. She was very pretty, quite fast asleep. He kissed her awake and then into his arms.

When he left Rob was waiting outside.

'Been there long?'

'Just a minute or two.'

'Let's go and find some breakfast,' Harry said, 'this kind of thing makes me hungry.'

At the nearest hotel there was coffee and eggs and bacon and toast and honey. Harry glanced across the table.

'You're not eating. Wasn't it a good idea after all?'

Rob grinned suddenly. Harry hadn't seen the light in his eyes for a long time and smiled back, pleased.

'Like that, was it?'

'Oh God, Harry, she is so beautiful. I could almost have believed she wanted me there, she was so good. She's dark like Sarah.'

When they had eaten they walked a little way on to Elvet Bridge and stopped there, looking down at the ducks that were paddling near the edge. Snow began to fall.

'I hate Christmas,' Rob said.

'Don't you find that everybody over the age of eighteen does?'

'What was the other girl like?'

'Nice. They're always nice. I always like them. I wish that just once I could meet somebody and think, "God, yes, that's her," the way that you did with Sarah. I'd like that.'

'It'll happen,' Rob said.

'I don't think it will. I've been getting out of women's beds on Sunday mornings for so long now I don't know what I'd do if I got married. I'd have to pretend I had an appointment and leave.'

Rob smiled. Harry put an arm around him.

'Did you ask to see her again?'

'Saturday.'

'Good. Do you think we'll be having cabbage again for dinner?'

'I expect so.'

'And that yellow stuff?'

'That's turnip.'

'No, it isn't. Turnips are tiny white and purple delicate things that look like snowballs on your plate and melt on your tongue. That stuff is what you give cows.'

'What in the hell do you know about farming? You come from London.'

'I know turnips when I see them, and those aren't,' Harry said.

When Rob had gone Susannah lay down for a while, but she didn't sleep. The sunlight was dazzling where Rob had pulled back the curtains to enjoy the view. She got up and washed and dressed and went downstairs to the kitchen. Claire had just lit the kitchen fire.

'We ought to get a maid,' Susannah said for perhaps the hundredth time.

'I don't want nobody talking about us. We'll manage. Do you want some tea?'

They sat by the kitchen fire and drank their tea.

'I wish I could make that much money every Saturday night,' Claire said. 'I'd give up the rest.'

'Generous?'

'I think he likes women.'

'And you liked him?'

'Some poor cow will marry him and never know a moment's peace for the rest of her life.'

Susannah laughed.

'What was the other one like?' Claire said.

'I don't think he ever paid for it before. I think he might be married.'

'He wouldn't be coming to you if he was. Can you imagine being married to a pet like that and telling him you've got a headache? I'd never have a headache again.'

'If I could have him – I mean if I could really make him want me, I could get rid of the others.'

Claire looked hard at her.

'A rich man's mistress? You could have had that before.'

'I didn't want to then.'

'Do you think he might do that? I'd be happy to sleep on my own for the rest of my days.'

'If he'd never paid for it before there must be a good reason for him doing that now, don't you think, Claire?'

'Did you like him?'

'Not particularly, but he's young and rich and good looking. I'm so tired of smug, fat, old men.'

Claire was looking at her.

'You do like him,' she said.

Susannah gave in.

'Oh Claire, nobody made me feel like that before. When he took me into his arms . . .'

'That's very dangerous,' Claire said.

'I know, and I know that really he's probably just like all the rest. He couldn't have made a lot of money without being selfish and ruthless and horrible.'

'You shouldn't see him again,' Claire said, and sighed. 'All that money though. It would be a shame to waste it.'

Seven

Rob's father began to get better so Faith and her parents were invited to dinner. Faith didn't want to go. She hadn't seen him since he had come home, she had deliberately stayed well away from the house.

'I don't think I can bear to be in the same room,' she told her mother.

'You only have to be polite to him for an hour or two, Faith,' her mother said. 'It won't kill you.'

Faith put on her oldest dress. It was blue and mended. It had the kind of big sleeves which were no longer fashionable. It had been John's favourite dress. She put up her hair in the most severe style and then she walked across and down the street with her parents, with thumping heart and uneven breath.

Nancy did not open the door. There was a new maid whom Faith did not recognise. Rob's father and mother were sitting by the fire, and in the room were the two most stylish men Faith had ever seen. She began to wish that she could have changed her hair, her dress and several other things.

Both of them were tall and dark and they stood up as she walked into the room. One of them had eyes which were the nearest thing to chocolate, and the other had smoky eyes and, but for that, looked exactly as John Berkeley had looked the last time that she had seen him alive. He was John to her, she wanted to run across the room and throw herself into his arms. Faith remembered Rob careless and laughing, she didn't remember him like this. He said hello quite naturally and introduced her to Harry Shaw. They were both so well bred and easy that Faith didn't know what to say. She sat opposite Rob at dinner and didn't lift her eyes. She wished more than anything that he would turn back into the horrible person she felt sure he was. It was as though some evil fairy had cast a spell and Rob had died and John was sitting across the table, eating his dinner with total unconcern. She tried to talk to Harry. She watched him approach his plate carefully.

'Aren't you hungry?' she said.

'It's the cabbage,' he said. 'It's such a pedestrian vegetable, don't you find?'

'People around here are glad of good food. Are you from Nottingham, Mr Shaw?'

'I'm from London. We live in Nottingham most of the time though we do have a house in London.'

'And what do you do?'

'We make things, like you do here. We manufacture goods. My father and I are engineers. He builds railways, at least bits of them, and bicycles and . . . other things.'

'He must be very clever.'

'He's a cantankerous, demanding old fool as a matter of fact, but he had a teacher once who called him a genius and he's never recovered.'

Faith was shocked again at Harry's free way of talking. No man that she knew would have been as rude as that about his own father. She thought it was particularly tactless when Rob's father was so ill because of Rob.

'What does he think about you coming here?' she said.

'Not much.'

'If Robert had come home earlier it wouldn't have been as bad as this.'

Harry, wisely Faith thought, said nothing to that and her cheeks burned for a moment or two because she had not meant to say it.

After dinner the older people went off to the sitting room to have tea, but Harry and Rob seemed inclined towards the little back sitting room where the maids would have sat, had there been any maids. Here Theresa, the new help, had left coffee for them. It had obviously become something of a ritual and, since Harry was polite enough to ask Faith to go with them, she went.

Faith was determined to have Rob as she had imagined

him and not as her shaking hands told her he was now. When he gave her coffee she said, 'I was beginning to think you weren't going to come back at all.'

'I wasn't.'

'What about your father and all the people of Berry Edge who would be put out of work?'

'I didn't think that was anything to do with me.'

'It's very much to do with you. If it hadn't been for you none of this would have happened.'

Harry sat forward in his chair.

'Miss Norman—'

'It's all right, Harry, I know what Faith thinks of me.'

'After ten years?' Harry said.

'It was John's birthday last week.'

'I didn't forget,' Rob said softly.

Faith looked down into her coffee cup.

'You've altered,' she said.

'You haven't. I thought I might have come back here and found you married with children—'

'That would have been easy for you, wouldn't it?' Faith looked at him suddenly. 'Is that what you tried to think when you were away? That everything was all right, possibly even that the accident had never happened, that you and John had not quarrelled, that he had not drowned, that John and I were married and happy here?'

'I just hoped that you could have gone on by now.'

'I couldn't marry anyone, not after John. You should know

that. The only person in the whole world who is anything like him is you, and it's so cruel because you only look like him, you're nothing like him at all, you were always – always jealous of him. He was everything you weren't, kind and generous and clever and . . .' Faith ran out of words. Harry was startled but Rob wasn't looking at her. When he did his grey eyes were icy.

'How long have you had that dress?' he said. 'I think I remember it.'

Harry Shaw closed his eyes for a second. Faith didn't understand why, or Rob's question.

'What?' she said.

'Whatever possessed you to wear it? Are you frightened in case some man might think you look pretty?'

Faith nearly choked.

'I considered over dinner,' Rob said, 'that no woman who thought any good of me could have appeared in such a dress.'

Faith burst into tears.

'I hate you!'

'My dear girl, where are your manners? You didn't really wait ten years to say that to me? I don't understand what you're doing as an old maid. The whole thing is quite ridiculous. My mother tells me you go to his grave every week and put fresh flowers there. It's as though you're keeping him alive with your good works and your dowdy looks—'

'Dowdy?' Faith stared at him through her tears.

'John's dead, Faith, and all your misguided loyalty will never bring him back.'

'I don't know how you dare speak his name. He's dead because of you. It was your fault, you did it!' Faith was on her feet now. What she wanted more than anything in the world was to go over and hit him so that he wouldn't be John. This was exactly the way that John would have reacted if anyone had attacked him verbally, Faith felt sure, all intelligent and cold. Rob wouldn't have. He would have laughed and yelled and maybe even hit her before now like he had when they were children. Rob had had a seriously bad temper, and the fact that she was a girl had not made much difference.

'I never liked you,' was all she could think to say.

'I never liked you either. You were always in the way. Our John would never play with me because you were there.'

Faith hadn't heard the familiar use of John's name in years and it sounded very strange.

'You sat me in a puddle once.'

'Faith, if there was one near enough I'd do it now.'

Faith actually smiled. She tried not to. Rob came to her.

'Won't you be friends with me?'

'No.'

'Not even bad friends?'

'I can't,' Faith said, and she ran from the room.

When she had gone Harry poured some more coffee. Rob refused. Harry didn't drink his.

'It's funny how it works,' Rob said. 'I hated him but I miss him so much. It's like a lost opportunity, we could have been different, should have been but we weren't. It's almost as though that was how it had to be, like it was mapped out—'

'I thought you didn't believe in fate.'

'I don't, at least I didn't. I don't know now. I have the feeling she's crying her eyes out in the hall. Go and look, will you?'

Harry put down his coffee cup and saucer and ventured into the freezing dimness of the hall. Sure enough, there she was, standing in the draught by the front door, crying into the coats. He had no idea what to do. Sarah would never have made such a performance, but then Sarah had never had to face such a thing, and his only experience of loss was his sister.

Faith was not the kind of woman he was used to. His mother was open about her hurts and feelings and other women were too remote for him to be concerned. Faith had been quite a surprise to Harry. He couldn't have imagined a brother of Rob's falling in love with and wanting to marry such a skinny, plain, badly dressed woman. She was offensive, unmannerly, pious, sanctimonious and she had attacked one of the few people whom he loved, but she was standing there crying and hanging on to the coats, her face buried in the material, with no regard that anyone should hear her. Harry ventured nearer.

'Perhaps you would like to go home, Miss Norman?' he said.

The crying stopped instantly, silenced in embarrassment

because she had suddenly realised that he was there. She cleared her throat hard.

'No, I . . . no, really I . . . it's just across the way.'

'Is this your coat?'

Faith moved back to see the one he indicated and wiped her face ineffectually with her fingers.

'No.'

'This one?'

'No, it's . . . it matches my dress.'

'Oh yes.' Harry didn't look at her. He well knew by now that women were made ugly by crying and Faith was bad enough to begin with. He didn't want to see her spotty face and red-rimmed eyes, even less her moist nose, but he helped her on with her coat and was quite surprised. Her wet eyes were a shade between green and brown that only an unimaginative man would have called hazel, her eyelashes were darkened with tears, her mouth was pink and trembling and her nose was her most attractive feature to begin with so it wasn't a problem.

Harry put on his own coat and went with her. The night was icy. He put her hand through his arm without asking, the streets were treacherous. She fastened her hands around his arm and he felt in those seconds a real desire to protect her which he had never felt before for another person. He didn't think he had ever met another person who needed protecting. His mother had his father, his sister had had Rob and all the girls he knew were from families who looked after them. This woman was small and hurt and vulnerable. When they reached her front door he turned her to him.

'You won't cry any more, will you?'

'I'm so ashamed. What must you think of me?'

Faith smiled just a little and Harry thought her eyes were really quite beautiful.

'I'm sorry,' she said before she went inside.

Harry walked slowly back down the bank the short way. There were sounds of revelry from the pub at the bottom of the bank. Rob was standing by the fire in the little back room.

'If you ever take up sword-fencing you'll kill somebody,' Harry said as he walked in.

'She thought I was John.'

'What?'

'I look like John.'

'Very like him?'

'Almost more like him than he did as far as Faith's concerned now. John looked older than he was and, God forbid, I think I look younger.'

'And what was that meant to be, disillusionment?'

'What was I supposed to do?'

'I don't know. God almighty, Rob, that dress. It has a matching coat, you know.'

'It doesn't, does it?'

'I've got some brandy in my room,' Harry said, 'I could go and get it.'

'It's the best idea you've had all day,' Rob said.

Eight

Rob had forgotten what his home was like, the house seemed so small, the people so intolerant and insular. He could remember being sent away to school because he had turned into that worst of things, 'an impossible child', and wanting to come back to Berry Edge so much that he thought he would die if he didn't. How could he ever have loved the foundry and the countryside? He remembered breaking out of school, and the various ways that he had contrived to come home, because he knew that however bad things got he could not live without the town and the moor where he had been brought up. No matter what happened, no matter how often he was beaten and banished or hurt, he would spend his last breath crawling towards the fell that belonged to him.

All that was gone now. There was nothing here that had anything to do with him, and in some ways the life that he had found for himself with Vincent Shaw and his family made coming back here all the more impossible. It didn't seem strange that the mother he hadn't seen for ten years shouldn't want to kiss him or hold him. Ida kissed him and touched him so much that it should have been odd when his own mother did not, but his mother had never touched him. Ida treated him just like she treated Harry. She called him 'young man' when she was angry with him, whereas in fact he had been almost twenty-two when he met her so she had never known him young. Ida was his mother now and he adored her. John had been dead for almost a year when he met the Shaws and Rob was already a different person.

He had travelled a lot that first year, working in various foundries but moving on after a few weeks because there was no reason to stay until he reached Nottingham, and there Vincent Shaw and others were building yet more railways and setting up businesses. Rob was fascinated.

Nottingham was everything to him that Berry Edge was not. The city was so exciting and everybody was in work. They were making lace, stockings and bicycles. There were foundries and factories producing parts for new machinery. Jesse Boot had already overturned not just the pharmaceutical industry but the whole concept of marketing with his new ideas of buying in bulk and selling cheaply to the public. He had changed the face of shopping.

Girls there were independent because they worked in the lace and hosiery factories. He would listen to their confident voices and see their uplifted, laughing faces and be glad.

Nottingham had its slums, it had its back streets, but it was going forward at a great pace and Rob wanted to be there among it all, the hum of a hundred interdependent industries, the people who were making money, the prosperous shops in Angel Row and King Street. Nottingham was all contrasts, woods and fields, busy streets, work and leisure, there were music halls and pubs and places you could take pretty girls dancing. There was the famous Goose Fair in October which had once been a place for farmers to hire help and buy and sell stock, but was now a huge entertainment for the entire area. There were rowing and pleasure boats on the River Trent, cricket at Trent Bridge, new schools and public buildings. Nottingham and its surrounding towns and villages was the place that Rob decided he wanted to stay.

Vincent was an engineer, a successful, flamboyant person who already had a number of businesses. He lived in a big detached house on the outskirts of the city overlooking a park. Rob would have given a great deal to talk to him. He hadn't talked to anybody for a long time other than necessary conversation, but Vincent was clever and educated and had nothing directly to do with the workmen in his foundries and factories. It was one of his biggest failings, Rob thought. Vincent lacked the imagination to see that he kept his workforce poorly in almost every way, and now that Rob had been in so many places he had seen good masters and bad. He knew that although Vincent paid his people fairly he could have done a great deal more for them, and they would have repaid him by working more competently and turning out better goods.

Once a year he invited them to his house. Each winter he provided a party and there Rob went.

He was fascinated by what he had heard about the Shaws, and because they were so prosperous and unconventional the whole town talked about them. It was well known that Ida Shaw, Vincent's wife, had come from a rich, titled family, and that when she married him her family had been shocked because he was so far beneath her. Although his family had been respectable, they were trade, and Vincent was a man who abhorred idleness.

They had a huge London house which had belonged to his wife's parents and from them she had inherited a vast fortune, but Vincent Shaw was the kind of vulgar man who had made his money when he was very young, and it was rumoured that not only did he not care for the aristocratic idlers but that they would have little to do with him. Sarah Shaw, his only daughter, was admired, had come out in London and become engaged to the kind of man her father most deplored. Rob was eager to catch even a glance of any member of the family and he walked slowly around the house taking in everything he saw.

In one of the rooms there was a painting over the fire-place. Rob was drawn to it, having seen it from the hall, and as he went nearer the painting seemed to come alive. It was a country scene, a farmhouse and the fields, a man with a sheepdog and some sheep, quite a simple painting but it reminded Rob so much of the countryside around Berry Edge that he felt sick to go home.

'What are you doing in here?'

Startled by the sharp voice, Rob stepped back and Vincent Shaw came into the room.

'Stealing, are you, boy? Turn your pockets out.'

Rob knew very well that he didn't look his twenty-two years. He was thin, the suit he wore was old and shiny with use, and his hair was too long. Under Vincent Shaw's steel gaze Rob turned out his money and a handkerchief.

'Is that all?' Vincent roared.

'Yes, sir.'

'So you work for me, do you, boy?'

'Yes, sir.'

'And what great service do you render me?'

'I'm a moulder, sir, in the foundry.'

Vincent laughed. Rob watched him.

'A moulder? You're a bloody liar, boy. You're not old enough to use a bloody wheelbarrow. The moulders in my foundries are clever, skilled men, not pathetic little lads. Get out of my house, and keep your bloody hands in your pockets!'

It was cold outside. Rob hadn't eaten anything and it was a long walk back to his lodgings. It snowed. It always snowed, Rob thought. Any time when you'd had enough, it snowed and made things worse.

On the Tuesday of that week he was called into the offices. Rob had never been in the office building and it was sumptuous. Up where the important people were, there was a thick red carpet and chandeliers, and a lot of shiny wood; and above all the rest, at the end of a long corridor, was a huge office with a big desk and a view that seemed to him to take in most of Nottingham. Rob couldn't help but think that Vincent Shaw could have spent less money on his offices and a great deal more on his factories. He stood behind the desk.

'Robert Berkeley,' he said.

Rob felt sick. He didn't understand what he was doing here. Vincent Shaw didn't dismiss his workmen himself and there could be no other reason for his being here. Rob liked Nottingham, he wanted to stay there. All he had now was his work.

'I didn't do it,' he said.

'What didn't you do?'

'Anything. I didn't . . . I didn't do anything.'

'Is somebody accusing you of something? My man in the works who tells me these things tells me that you are in fact a moulder, that you are not the pathetic little runt I thought you were. In fact you even seem bigger than I thought you were. I understand that you are the best moulder we possess. I apologise, Robert Berkeley, from the bottom of my rather shallow soul. Where did you learn?'

'Durham, sir.'

'And you speak the Queen's English, other than that appalling accent. How interesting. What have you run from, I wonder? A woman? A baby? A prison sentence?'

'I left home.'

'And what did you do to occasion this leaving?'

'My brother died. We had an argument, a fight. He drowned. People blamed me.'

Vincent Shaw said nothing. Rob listened to the silence in the room and he thought of his work in Vincent's foundry and the losing of it. He had never told anyone before what had happened, he had not expected that he would tell a man like this, a pompous, unfeeling, bombastic master like Vincent Shaw who would surely dismiss him.

'How long ago was this?'

'A year. I went to Sheffield for a time and then I went to London.'

'And now you're gracing Nottingham's fair city with your presence?'

Rob gave him the requisite number of 'yes, sirs' after that and then he went back to his lodging, packed his things and left. He hadn't been at the station for many minutes when a tall, dark-haired man with a long flowing coat grabbed him by the shoulder.

'Where are you going?' Vincent Shaw demanded.

'The next train.'

'No, you're not. How am I meant to manage without my best moulder? You're coming back with me.'

'Back' meant the Shaw house which he had been so lately dismissed from. There the family were just starting dinner, the smell of food was wonderful. Vincent propelled him in and said, 'This is young Berkeley. He missed his meal last time he was here. Robert, this is my wife, Ida, and my son, Harry, and that exquisite creature at the far side of the table is my daughter, Sarah. Sit down and don't talk with your mouth full.'

Sarah Shaw was everything that any man could ever have wanted in any woman and Rob fell in love with her at that very moment. She was nineteen. Rob had never been in love before, but he recognised it for what it was when it happened. He even felt rather sorry for himself for a few moments. Sarah Shaw was as beyond his touch as though she had been royalty. Worst of all she seemed to like him, in the friendly way which Rob discovered the Shaws had. They were open, sociable people who had many visitors at their house, and that evening, when Vincent and Ida left the room, Sarah and Harry stayed and talked until it was late. Rob had never been in such company before. He liked it. They were educated and enquiring, interested and interesting, well read and well travelled and Harry Shaw was an engineer, not like any rich man's son that Rob had ever seen before.

After that evening Harry called in at Rob's lodging and asked him out and, having discovered that Harry had a liking for his company, Rob went out and had his hair cut and bought a new suit. Harry was careful with Rob too, Rob noted with some amusement. He never took Rob anywhere that he couldn't afford or talked about things in which Rob had no part. Harry smoked and drank and went to Doncaster races and slept with high-class prostitutes, so Rob was told, but two or three evenings a week they just sat in the nearest pub over a drink and talked about work. Rob knew that Harry wouldn't have kept on seeing him if he had been bored.

Harry was kind too; he introduced Rob to those of his friends he thought might be informative, helpful or entertaining, and quite often he took Rob home to dinner or later just for a drink and to sit by the fire.

Sarah was to be married the following spring. That autumn the young man came to Nottingham to see her, and there was a party at the house. Rob had not expected to be invited, but Harry said he wasn't going if there was nobody to talk to, and Lawrence Carlington was said to be bringing friends with him for the weekend.

The evening of the party Rob was quite happy with Harry and his friends until Sarah brought Lawrence over and introduced them. Lawrence turned merry eyes on Rob.

'You're from the north, I understand. My family has pits there. You aren't a pitman of course?'

'No,' Rob said. 'My family has pits and a steel foundry.'

'Pitmen are small like goblins. They never wash, I understand, and they keep coal inside their houses. Very strange.

You must find Nottingham extraordinarily civilised, though of course there are pits here too. Even this is a little far north for my taste. I have told Sarah that after we are married she will have to invite her family to stay with us. The fascination for industrial towns escapes me.'

Rob was watching Sarah Shaw just behind her fiancé. She had blushed quite pink by now.

'Your accent is very interesting. Say something,' Lawrence said.

'Lawrence, you're an offensive bastard. Bugger off,' Harry said.

Lawrence stared at him and then frowned.

'If you weren't about to become my brother-in-law, Harry, I should knock you down for that.'

'Do try,' Harry said.

'Dance with me, Rob,' said a beetroot-faced Sarah.

'I don't know how.'

'Don't be trivial,' she said and grabbed his sleeve.

'You promised me this dance,' Lawrence said.

'You've insulted my guest,' she said and dragged Rob away even as Lawrence protested that he hadn't meant to.

'Don't you really know how to dance? I would have taught you if you'd said. Put your arm around my waist.'

'Are you sure?'

'Certain. You can't dance with me if you don't hold me.'

It was the most delightful way Rob had ever spent a few minutes and probably he reasoned, the closest that he would ever get to Sarah Shaw. She didn't seem to notice him looking at her or holding her because she was concentrating on giving him instructions.

'I don't think you're ever going to be much good at dancing,' she said when the music ended. 'You didn't listen to what I told you. I'm sorry about Lawrence, he really doesn't mean it. My father thinks you're very clever.'

Rob looked at her.

'Your father does?'

'Yes. He's not going to leave you in the foundry. He thinks you'll make a designer. We get big doses of you at mealtimes.'

'How awful,' Rob said.

'I wish he would talk about Lawrence.'

'Lawrence doesn't have anything to prove.'

'He does to my father. My father thinks everyone in the world ought to be an engineer. Lawrence doesn't have to work and Father hates him. It's so silly. His family is horrified that I come from a family that works. I'm socially beneath him. Harry doesn't like him.'

Rob was aware of this. Harry had called Lawrence 'that stupid bastard' just the day before, though not within his sister's hearing.

'It's probably just because they're different. They'll be better later when they get to know each other.'

'There you are,' Lawrence said. 'Don't you know I'm waiting for you?' And he dragged Sarah off into the middle of the room to dance.

'Wondering what she sees in him?' Harry asked as he sauntered over.

'High position, a country mansion, breeding, good looks, education.'

'You left out charm,' Harry said dryly. 'I wonder how long it will be before she comes to her senses. Her wedding night, I shouldn't doubt. Lawrence will have all the finesse of a bull.'

'Don't talk about it.'

'I see. What would you like to talk about?'

'Have you finished with those sketches I gave you?'

'I want my father to see them.'

'He won't be interested.'

'He might. They're just in the library. You can get them. I promised to dance with the lovely Miss Byatt. I'll see you later.'

Vincent was in the library. Rob was surprised. Vincent didn't usually spend much time there.

'Robert,' he said, looking up and beaming approval. 'Enlighten me. What are these?'

'They're mine.'

'I gathered that, yes, that tiny meticulous handwriting is unique.'

'I brought them to show Harry. He said you never use the library. I didn't think you'd mind.'

'I knew it was a mistake to let you spend so much time with my careless son. Do try to keep up. Shall I repeat the question?'

'They're . . . alterations for the bicycle works.'

'And when were you at the bicycle works?'

'I went with Harry.'

'I said, "When",' Vincent repeated sharply.

'Three times lately.'

'Why?'

'Just out of interest. I hadn't seen a factory like that before.'

'And knowing nothing about it you decided that it needed altering?'

'Well, I—'

'Yes or no? I had experts to design that building and set it up. It is considered a model of its kind.'

'I don't think it is. It could be much better.'

'To the point at last. Show me.'

Rob picked up his drawings one by one.

'It's nothing like a good factory should be. Other people have designed much better things. We went and looked. It's cramped, it's dark, it's in the wrong place. Harry said you have a big piece of ground on the edge of the city and it would be ideal for this. You could have big windows like this and glass in the ceiling so that people could see better, making the most of natural light. You could have gardens around it like this so that people could go outside during breaks and have fresh air. There would be a dining room for them, a big room so that they wouldn't be crammed in and perhaps a drying room here where hats, coats and 'shoes could be left in wet weather. These are baths and wash houses.'

'And what's this?'

'Electric lighting.'

'That would cost a fortune.'

'You make a great deal of money and the demand for bicycles is growing. It would be a drop in the ocean. Other people have done these things and they run at a profit, partly because the people who work for them are properly looked after. Some factory owners build good houses, schools, places of leisure. You could do all that, Vincent, if you wanted to. It would pay you to. I've done some figures—'

'Something told me you had,' Vincent said. 'Let me have a look. Come and sit down. Would you like some whisky?'

'No, thank you.'

They sat in big chairs behind the desk and Vincent studied the figures and the drawings. Suddenly he looked up.

'You called me by my first name.'

'I'm sorry—'

'No, I think I like it,' Vincent said.

Vincent took Rob out of the foundry and kept him close. Rob admired Vincent Shaw as he had never admired another man in his life, but it was more than that. Vincent taught him, showed him, educated Rob in all kinds of different ways, but best of all Vincent took his ideas seriously and began gradually implementing them and encouraging other industrialists to do the same.

He took him around the various foundries and factories, and Rob found in Vincent the kind of person he had wanted to find in his father. Vincent encouraged him, praised him, treated him as one of the family. More and more in the evenings because he wanted to talk about work, Vincent took Rob home with him and the Shaws were open about how much they liked him. Ida began to kiss him as he walked in the door, to treat him like she treated Harry. He nearly always stayed for dinner and their house was so comfortable. The meals were good and the conversation was interesting. At weekends when they had dinner parties they invited him, and Rob got to know other people in Nottingham.

Vincent began to pay him much more so that he moved into better lodgings. Rob could not believe his good luck, that people like these accepted him as an equal.

Lawrence was often there, and sometimes Sarah was not because she had gone to stay with him. Rob tried not to think about her. He did not want to hurt anyone, he had learned that lesson well. He pretended to himself and to her that he cared no more for Sarah Shaw than he cared for any other young woman he met.

Her mother took her to London to buy her wedding dress. When Sarah was there Rob was happy. He didn't even have to touch her, just to see her, to talk to her, to be there at the dinner table, to watch her laughter and join in the talk was enough. Rob was happier than he had ever been in his life. The best part of all was when he, Sarah and Harry sat over a big fire late at night, or when the weather grew warmer in the conservatory and finally in the garden until Sarah's wedding was only weeks away. Lawrence even bothered to be polite to Rob and Harry, though Harry said privately that he couldn't bear him, and Rob cared too much for Sarah to like Lawrence.

She seemed to Rob that early summer to become less and less happy. Ida was so concerned that she went to Harry and Rob.

'I can't talk to your father about it because he can't be rational when it comes to Lawrence. I don't know what's the matter with the girl. She says she wants to marry him, he's her own choice, goodness knows he wouldn't have been mine, but she's got less to say than a china doll and she's starting to look like one.'

Harry tried to talk to her.

'I got nowhere,' he said flatly. 'You try.'

'Me? No. You know I can't do that.'

'If you cared about her you would.'

'Harry—'

'Well?'

In the end Rob went looking for her. She was sitting on a swing in the rose garden, wearing a bonnet that would have made any girl look pretty, and a soft white summer dress. It was a glorious June evening. She looked waspishly at him.

'My mother sent you. Really Rob, first Harry and now you. What is this?'

'She's worried about you.'

'I know. Push me.'

'What?'

'Push me.'

'How can I talk to you if I'm behind you?'

'Just do as you're told, Robert.'

So Rob pushed the swing. She complained.

'Higher than that.'

'You'll fall off and break your neck and then you won't be able to get married.'

'Is it anything to do with you?' she said rudely. 'Push me!'

Rob got hold of the swing and stopped it and hauled her off it. She hit him on the arm with one neatly gloved hand.

'What is the matter with you?' Rob said.

Sarah pulled off her gloves and her hat. Half the pins came out of her hair.

'I'm not going to marry him,' she said.

'Have you told your parents?'

'I haven't told anybody. I haven't even told him yet.'

'But why?'

'I don't think that's any of your business, Rob.'

'You have to tell him.'

'I tried to. He just laughed, and who could blame him? He's such an incredible catch.'

'Do you need an incredible catch?'

'Of course I do, I'm an industrialist's daughter, even though my mother is quality. To sit at the top of the heap I need to marry well. Lawrence's family will be relieved. Marrying trade. Dear, dear.'

'And is that what you want?'

'What?'

'The – the top of the heap.'

'There is an extremely ignoble part of me that very much wants that. Unfortunately I couldn't stand the idea of Lawrence in the end. Lawrence thinks the art of conversation is to recount the day's hunting. Having been brought up with my father all I can think of at these times are shockingly sarcastic remarks or the kind of language which would appal a stableboy. And it's very bad form. I ought to have been content to marry well and breed like a dairy cow. I find I don't have the class. I shall be obliged to marry an engineer.'

'Nottingham's full of them,' Rob pointed out. 'What did he do?'

'Why should he have done something?'

'He did though, didn't he?'

'He tried to make love to me.' Sarah looked down at the bonnet in her fingers. 'I didn't realise that I was going to be disgusted. I just couldn't. He called me names, things even I hadn't heard before . . . and some that I had, very insulting with the indication that I was middle-class and extremely small minded and innocent in a – in a very stupid way and then I discovered that he had not . . . that he didn't love me, that he would never love me as my father loves my mother. I was to be useful and made use of to produce heirs, and I knew then what kind of a man my father is, that I wanted someone like that. My father is a good man, mostly, and especially towards my mother. That's what I want. Now I'm going to go and sit on the swing. I want you to push me.'

'I'd be glad to,' Rob said. 'After all, it doesn't matter if you fall off and break your neck now, does it?'

Sarah pulled a face at him.

She sat down again on the swing but Rob didn't push her and she didn't move.

'I think you ought to go and tell your mother.'

'I can't tell her about that.'

'You don't have to say that, just tell her you changed your mind, you don't think he's the right person.'

'She's spent a lot of time on this wedding.'

'Sarah . . .' Rob got down beside her. 'If you married him and then found out you didn't want him it would break your mother's heart.'

Sarah was not listening and proved it moments later by putting one arm around his neck and kissing him.

'Don't just sit there you dolt,' she said, 'kiss me.'

'Your father would kill me if I touched you. You're just upset.'

'You still don't understand, do you? You're the reason I'm not going to marry Lawrence. The minute I saw you I wished I'd never set eyes on him. I tried to convince myself that marrying him was right for me. It seemed so stupid. I told myself that it would pass, that it was just because I was engaged. I'm going to expire if you don't kiss me.'

'Sarah, I've got nothing, nothing to offer anybody.'

'My father says you have the finest mind of any man he ever met.'

'That's not true, he's just an enthusiast for his own discovery.'

'Oh, do shut up and kiss me,' Sarah said, so he did.

Nine

Rob thought a great deal about Susannah Seaton during the six days before he saw her for the second time. It occurred to him uncomfortably again and again that because Susannah was physically similar to Sarah he could be confusing the two, but he decided that it was not so. His wife had been educated, impeccably brought up, cultured, well loved, confident. As far as he could judge Susannah was none of those things.

Each day he wanted her more badly than he had done the day before. The week was like six even though every waking minute was filled with work and important decisions. By the end of the week he could hardly sleep.

He made himself not go early but it was difficult. Up the hill a little way from the bridge and there they were, the steps of Susannah's neat house. Claire answered the door and this time she was smiling and welcoming.

He walked up the stairs just as before and into the sitting

room, and he got a shock. This time she looked what she was. She wore make-up, he could smell perfume, her hair was elaborately dressed and she wore a thin robe on top of what Rob knew was underclothing which would reveal her beautiful body. She came to him and put her arms around his neck and kissed him and then looked at him.

'It doesn't please you? I can change.'

'No, it's fine. It's just that you didn't look like this last week.'

'Last week I wasn't expecting you.'

She led him into her bedroom, and when she took off the robe she was wearing black. Rob had never seen such underclothing on a woman. He wasn't sure he liked the way it made him feel. He had expected this to be something slowly enjoyed, conversation, wine, to wait just a little more because the week had been forever and now he was here with her. He had thought to look at her and admire her and tell her how he had longed for her but the feeling of wanting her was overcoming the other ideas.

She started to undress him and then he began to kiss her and touch her. He thought that it was no wonder she made so much money. She acted as though she was trying to stop herself but couldn't, as though he was the only person in the world she had ever needed or would ever need.

In the world he came from he had been to parties where there were beautiful women, and he had wanted them, but he knew quite well that unless they were unhappily married the women in his social sphere did not let men have them without a wedding ring. There were plenty of married women, there were affairs, but somehow that didn't seem right for him either.

He couldn't believe that this woman was going to let him have her. Even dressed like this, looking and smelling of perfume like the whore she was, she was so beautiful. Her body was soft and flawless and rounded in all the right places. She didn't stop him doing what he wanted to her, she even helped with his clothes and with hers, but he couldn't tell whether any of it pleased her, whether she was just pretending. He had the awful feeling that she was still halfway through her Dickens novel and would have been much happier sitting by the fire reading about Estelle and Pip and not having her body used quite so completely and thoroughly for somebody else's pleasure.

Last week he had been almost too hungry to think about that. This time he tried to be kind, but all he could think was that she was not Sarah, she was not his wife, that she was not with him for any other reason than because he was paying her a great deal of money for her to give herself to him like this, to pretend to him, and he couldn't help wanting her.

Rob hated himself for being so weak and stupid. He was a little sorry for himself too because Sarah had been rather like this, brought up by modern parents, allowed a free mind and a good education which made her feel that she was a man's equal. Sarah had not held back in bed as he knew many women did. This woman didn't hold back either and it made him miss Sarah more. Sarah had loved him, had wanted him, but only the money he was paying her held Susannah Seaton here in his arms. He knew that it was disgusting to her, and that was why she had dressed like a whore, so that he would lose control of his senses and want her very badly, unable to refuse. Now he hated himself. If they had been true lovers then it wouldn't have mattered, he could have lost himself in her because there would have been nobody to lose and nobody to win, it would have been equal, fair and wonderful, but it wasn't. He could no longer remember how to be kind to her, he couldn't remember anything, he couldn't think, he wasn't even sure that eventually he didn't hold her down. The whole thing was completely savage and mindless, that was the only way he wanted her and that was the way she had planned it, so that she could hate him for his stupidity and he could hate himself. That was the way she won.

Susannah had thought about Rob quite a lot that week, and she was frightened. He was the only person who had ever breached her defences in that way. She had considered sending him a note telling him that he could not come back, but she couldn't bring herself to do it. She decided that she would break the liking she had had for him. All she had to do was make him lose control. Then he would be like the others, she would care nothing for him, she would act for him, pretend, think of other things when she was with him, and it had worked. He had had her mindlessly, thoughtlessly, without restraint, but she felt no triumph. She had not counted on her own reaction. Her body remembered him, she felt safe with him, glad, smug even. This had never happened before. No other man could have held her down like that, no one would have dared and she would never have let herself get into such a situation. Her body had thought it was a lovers' game. She had not felt threatened, just deliciously surrendering the responsibility as never before.

Susannah trembled for her own stupidity and turned what she hoped were angry eyes on her guest, ready to tell him to go and not come back, but she didn't. He had buried himself almost completely in the bedclothes and pillows. All she could see was the darkness of his hair. Susannah felt what she thought she would not feel for a man again, what she would have sworn she would not feel for a rich, powerful, good looking young man. She was sorry.

He didn't move for a long time and Susannah didn't dare touch him. Finally all she said was, 'Rob . . . ?'

He threw back the bedclothes and got out of bed and began dressing. Susannah gathered the sheet up against herself and watched him. She wanted to say something more but she couldn't because it was taking all she had not to cry. He threw money down on to the bed and made for the door and Susannah ran after him, the tears falling suddenly and fast. She got hold of his arm and then put herself against the front of his shirt.

'I'm sorry.'

Rob reacted, to her surprise, as though she had done something unacceptable at a polite party.

'No, really,' he said, 'it's not your fault,' and tried to move round her. Susannah got hold of his shirt. Watching him retreat behind cold eyes and a distant manner she could well see now why he was so successful. He understood completely what she had done to him and why.

'Don't go,' she said.

'I shouldn't have come here, it was miserable of me. Please accept my apology.'

He would have gone but Susannah didn't let loose.

'Susannah, you're ruining my shirt.'

Susannah released him but it was only to put both hands up to his neck and kiss him on the mouth. It had been so many years since she had done such a thing that she couldn't quite believe she was doing it, but she was, and it tasted wonderful. He didn't do anything at first. He didn't try to leave, he didn't stop her, he didn't kiss her and then he put one arm around her shoulders and the other under her knees, picked her up, sheet and all, and carried her back to the bed.

Ten

Christmas came. Michael bought fruit and sweets and a small toy each for the children. Nancy made dinner for Alice and Michael. She only wished she had had to go to work so that she didn't have to invite them. Mrs Berkeley said that they were going to spend the day with their friends across the road, Mr and Mrs Norman and Faith, and after that the two young men were going back to Nottingham for New Year.

They hadn't wanted to go back to Nottingham, Nancy knew. She had heard Harry Shaw complaining bitterly to Rob about it. Mr Shaw's father had demanded they should go when they had a great deal of work to do here. They talked in front of her, almost Nancy thought, as though she was not there, not in a nasty way but as though they were used to talking in front of servants, and more than that somehow, as though they trusted her. Nancy couldn't think what sort of a house they came from. Around here you didn't discuss private matters when the help was there, and you certainly didn't talk like Mr Shaw did. His language was fit to turn the air blue. He talked about his father, his father mind you, Nancy thought, like nobody she had ever heard before. He called him by his name and 'that awkward old bastard', but however much they complained they minded him all right and they were going. The works wouldn't be shut except for Christmas Day, it was too dear to shut it, Rob said.

Nancy liked Rob. She hadn't thought that she would considering his reputation in Berry Edge. He wasn't as foul-mouthed as Harry for a start off. She felt sorry for him too. Whatever he had done it was a long time since, and he was family, but his mam and dad didn't treat him like family. They hadn't a good word to say about him to anybody or to his face, and now that his dad was getting better and could come down to meals he went on and on at Rob about the blessed works, and he was nasty about it. Not that it seemed to upset Rob. Nothing upset him. He was not like Mr Shaw, getting cross all the time. He just got on with his work, he was there nearly all the time from what Nancy could judge, and so was Mr Shaw.

Nancy suspected that Harry didn't like Berry Edge and that in particular he didn't like the Berkeley house, that he was used to much better things. He didn't eat a lot, he very often, as far as she knew, went out and stayed out all night, and there were empty brandy bottles in his bedroom. He was untidy and caused Nancy a lot of work, and there was

so much washing that they had to get somebody extra in
to do it in spite of the new maid, Theresa. She didn't think
Mr Shaw noticed all the work. She had never known people
go through as many clothes as those two men did. They
didn't seem to think that somebody had all the washing and
ironing to do. If Nancy had been Mrs Berkeley she would
have talked to them about it, but Mrs Berkeley was too
busy looking after Mr Berkeley and didn't often talk about
anything.

Nancy was dreading Christmas Day, but it was better
than she had imagined. Michael was good with the children.
They never got fruit or sweets, and a new toy was something
very special, so they were happy. The dinner was perfect to
Nancy's surprise, even Mr Shaw would have eaten it, and
the day was mild.

After dinner the children sat happily by the fire, Alice was
content to stay in, and when Michael asked her if she wanted
to go and get some air Nancy was pleased to. It wasn't often
that she got a walk.

They went up on to the fell and it was a perfect day up
there, with a blue sky and, as the afternoon began to draw
in, the clouds were all grey and blue in big shapes and the
sun made a silver-gold outline on the fell top as though it
was trying hard because it was a special day.

Michael wasn't anything like Sean to be with and he was
the only man Nancy had ever gone walking with, in their
courting days. Sometimes in her mind she imagined herself

going for a walk with Rob (never Harry because he was the sort who would probably grab you when he got you there), but Michael was nice to be with. It was lovely up there on the fell top.

'Did you go to Midnight Mass last night, Michael?' Nancy asked him.

'No.'

'Some people only go to church for weddings, funerals, Easter and Christmas.'

'I don't go at all.'

'Why not?'

'I don't believe in God.'

'Holy Mary, don't say such things. Thank goodness the bairns aren't here.'

'Do you believe in him after the life you had with our Sean?'

'Am I supposed to blame the Lord for that?'

'Don't you think people are entitled to a little happiness?'

'I think people are entitled to die in a state of grace and that's all.'

'And do you think our Sean was in a state of grace?'

'No, I think he was in a state of intoxication,' Nancy said quickly and then wished she hadn't. It wasn't right to speak ill of the dead, Sean wasn't there to defend himself. She looked at Michael but he didn't seem shocked. They were sitting on the edge of the fell, looking out over Berry Edge. They could see the houses and the chimneys and most of the works from there and it was a really big expanse. You didn't often see how big it was.

'It would be like going straight to hell with nothing in between, wouldn't it? You can't think how many times I've brought it back to me, that he was paid out for the way that he treated me. Do you think God did that, Michael?'

'No, I think it was just an accident.'

She began to cry, she didn't know why. She had never cried over Sean, he had never deserved it, so perhaps this was just for herself.

'I was glad he was dead.'

'I was glad he was dead too,' Michael said. 'How could you not have been?'

'Isn't it a dreadful sin to hate people who are dead?'

'It's hard though when you hated them so much when they were here. It takes a bit of getting used to that they aren't going to hurt you any more.'

She laughed through her tears, that was the Irish way, and just for a moment Nancy wished that she could be somewhere she had never been, somewhere her grandparents had spoken of with love and hate. The most beautiful place in the world that was their home which had never belonged to them while they had always belonged to it, where the people had starved and died or left and died somewhere else, except for the strongest ones. They had gone places and been hated because they would do anything for enough food to survive on. They would not fight or strike or take up a position. They would live without education, without ambition, just to be there because anything was better than starving to death, which many of them had done back in Ireland. To find a place like Berry Edge was luxury. Here you could have a house that went with your job, a roof, coins in your hand and enough left over so that you had to decide what to spend it on when the food was bought. It was untold wealth, it was Paradise. This dirty little town with its iron and steelworks, its moors unlike anything else in God's creation, it was heaven.

She wondered whether it hurt Michael to see Sean's children. They were all that was left of his brother and they might make something good of what he had given them. They were in a way the children of luck, they would grow up hopefully. They would not know what it was like to want, to starve, to have nothing, to lose their home. They would even have education.

'Nancy, can I just say something?'

'What?'

'I want to help. I've got enough money—'

'No. Mrs Berkeley pays me. Keep your money, Michael, it's yours.'

'I don't need it.'

'You will one of these days. You'll find a nice lass and want to settle down and have some bairns. I never met a man as good with bairns as you are. If you have something put by it helps. Keep it and thanks.'

Nancy was quite proud of this little speech. Being with the Berkeleys all day she was learning how to say exactly what she meant and in pretty terms. Somehow it was lost on Michael.

'You shouldn't have to go out and leave the bairns, it's not right. I'm making good money. Why not take it and stop working?'

'I like my work,' Nancy said.

'They're left either with my mother, and you know what she's like, or with Vera. They must be starting to think Vera Ridley *is* their mother,' he said.

'Nothing of the sort,' Nancy said. 'Besides, what would I do stuck in the house all day?'

'Some women would be glad of it.'

'Well, I wouldn't.'

'It's your place.'

'My place? And who are you to tell me what my place is, Michael McFadden?'

If he had been Sean he would have clattered her for that, Nancy thought. He would have held her eyes with his fierce black gaze and then knocked her sideways. Michael sat there looking like Sean and just as angry, she knew somehow, but not meeting her look. Nancy was frightened at first. His doing nothing unnerved her. She understood violence. She didn't understand restraint. And she had to sit there and convince herself that he was not about to look up and then wallop her. She couldn't breathe normally, she was so frightened, but he just went on sitting there doing nothing and gradually she stopped being frightened and remembered with relief that he was not Sean. Sean was dead and Michael, she admitted to herself, was really nothing like him. He looked like him, yes, and even then not so much as she had thought, but that was all. Since his set-to with Rob, as far as she knew he had not got drunk or had a fight and he had never, again as far as she knew, lifted his hand to a woman in his life. She also remembered for some reason now the younger man that he had been, and she knew that if Michael had been born into different circumstances he would be living quite differently than he was, that he could have been some kind of an artist. There was no room for artists in Berry Edge, there was no time and no money and no opportunity. Michael would be a pitman for the rest of his life because of it, but at least she saw him as he was now. He had, Nancy thought ridiculously, eyelashes you could practically have sledged down. She didn't know what to say.

'I don't want any man in my way,' she said, and her voice trembled.

He looked up then. She didn't learn anything from the look, his eyes were like great big dirty puddles.

'I'm not trying to get in the way, Nancy,' he said.

'Good, because one McFadden in my road was quite enough.' She didn't like saying these things to Michael, because he was kind to her and the bairns, and she knew by now that he was as unlike Sean as he could be, but she was too afraid to try again. She would never forget Sean. Nothing could wipe out what he had done to her. Nobody would ever again take up all the room in bed, sit on the only decent chair, and get her to run about after him. Never, she swore, never.

Rob and Harry went home for New Year. Harry had rarely been as glad of anything or as angry with his father for insisting. They reached the house in time for dinner, and Ida, who had obviously been watching for them, came out of the house and ran down the steps to the carriage. Harry got out first. She hugged and kissed him several times, and did the same to Rob, and said, 'My darling boys, I have missed you.'

Harry regarded his home affectionately and then said, 'For God's sake, Ida, stop slavering all over us. We've only been gone a few weeks.'

She looked up.

'You get more like your father every day.'

'Who am I supposed to get more like, Mother, the gardener?'

They went inside. Vincent was standing by the drawing room fire.

'So,' he said, 'you came back.'

'We didn't have much option,' Harry declared, pouring himself a whisky. 'We could hear you all the way to Durham.'

'I need Rob here.'

'Well, thanks. We had a wonderful journey, freezing slush and inedible food.'

'Where is he?'

'I don't know. Perhaps he paused for a moment to take off his coat.'

Rob came in then, closely followed by Ida.

'You've lost weight,' she was saying to him.

'I have not.'

'What you need is a good meal,' she declared. 'I'm going to go and see if they can speed up that dinner,' and off she went.

'And how is the great northern venture?' Vincent asked.

'Fine.'

'Really?'

'It would be if we didn't have to come back here every five minutes,' Harry said.

Vincent was looking hard at Rob.

'How much?' he said.

'A lot.'

Vincent shook his head.

'Let it go,' he said.

'I can't.'

'Is that you can't because you think it's going to make a profit, or are we talking sentiment?'

'Do you want a whisky, Rob?' Harry said.

Rob nodded and Harry poured out the golden liquid.

'Answer me, damn you!'

'I think it's worth trying to save, yes.'

'You think! All you're any use at is bedding women and drinking my whisky, the pair of you. I suppose you think it's a good idea as well, do you?' He glanced at Harry.

'No, I don't think it's a good idea—'

'Well, a little light in the darkness.'

'—but I'm going to back him anyway.'

'You're going to help finance something you think will fail? Are you my son or is your mother not telling me something?'

'I wish she would,' Harry said. 'Having a father who is completely devoid of dress sense is a great burden to us all, and perhaps my father was a gentleman.'

'And what does your father think?' Vincent asked Rob.

'I don't know. He didn't tell me.'

The dinner was wonderful but Harry didn't enjoy it, because all the way through, Vincent told them how stupid they were, how incompetent they were. Harry thought of the way that Rob's father had treated him and didn't understand that Rob could go on calmly eating cheesecake as though there was nothing the matter.

'Why don't you shut up?' he said finally.

'Harry!' Ida said.

'You don't know what it's been like for Rob going back there—'

'He didn't have to go.'

'He did have to go. How would you feel?'

'Harry—' Rob put in.

'His brother's dead, his father's ill, the place is dropping to pieces and the people there depend on it for their work. It'll destroy the whole town if somebody doesn't do something about it.'

'Such heat,' his father said. 'I'm surprised you became involved. If you want to throw your money away I can't stop you but don't ask me for any.'

'I wouldn't ask you to pass the salt,' Harry said, and he threw down his napkin and got up and left the room.

Rob found Harry in the library, drinking brandy and sitting with his feet up on his father's desk. Rob sat down on the desk. There was nothing on it but Harry's feet, Vincent never used the library for its real purpose.

'He doesn't mean anything,' Rob said. 'He's worried, that's all. He doesn't want us to make a big mistake. If you have misgivings about it then stay here.'

'And put up with that bastard telling me what to do all day? No thanks. Besides, I like it.'

Rob laughed.

'What do you like most about it, the cabbage or the cold bedrooms?'

'I don't know, there's just something, and I like the idea

of working on something without him there trying to keep us right all the time.'

'If you want to be free you could start up something yourself.'

'I know that, but this is interesting, the not knowing gets to me. I want to watch myself at a distance and see how hard I try to succeed. I want to see myself struggle. I've never done that, he would never let me. Things have been so easy, I always had everything I wanted and school was easy and so was university and . . . Vincent did so much, he made so much money. I felt like there was nothing left to try and he doesn't want me to try, he wants me trailing around after him being astounded at his genius. He'd like me to wear those dreadful checked suits like he does. I'm tired of being his son and at Berry Edge I'm not, I'm just some foreigner with weird ways and ideas. I like it there, it feels right. I didn't want to come home. Only the idea of decent food and a nice bed persuaded me, and even that lost its savour when Vincent shouted at us all the way through dinner. I'd go back tonight if I could.'

'You can't, I need you here.'

'Christ, you're starting to sound like him. You need me at Berry Edge and that's where I should be.'

He should be there now, he thought. Leaving Berry Edge was already a wrench and he was convinced that things would go wrong at the works when he was not there to see to everything. He and Rob had worked every day up 'til

Christmas and it had been strange being away from home at the time. He had never done that before. Usually they went to London for a few days to see friends there and go to parties and the theatre. Sometimes people came to the house in Nottingham to stay, but since Sarah had died at Christmas two years ago there had been no celebrations, so in a way he was glad to be in a different place. The not being there made things much easier.

It was funny too that he should have enjoyed himself because nothing lavish was arranged up there in Berry Edge. There was to be Christmas dinner with Faith's parents. That meant no alcohol and a lot of polite conversation.

Harry had been brought up to buy gifts for people and so he bought Faith a muff and a pair of pretty pearl earrings. She was clearly astonished when she opened her presents and blushed so much that Harry was rather pleased with himself. It was obvious that no man had bought her anything in years. She wore a green silk dress that day, much prettier than anything he had seen her wear before. He thought that the earrings and the dress together brought out the colour of her eyes, making them quite definitely green. She put the earrings on, saying that he should not have bought them, but it made Harry feel good being able to produce such pleasure with so little effort.

After the meal she announced that she was going out and he offered to go with her, thinking that she meant a walk because it was such a nice day, clear and warm for

December. But she said softly, 'I'm only going to the church-yard,' and went.

After a little while the day changed and became foggy and he wondered whether she didn't feel strange in a graveyard in the fog, so he set off after her.

There was nobody about in the short afternoon, only her beside the grave, and it was difficult to see more than a few feet around you.

'It's just me,' he said, so as not to startle her.

'I was thinking about you. I'm sure this seems very dull to you. Didn't you tell me that you usually spend Christmas in London? That must be very exciting.'

'Not unless you can get away from my father. He wears thick yellow checked suits.'

She laughed. He liked to hear her laugh, she didn't do much of it.

'I don't believe that.'

'It's true. Ask Rob.'

She looked down again at that.

'It seems awful laughing here.'

'You suit those earrings.'

'It was very kind of you and quite unnecessary.'

'How could it be unnecessary? It's Christmas. Would you like to spend Christmas in London?'

'I should like nothing better.'

'I think next year my parents will probably go, and if they do I shall ask my mother to invite you. She loves company.'

'I couldn't do that, I don't know them.'

'Yes, you could. You know Rob and me.'

'He would be there?'

'I should think so.'

'You spend a great deal of time together. Is that because Robert works for your father?'

'He doesn't actually work for my father. You could say that we both work with him.'

'And you're both going back to Nottingham in a day or two, I understand.'

'Only for a few days. My father gets nervous when Rob's not there.'

'Don't you resent him?'

'Of course I do, he's an old fool.'

She laughed again.

'I mean Robert.'

'Rob? Hell, no, he's the brother I didn't have.'

The moment the words were out Harry tried to drag them back but they seemed to hang in the air like washing. Even so, above John Berkeley's grave he added, 'We've had so many good times together. I'd shield him from the lightest rainfall.'

Faith tried a smile. 'Men in Berry Edge don't say things like that.'

'I know. We went into the Station Hotel. Did I tell you about that?' She shook her head. 'There was this great big man in there who didn't like Rob. Rob floored him. It was beautiful. The place was full but they cleared like the Red Sea parting.'

'He always was good at fighting. Everywhere he goes he creates trouble,' she said.

'You could try forgiving him, you're big on religion.'

'I doubt he cares.'

'No, I meant for you.'

'For me? How would that benefit me?'

'You could stop kissing a ghost and try for somebody real.'

'I don't . . . you have a strange way with words. I could never find anybody I liked.'

'How hard were you looking? The world is full of men.'

'Not men like John.'

'Was he really like that, Faith, or is it just that you choose to remember him like that?'

'What do you mean?'

'Well, can you think of anything you didn't like about him?'

'I loved everything about him.'

'You couldn't have done. He must have had at least one unendearing habit, every man has.'

'Do you?'

'A dozen.'

'Like what?'

'I'm sarcastic, impatient, I swear, I drink a lot, I smoke cigars, I tread on people's toes when I dance . . .'

Faith was smiling.

'I don't think those are particularly unendearing,' she said.

'Don't you really? No wonder John seemed a paragon. So must every man. Perhaps you didn't give anyone a chance.'

'I just know that I couldn't love anyone again.'

'You've decided.'

'No, I haven't decided.'

'Wasn't there anything else you wanted to do?'

'There was a time when I wanted to go to college. I could have gone to St Hild's in Durham but my parents wouldn't hear of it. They thought it was unladylike.'

Harry screwed up his face.

'What do you think about education for women?' she asked him.

'Education at its best is enlightenment. How could it be wrong?'

'I'm too old. I feel as though everything has gone past me. I just keep busy.'

'You ought to marry Faith,' Rob's mother said to him that night when they got home.

'What?'

His mother looked at his father.

'We think you should,' his father said. 'She hasn't married and neither have you. I think the reason for that is because there's no one else you could marry. You owe her that much.

She'll never marry anyone else now and you could hardly expect her to go to her grave a spinster.'

Rob said nothing. He was only glad that Harry was there. The evening was unendurable. When it ended and he went to bed, Harry followed him into his room within minutes, enquiring as he shut the door,

'Are you all right?'

'Do you think it's going to snow? It looks so heavy.'

'How can you see anything?' Harry went to the window. He stood for a few moments and then turned to Rob. 'You haven't told them anything about Sarah, have you?'

'No.'

'Don't you think it would alter things if you did?'

'It's nothing to do with them.'

'They probably wouldn't expect you to marry Faith if you told them.'

'I don't think I could stand them knowing, asking questions or worse still not asking them. They don't care about what I've done and I don't want to spoil my memories of Sarah – people talking about her who didn't know her.'

'Would you seriously consider marrying Faith? She hates you.'

'Nothing on earth would make Faith marry me but I'd like to make peace with her, I'd very much like that.'

'And what about Susannah?'

Rob didn't answer that.

'You love her, don't you?' Harry guessed.

'I didn't want to tell you because of Sarah.'

'Why not when it was my idea to go there in the first place? From what I hear dozens of men have fallen in love with her and most of them weren't allowed anywhere near. Does she love you?'

'I don't know. I hope so,' Rob said.

Eleven

While they were in Nottingham they worked. Vincent tried to make it obvious that he couldn't manage without them whereas Rob felt certain that if he had tried he could have. He had plenty of competent men around him in his foundries and factories, and everything ran smoothly because Rob had spent years making sure that it would. When things did not, Vincent could cope alone, at least for a while. More and more he felt as though he should be back in Berry Edge where nothing was going right and he knew that Harry felt the same. Whenever they were alone they talked about the Berry Edge problems, but never in front of Vincent. He didn't want to know.

On the second evening after dinner they were sitting by the library fire talking, and when he came in they stopped. Harry even got up and walked out.

'Do your parents know anything about us?' Vincent said.

'No.'

'Do they know anything about your life or the work you've done?'

'No.'

'Why didn't you tell them?'

'They're not interested.'

'You let them go on thinking that you're the stupid person who let your brother drown.'

'I *am* the stupid person who let my brother drown.'

'People die every day. Do you think other people have to take on the responsibility? What are you going to do, carry the guilt to your grave? How could your father love you so little, and how could you feel so bad that you go to that godforsaken place to rescue some badly managed foundry which is nothing to do with you?'

'It is to do with me, Vince.'

'Let him fail, for God's sake.'

'He's old, tired and hurt.'

'So are we all before we're through. Why can't you let it go?'

'You don't need me here that much, Vince.'

'I miss you. Sarah seems even less here when you're not here,' Vincent said steadily. 'I was afraid that you would go back there and stay for good. I didn't know whether to be more afraid that your father would take you back affectionately because I didn't want to lose you, or that he would treat you like he has and you would stay anyway because you think the debt is insuperable. And now I've lost Harry too.'

'He's thirty, Vince, he had to leave home sometime.'

Vincent stood there for a few minutes by the fire and then he said,

'So, are there any decent women in Durham? You must be screwing somebody.'

'Vince—'

'Go on, tell me you're not. I'll kick your bloody arse through the door.'

Rob grinned suddenly.

'I love you, Vince,' he said.

'Oh, go and bugger yourself,' Vincent said.

Ida had planned a New Year party.

'I've invited several young women and I don't want you two to do what you did last time.'

'Which was?' Harry asked.

'Pissed as rats,' Vincent said.

His wife looked hard at him.

'Vincent, I will not have that kind of language in my drawing room.' She looked severely across the room at Rob. 'Promise me. I have invited several of the most beautiful young ladies in the county, and you will dance with them.'

Rob said nothing. Vincent waited until the two young men left the room and then he said, 'You're pushing him too hard, Ida.'

'It's been long enough,' his wife said. 'I won't have him

grieving the rest of his life over it like he has done over his brother. I won't have it, Vincent.'

The following afternoon the guests arrived. Most of them were staying and had come while it was light. Some of them had been there for lunch. Rob had never seen so many beautiful young women. That night he danced with as many of them as he could, one dance each. He didn't drink, he didn't leave, he made conversation and when the night was almost over and he was able to go to bed, he wished more than anything in the world that he could just go to Susannah's and lose himself in her. She didn't laugh at what she thought were meant to be amusing remarks, she didn't agree all the time and turn widened eyes on him. He thought of Faith and how beautiful she had been once. Some of the girls here tonight were ten years younger than her, and he could have had any one of them because he was rich. Faith would have looked plain and old beside them, their sparkling eyes and sweet smiles, their giggles, their pert figures. At least Faith knew how to make conversation. This was another world. Faith would have been at one of her Bible classes that day. He wondered how long it was since she had danced, whether she had ever drunk champagne. He doubted if she had been kissed in ten years. It was strange to think that the last person to place his mouth on hers had been John. She was too old to marry now, everybody was married around her. There was no one left. If he didn't marry her she would live at home with her parents, lie in her own bed for the rest of her life because of him.

Rob tried to talk himself out of this line of thought because he knew that he wouldn't sleep, but his mind conjured him the children Faith would not have, the marriage she had not known, the wedding day, the man, and then again, for the thousand upon thousandth time, that drunken evening in Durham when he and his friends had been partying all afternoon, and John arrived, and Rob encouraged him to have a drink. John wouldn't, but somebody laced his lemonade. It had seemed so funny, John happy like that, John almost on his level, not the aloof young man he had turned into. John had long before that time learned to despise his brother who worked in the foundry. John had been brilliant at university and had tried to stop Rob from drinking, gambling, partying all night. He hated those things, so it seemed the funnier for John to be drunk. John hadn't thought it funny. They had argued, and then fought. John was no good at fighting, he had never done any. Rob gave up in disgust. John was so drunk, swaying, shouting at Rob how much he hated him. Rob had left, gone into the pub with some friends and John, drunk and upset, had lost his balance, gone over the bridge into the water. Rob went in after him when somebody ran inside and told him, but it was too late. John was knocked unconscious and had drowned by the time Rob got to him.

Rob left the dying fire and went to the window. He pressed his face up against the cold pane. The road to Berry Edge was his nightmare, but he had to go back. His parents would never forgive him for what had happened, but that didn't matter. He had to try to save the works somehow.

The following morning Ida was down to breakfast. She and Rob sat there alone and she said, 'What did you think of Miss Castleton?'

'Which one was she?'

'You could hardly miss her, Robert, she was the beautiful blonde girl with the blue eyes and—'

'Oh yes, she had a dress you could see down,' Rob said. 'Very nice.'

Ida looked disapprovingly at him.

'She's a very clever girl. She plays the piano and can talk French. Didn't you like her?'

Rob looked up.

'I have no desire to talk French, Ida, or to listen to fetching young women mangling Beethoven.'

'You didn't like her then?'

'The only interesting thing about her as far as I could judge was the fact that she had perfect breasts. I had a hell of a job keeping my hands off them.' Ida was silent. 'And if you think that parading half the beautiful girls of Nottinghamshire and Derbyshire in front of my eyes is going to make me marry one of them, you're mistaken, Ida. I loved Sarah. I'm never going to love anyone like that again and I don't understand why you are apparently so keen to become my ex-mother-in-law.'

Ida said nothing.

'Talk to me, damn you!' Rob yelled, and she jumped. 'You began this wretched conversation.'

'Sarah's been dead two years. I won't have you ruining your life over it.'

'Do you really want me to bring another woman into this house to take Sarah's place?'

'If Sarah had still been alive you would never have left,' Ida said steadily.

Rob went to her, got down beside her chair.

'This is my home.'

'You say that, but I can see what's going to happen and then I will have lost all three of you.'

'I swear it to you, Ida, I'm coming back. I just want to get the place pulled together first. Will you stop worrying? And no more parties, eh? No more Miss Castletons with their breasts falling out of their dresses. Please?'

Ida smiled. Rob kissed her.

He and Harry were there two weeks. It was the shortest fortnight that Rob could ever remember, and the house and the grounds and the area around it were so precious to him.

He went to Sarah's grave and there was no reluctance in him as there had been in Berry Edge with John's.

He had had to watch Sarah die. He had had to watch her grow pale and thin until sometimes he thought that he could see through her. She had wasted from him in that autumn and early winter of two years ago. Nothing could stop it. The doctors, even the best London doctors, did not know what to do.

She had wanted a child, and when nothing happened became impatient. And then her monthly bleeding stopped for a while and she rejoiced, and then it began without apparent change of any kind. She began to tire easily, she did not want to ride her horse or go out in the evenings. Sometimes she fell asleep in the afternoons. She bruised when she knocked even slightly against anything. She seemed able to do less and less. She fainted. Rob insisted that she went to the doctor, because her mother had begged her and she had said that there was nothing the matter. When things got worse Rob took her to London but nothing helped. All she wanted was to go home.

The doctors prescribed liver sandwiches and a lot of rest. They thought it was something to do with the blood.

Raw liver sandwiches became the bane of Sarah's life. She loathed them so much that quite often she was sick either during or after so that it was almost a waste of time struggling to get them down. She did not get better. She became more and more tired, so that even when Rob came home she could barely make the effort to spend the evening with him. There were black shadows under her eyes.

That autumn Rob rarely went to work. They sat by the window in her bedroom watching the leaves drop from the trees on to the lawns below, the way the leaves turned orange and brown and fell, sometimes in twirling motions, sometimes gusted by the wind as the garden prepared itself for winter. The leaden skies and short afternoons were a pleasure to her when she could lie in front of a log fire and watch the dusk gather.

One cold December evening, snow began to fall as he and Sarah were sitting together by the window.

'Do you remember last year?'

Rob said that he did. Last year there had been a future.

'Would you carry me outside? I want to see it.'

'You can see it from here.' She was in her favourite place, even though her mother complained that it was too cold for her there on the chaise longue.

'No, I want to really see it. Take me. Please.'

He wrapped her up in a big rug and carried her down the stairs and along the hall and down the outside steps that she used to run down and never would again. She insisted on going right across the lawn to see the trees. The snow on the branches was already weighing them down and some of it was falling off. There were drifts beside the wall, graceful slopes. She lifted her hands and put out her tongue like a child and laughed at the feel of the snow.

'We could have a white Christmas, Rob. Just think how that would be. The children will go sledging and everything will be so pretty.'

'We should go back inside. You'll catch cold.'

'Just a minute longer.'

'Not another second,' Rob said.

They did have a white Christmas, but Sarah didn't live to see it. On Christmas Eve, with the snow piled high outside the window, Vincent Shaw took his son-in-law into his arms.

'It's all right, Rob, I've got you,' he said.

When Rob and Harry went back north there was snow in Berry Edge. Being so high it got more snow than almost anywhere else, and all autumn and winter and early spring people went around in thick coats, and the women wore scarves and boots, because the wind bit across the moors and didn't stop just because madmen had placed a town there. As they drew further north it became colder and colder, and he thought the place had never looked as bleak as when he finally arrived again at the gates of the house where he had been born. He had no desire to be there. He longed for the abbey and its comforts, but Harry was with him, and later, when his mother and father went upstairs, he and Harry sat by the fire and drank whisky which Harry had brought with him from home. It was single malt and superb. Vincent had bought it specially.

'I miss him already,' Rob said.

'I couldn't wait to get away from the old bastard. When are you seeing Susannah?'

'Saturday.'

'There are certain things about Durham which Nottingham doesn't have,' Harry said, and grinned.

Susannah was dressed as she had been that first time, as plainly as she could be. It made him smile though against himself.

'You dressed for me.'

'Of course.'

She got up and kissed him briefly as though they were friends, and gave him wine and asked him about Nottingham. They sat by the fire on a big sofa. They made love on the sofa and then on the rug in front of the fire, and she wasn't defensive or controlled. Her eyes were lit for him. They went to bed and she lay there in his arms half asleep, and Rob remembered what being happy was like, how he had not wanted to be with any woman since then as he wanted to be like this with Susannah Seaton now.

The fire was burning brightly. It was long after midnight. The curtains had closed out the cold night, the lamp was burning. She moved back and opened her eyes.

'There's something the matter, isn't there?' she said softly. 'Did something go wrong in Nottingham?'

'Susannah, have you ever been in love?'

She smiled in surprise and didn't answer immediately.

'Do you mean am I in love with you?'

'No—'

'Do you mean do whores ever do it free? Am I costing you too much?'

'No. It doesn't matter.'

'It's all right, I'll tell you. I thought I was in love once, he was called Sam. When I think about it now I think that it was never real, that it could not have been because I could never have loved somebody so . . . He didn't love me, I don't think that he had ever loved me but then . . . men see me and then they think that's love. Men don't love women, they admire their beauty and try to gain it for their own benefit.'

'What did he do?' Rob asked her softly.

'He did the worst thing that he could ever have done to me. He betrayed me.'

'With another woman?'

Susannah smiled.

'Only a man would think that. We were engaged to be married. He had a farm up near Hexham, it was the prettiest place. The house was old and had small square windows, and the fields around it were small and square too, and he was . . . he was rather like you, young and very nice to look at, dark. We were going to be married in the summer and I could see us there, having children, living the days out. And then one night just after Easter I was set upon by two men. I was living in Newcastle at the time. It was late and I was going back to the house where I worked as a maid and they . . .' She stopped and looked sharply at him. 'What am I doing telling you this? I never tell anybody.'

She got out of bed and fastened a thick dressing gown around her and went over to the brightly burning fire.

'They took from me what no man had ever had and after that he refused to marry me.'

'Didn't you have anyone to help you?'

'No. My parents had died. They were good people. My father was named Mathias, he was quite religious. He called me after John Wesley's mother. When . . . when something awful like that happens to a woman, people somehow assume that she caused it. I was so distressed that I allowed people to know what had happened to me, and after people knew there was a kind of terrible shame. I lost my work and my friends, everything. I spent the money I had left on fine clothes and good food and a room and I waited until I found a gentleman. I got him to pay me what seemed such a lot of money to have me. Not nearly as much as I get now of course. You learn.'

She looked at Rob.

'I don't learn some things though. Since then I've never told anybody that except Claire. I've especially never told a man. You're a very dangerous person, Robert Berkeley. You seem so nice, and beyond that niceness . . .'

'What?'

'I don't know. Can I ask you something?'

'Certainly.'

'What is your wife called?'

That knocked Rob, he hadn't expected it. 'Sarah.'

Susannah looked long at him and when she spoke again a hardness had come into her voice.

'Don't you love her any more that you come to me?'

'I loved her very much. She died the winter before last.'

'I see. I'm sorry, I didn't realise that.'

'Susannah, if I were to pay you sufficient, would you give the others up?'

'I might, if it was enough.'

'And I could come and see you any time I wanted?'

'Any time.'

Rob smiled. Susannah came back to bed, and he took her face in his hands and said, 'I'll never let anybody hurt you ever again, I swear it to you.'

'Oh, Rob, don't swear. Don't tempt fate.'

'I love you.'

'No, no.' Susannah put her hands over her ears but Rob dragged them away.

'Don't you care for me at all?'

Susannah looked at him. 'I didn't want to. I thought you were married. I was sure that you were.'

'Don't pretend to me. Tell me. Is the past too much in the way? Can't you love anybody, Susannah?'

'I don't want to. You can see why I don't want to.'

'But I'm not like that, and I love you. I'll take care of you. There'll be just you and me if that's what you want. Is it?'

'Yes.'

'Really?'

'Yes.'

Rob kissed her and held her and whispered words of love into her ears and Susannah was soon blind and deaf, lost to the world.

Twelve

Harry didn't miss his home at all once he got used to Berry Edge. The last two years, since Sarah had died, his parents had concentrated on him more and more as though he was about to disappear, so to actually leave and have his freedom was a heady feeling.

He regarded everything about Berry Edge as a challenge. He and Rob didn't go home again, and his father became used to the idea and more fair and stopped asking them to. It was a hard winter; when it was cold the wind blew relentlessly, and when it was less cold it snowed heavily. Rob's father became so ill that he didn't leave his room; that made mealtimes much better without the old man complaining and Rob's polite silences. Often Mrs Berkeley would take her meals upstairs on a tray in her husband's bedroom and he and Rob would have the dining room to themselves. Harry liked these times, talking over the work, making plans for the future. One cold February evening when they had finished dinner and were sitting around the table in the way that he liked, talking idly for once, he said, 'Do you think we should take Faith out somewhere?'

'Faith? Whatever for?'

'She doesn't seem to go anywhere.'

'She likes her dull life.'

'Does she?'

'We could take her out if you like, but it won't alter things, Harry.'

'How do you know? It might. We could try. We could take her to a concert. There's one on Saturday. Let's go over and ask her.'

They went. The Normans' house was a disappointment to Harry; it was even plainer than Rob's parents' house. Faith was wearing yet another boring dress which didn't suit her. It was an awful colour between grey and off-white and, to Harry's experienced eyes, years out of fashion. No wonder she didn't attract anybody, he thought. Her hair was pulled back severely from her face; she wore no jewellery except a cross around her neck.

Her father and mother were polite to him and welcoming to Rob, and it was obvious to Harry that they thought part of Rob's duty in coming back to Berry Edge was to marry this cold female. He began to regret having thought about her.

She watched Rob a lot but she didn't see him, Harry thought. She wanted to see John so that was what she saw.

It was strange. In Nottingham neither of them would have given her a second glance. Here in Berry Edge they were asking if she would go out with them. Her mother had gone to make some tea – Harry was beginning to hate tea, there was so much of it drunk here – and her father had gone to find a book which he was convinced they ought to read, and which Harry had already decided would be too boring. Rob asked Faith about the concert and she turned him down; she took pleasure in doing so, Harry could see, and it annoyed him because he had had to persuade Rob to ask her in the first place, and because he knew how much Rob wanted to make things up with her.

'What are you doing that evening, polishing the Chapel?' he said. 'I think you're very rude.'

'I'm rude?' Faith stared. 'There's a special meeting—'

'You could miss it for once. The place wouldn't fall down.'

'I said I would help with the tea.'

'I'm sure there's somebody else who can pour tea. Would you rather do that than go out with us?'

She didn't answer, she wasn't even looking at him. Harry had a great desire to smack her face.

'Well?' he demanded.

When she still didn't answer, Harry got to his feet. Faith actually left her chair and retreated a step or two. Harry was angry and he didn't understand why. She was an old maid. Nobody would ever want her, nobody would ever marry her. She would go on fussing with her small life, filling her days with Chapel teas and Bible meetings forever. Why should he try to change that? Socially she was far beneath him even if she didn't know it.

She looked as though at any moment she was going to turn and run for the door, not like a woman of thirty. In Harry's world women of thirty were fashionable and sophisticated, married to powerful men, running households, having children, talking of art and literature and music. Sarah had been like that. How strange it must be for Rob to come back here and be faced with this plain, diminutive woman who was holding her hatred of him because she had so little else in her life. She spoke of John Berkeley as though he was still alive, and her speaking of him kept him alive in her mind.

'Faith doesn't have to go with us,' Rob pointed out softly.

Harry had sense enough to say nothing before her mother came back in with the tea tray. As they walked slowly across the road some time later he said, 'I've been turned down for another man, I've been turned down for another day, but I've never before been turned down for a Chapel tea.'

Rob smiled and put a hand on his shoulder.

'You have to come to Berry Edge for some things,' he said.

That Sunday, after Rob and Harry had come home for the big meal, Harry went to the churchyard. There was Faith, tidying up and putting greenery on John's grave. It was cold and wet; the trees in the churchyard dripped.

She looked up but she didn't speak to him, just went on with what she was doing.

'Will you let me apologise?' he said.

'I don't think so.'

Harry stared across the wet foggy day. Leaves were still there from the autumn winds as though an unseen hand had stuffed them down beside each gravestone.

'Are you going to hate Rob for the rest of your life?' he said.

'I don't hate him any more.'

'You must. You couldn't treat him so badly if you didn't.'

'You . . . you have no idea how difficult it is. He looks now exactly like John. When I see him I think it's John, only it never is. John was a good man, the best I ever met. He was a good Methodist. He didn't drink or smoke or— or chase women.'

'You can be a good man and still drink, smoke and chase women,' Harry said. 'Will you come for a walk?'

'It's not much of a day for walking.'

'What could be more depressing than a graveyard?'

'I don't find it depressing.'

'No, of course you don't. Your whole life is buried here; not only your past, but your present and your future. If you could take your meals here, no doubt your life would be complete.'

'You don't have to stay,' Faith said.

'Come and walk just a little. I want to talk to you.'

Faith finished what she was doing and they set off up the hill towards the park. Even in this weather, Harry thought, the park was congenial. It had been carefully planned, with so many different kinds of trees all set out to best advantage, that even bare of leaves the trees were still interesting.

'How are you? What have you been doing?'

'I'm fine. I went to Chapel this morning. Do you go to church?'

'No.'

'Why not?'

'I wasn't brought up to it, my father doesn't believe in God. He's essentially a scientist, I think.'

The park was deserted.

'I've never met anyone who didn't believe in God. Isn't he afraid of there being Hell?'

Harry laughed.

'He's completely fearless. I admire him more than any man I ever met. I'm very proud of him, and he's honest. Don't you think God would forgive an honest man? He's not afraid to die so he has nothing to fear. Do you think God will forgive you for hating Rob?'

'I can't help it.'

'You could tell him that you have.'

'It would be a lie.'

'Faith, he has been carrying this guilt around for ten years now. Surely, you could manage among your personal feelings a little deception on his behalf.'

'I have no idea what you're talking about.'

'Yes, you do. Don't give me that "I'm a woman and I don't understand" kind of shite—'

'Harry!' Faith said.

'Oh come on, Faith. Tell him you forgive him. What is it benefiting you? Try and be nice to him. You'll get it back tenfold, people always do with him.'

'I couldn't.'

They were standing under a tree. Harry had doubted the wisdom of this to begin with, and now it was steadily dripping icy water down the back of his neck. He moved forward out of the way and Faith, who was standing in front of him, moved back almost against the tree. To Harry's astonishment, as he looked at her he began to wonder what it would be like to kiss her. He couldn't understand his reaction. For years his mother had been trying to find a girl he liked. The truth was that he liked them all.

At twenty Faith would have been very pretty, but in Nottinghamshire society there were dozens of pretty girls. She was thirty and had lost her looks. She was religious and she had a flat, northern voice. She was unworldly, uneducated, she didn't even like him as far as he was aware. He couldn't understand himself. He turned away slightly in confusion so that he would stop looking at her mouth, and told himself it was just that here he was nobody and Faith didn't like him, whereas at home he was rich and eligible and could have anybody; her disliking him had needled his pride, that was all it was.

'Rob's changed,' Faith said. 'I couldn't believe it when I saw him. I couldn't believe that he was the same careless young man.'

'He isn't. How could he be? He lost everything when he left here – but he came back, Faith. Surely you can forgive him because he had the courage to come back. He didn't have to. He made a new life for himself and it's sitting there waiting for him any time he chooses to leave here. This isn't his world any more. He came back for his parents' sake, but he won't stay. You should have left.'

'I don't want to leave. It's not just because of John. This is my home. I belong here. I like being somewhere that I know people. I've lived here all my life. Don't you feel like that about Nottingham?'

'No. I don't care about things like that. Only people. Will you accept my apology now?'

Faith smiled a little.

'Yes.'

'And you'll have tea with us?'

'All right.' They turned and began walking back down the hill through the park.

Thirteen

Spring came slowly to Berry Edge. Rob had forgotten. He had thought that his father would get better as the weather warmed, but he did not. Rob and Harry spent their time at work.

They were comfortable at home now, and it was just as well, because at work things got better very slowly. The men didn't like Rob because the works had been left for so long to go down. They were not in the habit of changing their ways and took slowly to his new and strange ideas, to new machinery, to new bosses.

They liked Harry better because he joked and laughed and remembered their names, and also because they realised that he knew what he was talking about. He admired their work, encouraged them, and Rob was happy to let him do this while he did the difficult parts and the men went on hating him.

The orders began to come in. Many of the office ways

were reorganised. Rob employed women there. He found them capable and quick, and glad of the work.

The window in Rob's office looked into the works. He could see from there quite a lot of what was happening without actually going in and interfering. The place was very big, so there was also quite a lot that he couldn't see. He had taken on a number of men at the different mills to manage them, and although the works was so big it made him feel in touch. He hoped that it made the new men think that he might just be keeping an eye on them. In fact he sent Harry around to all the various workplaces. It was better than going himself because Harry was a stranger, good with people, even sounded different. Rob realised almost from the first that Harry was beginning to like the place rather as he had liked it when he was fifteen and had worked there alongside all the others.

Rob went often to the pits which were owned by the works. Sometimes at the Diamond pit he saw Michael McFadden. Michael behaved as though they had never met. Rob had learned to do the same. The memories of his childhood were tarnished now, all tinged with Michael lying on the floor of the Station Hotel where Rob had so efficiently put him. Rob knew also that the men were aware of what he had done and that it had done him no ill in their eyes. Every day in this place he had to prove that he was not soft. They didn't admire him for his mind, for his new ideas or his methods. They despised the men he put to be masters over them.

Rob wore old suits when he went to the works and to the pits. He spoke curtly and walked tall. He wasn't as big as Michael but luckily he was quite a bit bigger than most of the men. That made it hell in the pits, but was very useful otherwise. He could not be friends with any man, not even the managers. They were frightened of him and he knew it. They called him Mr Berkeley and were respectful – to his face. He knew very well that in the pubs of Berry Edge at night they called him other things, but it worked.

He went out all over the country for work and he sent Harry too in other directions. He sold the goods far and wide, he provided work and he interfered in the lives of his employees – as he would have despised his father or any man for doing before now – because if the steelworks was to succeed, everyone had to co-operate in every way. If they didn't come in when they should, he penalised them, and then if it continued got rid of them. If there were serious disturbances he had them thrown out of their houses. If they quarrelled he had it stopped. He was involved with the shopkeepers, the churches, the schools, he organised outings for the children, he sat on committees, he gave orders, he went to the mines and into the various shops and mills at work and he watched carefully. When the managers made mistakes, he took them aside in an office and gave them the kind of treatment that he had learned from Vincent. He had seen pure hatred in their eyes. Only late at night in his room did Rob stop being that man, and only on Saturday nights in Susannah's arms did he give in completely.

His father was not well that spring and his mother was too busy to see to the house, so Rob told Nancy to take on a third maid, and put her in charge. He gave her more than enough money to do so, and was amused at how carefully and economically she ran the household. She liked it, he could tell that she did. The only thing they both agreed that wasn't satisfactory was the fact that she was not there on Sundays. Rob and Harry contrived to be out most of the weekend so it was not a big problem. Nancy said again that she ought to be there to supervise the Sunday dinner.

'I think your children are more important than the dinner,' Rob said flatly.

He and Nancy were in the sitting room. Rob had been doing paperwork in there, since his mother was upstairs mostly. It was truly spring at last. The flowers were lifting their heads in the garden and the sunshine was actually warm through the window. It was Saturday afternoon, Nancy had come over especially to see Rob even though he told her it wasn't necessary. She liked the responsibility of making sure everything was going well in the household.

'Theresa doesn't get the dinner right, Mr Shaw says,' Nancy insisted.

'Mr Shaw has spent his whole life complaining,' Rob said, 'just ignore him.'

'Was the money correct, sir?'

Every week Nancy asked this about the expenditure. Rob had never yet looked at it.

'Nancy, it's fine, it always is.'

'You wouldn't know. You haven't set eyes on it,' she accused him.

'I don't think I have anything to worry about. Are the children well?'

'Yes, sir, grand.'

'What's your house like?'

'Sir?'

'Your house. Come and have a look at this.'

Nancy went over to the desk and on it was some kind of drawing.

'New houses. We're starting them this week now that the weather's better. They're long overdue.'

'I like the one I've got. It's near.'

'Yes, but if you could move into one of these, then have your old house done up so that it was really nice, and then move back, how would that be?'

'I can't see anything wrong with that. I like my neighbours, I don't want to move any place. We're near the shops and the school and the church. I like it.'

'They're not good houses, though, we can do better.'

'You are doing better, sir, you're doing grand.'

He hadn't realised that he was in need of reassurance, but Nancy had obviously sensed it.

'I hope I'm not this transparent when I'm at work,' he said, smiling ruefully.

Nancy walked home in the half light. Sometimes she found it difficult to reconcile the man whose house she ran with the man who ran the area, and he did run it. He was putting the wind up a lot of people in a lot of ways. At home he was courteous, generous, even gentle and funny sometimes, but Nancy knew very well that Rob was a different person outside the house. She was loyal to him, she didn't discuss him with anybody, and she could have. She could have told the whole of Berry Edge many secrets which Rob and Harry had, because they were less than discreet.

She had to protect them from gossip, and tried her best, but it was difficult. She had told the other two maids that if she heard anything which she thought had come from them, they would be sacked straight away.

Nancy knew very well that Rob was not at home most Saturday nights. Rumour said he kept a beautiful mistress in the city. She was also aware that he had been married. There were pictures in his bedroom of a pretty young dark-haired girl, in one of which she was wearing a wedding dress, but he didn't discuss his marriage – or, indeed, anything of his past, or anything important about the present, other than with Harry.

Nancy had a respect for Rob which she would never have for Harry. Though Harry flirted and laughed, talked to her and to the other maids, and was open and friendly, she called him and thought of him as 'Mr Shaw'. She called Rob 'sir', but always thought of him by his first name in her mind. They had, she knew, a special relationship, and Nancy was glad of that. Rob chose not to hide the fact that he liked her, that he was fond of her, and Nancy knew quite well that if she had any difficult problems in her life she could take them to Rob and he would sort them out. Harry liked her, but Nancy cared nothing for that; Harry was free with his favours. Even some of the men liked Harry, but nobody in Berry Edge liked Rob. Nobody had a good word to say about him, but Nancy could see what he had done and was doing. There was work, people were at the works and the pits full time now. He had begun to repair houses and build new ones, he had got himself on to committees and councils where he could be influential and make the difference, and Rob was effective. He was bringing Berry Edge back to life again. Everything seemed brighter to her somehow, and it was not just the spring arriving. Last spring there had been little work and less pay and no one had been in good spirits. Now the men cursed his name freely in the town, but to most of them that was good. They had not talked about Rob's father like that. They had disliked him because they felt he had let them down, that he was weak, but Rob was somebody they could fight with, fight against. It was not just the men alone Rob was in conflict with. He made everybody sweat. Vera's husband had come home with the satisfying message that the manager of the plate mills thought Rob was as big a bastard as his men did. Nancy was pleased about that.

Rob longed for Saturdays. Although now he could have gone to see Susannah at any time, he was far too busy to go during the week. But he liked the idea of her waiting for him, not seeing other men. He kept her lavishly. He liked doing so, and knew also that Susannah was keeping Claire with his money. There were no more men at the house and he was glad. Claire went out on Saturday nights. Harry had not been there for some time. It didn't surprise Rob. Harry always grew bored with women quickly.

Saturday nights made up for the rest of the week. She always ran down the stairs when she heard him at the door, he could hear her feet clattering, and then she would pull open the door and throw herself into his arms. It was so sweet that it made up for the difficult parts of his life.

One particular week in April everything had gone wrong. Orders had been down, castings had been badly made and sent back – and some were not able to be sent; men had stayed away from work, and some thief had broken into the offices and made the kind of mess which would take weeks to sort out. Rob's father had been too ill to come downstairs now for almost a fortnight. He had suddenly become worse and lost the use of speech and the whole of his left side. Rob tried to be sorry, but the most he could manage was a kind of polite sympathy for his mother and a longing to rush off to Durham and lose himself in Susannah's body. With his father so ill he had not seen her for two weeks. By the third week he couldn't sleep and could barely eat or work. He thought Saturday would never come. All he wanted was to come away and have her in his arms. He pulled her to him when she opened the door and crushed her there until she said she couldn't breathe. They went inside arm in arm.

'God Almighty, you look wonderful,' he said. 'I'm so sorry I haven't seen you. I adore you, I want you, come here.' He rained kisses on her. Susannah laughed and kissed him lingeringly on the mouth.

'I love you,' she said.

She unknotted his tie and the top two buttons on his shirt, and then he drew her back against him and cuddled her and sighed.

'We see less of each other now than we did before you kept me,' Susannah pointed out.

'It won't be for ever.'

Rob couldn't bear to leave her the next morning. They stayed in bed until the middle of the afternoon, and even then she kissed him at the outside door as though he was just arriving.

When he got home his mother came out of the sitting room.

'Where have you been?' she said, as though she had never noticed that quite often he was not there on Saturday nights.

'Out,' Rob said unhelpfully.

'Your father died in the middle of the night. You weren't here and nobody seemed to have any idea where you were. Sometimes I have great difficulty in believing that you were ever my son.'

Rob went into the study where Harry was working. He closed the door. Harry looked up.

'You couldn't have done anything,' he said. 'He was gone in five minutes. Your mother will be able to move her furniture into the churchyard now. You all right?'

'Yes.'

Harry got up, smiling.

'Must have been some night.'

'I should have been here.'

'Rob, you've been here night and bloody day for weeks. The old bastard probably chose last night to snuff it just because you *weren't* here. I'm not going to have this be your fault. After all, when it comes to a choice between screwing Susannah and drinking tea with your mother, I know where I'd rather be.'

'My mother—'

'I was here. She likes me better than you anyhow.'

'Why were you here on a Saturday night?'

'I can't find a woman to put up with me. I wasn't feeling

well. I didn't have a clean pair of shoes. What does it matter to you?'

'Thanks, Harry,' Rob said.

Nancy had never been to a Protestant funeral before, but she felt that she should go to Mr Berkeley's. She sat at the back and was amazed at how plain the chapel was and how casually people acted, not like it was a church. Mrs Berkeley cried a lot and Rob not at all, and Mr Shaw looked as though he would rather have been at the races (which Nancy knew for sure, because he had told Rob so earlier in the day). Nancy had got used to Mr Shaw by now, and had stopped being shocked at what he did. Somehow when he told Rob that and made him laugh, she was glad.

The talk around Berry Edge was that Mr Shaw was busy making up to Miss Norman and that no good would come of it, Mr Shaw being very free and Miss Norman as cold as you like. Miss Norman had managed to look very pretty at the funeral. She suited black. It was Rob that Nancy was concerned about, he was so thin and quiet and looked so good in black and white that Nancy had to make herself concentrate on other things. She wished that she could take him home and feed him soup.

*

They all went back to the house for tea and ham. Harry couldn't understand how people could eat after funerals. The only thing he wanted was a stiff drink, and that was obviously not going to happen unless he sneaked away. He didn't like to leave Rob; his mother had yet to speak a kind word to him. Harry wished that he and Rob could leave, he really wanted to go back to Nottingham at this stage.

Faith, he thought, was in her element here. She chatted to the minister and gave everybody cake. Harry pretended he didn't care what she was doing or who she was talking to, but as the cool wet afternoon went on he became irritated. She wore a smart black dress and hat and smiled at everyone, saying the right things.

Only when most people had left did he get her to himself, and that was in the kitchen, an area of the house that Harry had never had much to do with, and it confused him. He couldn't see what she was doing in there, the maids had cleared up.

'Harry, hello. I'm just putting cake into tins.'

It mystified him, the things that women did. 'The day's brighter. Would you like to go for a walk?'

'I can't. I have a meeting at the chapel at five.' She struggled to put the top on to a tin.

'It's the wrong one.'

'What?'

'It goes on that tin over there.'

'They're the same size, you wouldn't think it would matter.'

Harry ventured nearer. The cakes were small things in individual wrappers or whatever, with some sort of cream confection on the top and then two bits of cake stuck on.

'They're butterfly cakes,' Faith said.

'I never saw a butterfly that looked anything like that, thank God.'

'It's the wings.'

'How disgusting. Come and spend some time with Rob and me, Faith.'

'I can't.'

'Don't you want to see us?'

'I didn't say I didn't want to, I said I couldn't.'

'And do you want to?'

She didn't reply, and he took the tin out of her hands and jerked up her chin with his fingers.

'For God's sake, say something!'

'Don't touch me,' she said.

Harry let go.

'There is no point in this,' Faith said calmly. 'I dare say there are a dozen girls in Nottingham who would be glad of your company. Why waste your time?'

'I didn't think I was wasting my time.'

'And mine,' Faith said, as if he hadn't spoken.

'I thought we were going to be friends.'

'I'm never going to be friends with Rob and that's all you're doing it for—'

'His father's dead, Faith. Couldn't you—'

'I hear that he wasn't even there when Mr Berkeley died,' Faith said, looking straight at Harry. 'I know him quite well. He hasn't really changed at all. Saturday night, drink and women.'

'Neither of us had been anywhere but work for three weeks, the kind of work that takes up twelve or fourteen hours a day, every day. It was one night, and I was there with Mrs Berkeley.'

'That must have been a big comfort to her, Harry, considering that you're a stranger and a southerner.'

There was a long silence after that during which Harry considered whether to push her face into the remains of the sherryless trifle.

'Please forgive me,' he said. 'I didn't realise that I had been so offensive,' and he swept her a little bow and left the room.

He went through into the sitting room. Rob was there alone by this time.

'You don't want to go out and get drunk later, do you?'

'Do we have to wait until later?' Rob said.

It was well after midnight when Susannah heard the knocking on her door. She put on a dressing gown and ran downstairs, hesitating no longer when she heard Rob say, 'Open the door, Susannah, it's me.'

Susannah unbolted the door and let him in.

'I hoped you'd come. I've been so worried about you.'

'I'm fine.'

They went upstairs and Susannah watched him walk wearily into the bedroom and sit down on the bed.

'I'm sorry about your father, Rob. I would have come to the funeral . . . Would you like a drink?'

'No, thanks. I've already had several.'

Susannah went over and sat down beside him.

'Was it when you were here?'

'Yes.'

Susannah would have put her arms around him, but he got up and moved away.

'I've been thinking about things, Susannah. I want you to marry me.'

Susannah stared at him.

'How many drinks did you have?' she said.

'I mean it. I love you. I want us to get married.'

'It's been a bad day, Rob—'

'Do you love me?'

'You know I do.'

'Tell me. You never tell me except when I ask you to.'

'I love you very much, and that's not true.'

'Will you marry me?'

'Certainly not. You're upset and shocked and you've had too much whisky, I can smell it. In the morning you'll only wish you hadn't said such things.'

'I know what I'm saying.'

'And I know how you felt about your father. I won't have you hurt like this.'

'There's nothing anybody can do. It's finished now, it's over, he's dead. I want to start again.'

'You can start again in the morning. It's very late.' She went to him and loosened his tie. 'How much have you had to drink?'

'I don't remember.'

'You look so tired. Don't worry about things, it'll be all right in the morning.'

Rob undressed, fell into bed and slept instantly. Susannah lay awake for a long time holding him close and watching him.

When Rob awoke, he wished he hadn't. He had been having a particularly nice dream about Sarah, but just as he was about to kiss her he woke up. Somebody was drawing back the curtains and letting in an inordinate amount of sunlight.

'Don't do that, damn you,' he said and then realised that he was not at home, that he had not been at home for quite a long time now. It felt like forever. He wished himself in Nottingham. Then Susannah sat down on the bed with a cup and saucer in her hand and said, 'Early morning tea, sir?', in high affected tones as she evidently thought a maid might.

Rob sat up, trying to avoid the light, and took the cup and saucer from her.

'What time is it?' he said.

'Oh, good morning, Susannah. What a beautiful morning, and how lovely you're looking.'

'You've put sugar in it,' Rob said.

He gave her back the cup and saucer and closed his eyes and said again, 'What time is it?'

'Eleven o'clock, near enough.'

'I should have been at work three hours ago.'

'Then why aren't you?' she said, throwing his jacket at him.

Rob got hold of her wrists and brought her to him.

'Whisky,' she objected, turning her face away. He kissed her. 'And you need a shave. Go away.'

Rob pulled her down on to the bed, into his arms and kissed her again. Susannah pushed at him.

'Go away,' she said again.

Rob looked at her and then he let go of her, got out of bed and dressed. Susannah put his tie on for him and knotted it, gave him his shoes and then she kissed him.

'Come back when you're sober,' she advised him, and pushed him out of the front door.

Fourteen

When the funeral was over, Rob's mother went to stay with her sister in Ashington. The atmosphere in the house lightened considerably. She hadn't spoken to him since the Sunday before. Rob had made all the arrangements. His mother had gone to John's and his father's graves every day.

After she left they treated the house rather like an office. The ashtrays were always full of cigar stubs. There were papers piled in the downstairs rooms and Nancy complained about the glasses everywhere which had contained whisky or brandy. Other men came to the house for meetings, and there was more cigar smoke and more whisky fumes, and a great deal of food was consumed. Jackets were left over chair backs and shoes under sofas. It seemed as though part of the works had taken over the house.

To Rob's horror Vincent had written and announced that he and Ida were coming. He had not waited to be invited though, Rob reasoned, it would have been a long wait.

Rob only hoped they weren't staying long. Nancy had been horrified.

'Mr Shaw's parents? His mam and dad? Aren't they very rich with a big house? They'll expect everything to be right.'

'Nancy, this is our house. If Vincent doesn't like it, he needn't stay.'

'That's not the point, sir.'

'It is the point, Nancy. All you have to do is buy and cook more food and make up a bed. What could be simpler?'

'It might be simple to you, sir,' Nancy said and strode out of the sitting room.

It was the following afternoon when Vincent and Ida arrived. Vincent greeted both Rob and Harry civilly enough, but he looked around at the front of the house and said softly, 'My dear boys, I didn't realise you were living in a garden shed.'

'There's only the two of us here,' Harry said.

'Couldn't you have rented something larger?'

'Vincent, if you don't like it you know what you can do,' Rob said.

Vincent eyed him.

'Northern manners, Robert?' he said.

Vincent went inside and there he found Nancy in the hall. She gave him a sort of bob. Vincent beamed at her.

'I'm Vincent Shaw.'

'Nancy, sir. I do the cooking.'

'I'm delighted to hear it.'

'You haven't tasted it yet,' Harry said from behind him.

'He's very rude. He gets it from his mother,' Vincent said.

Ida came in with Rob and beamed as he introduced Nancy.

'I shouldn't say this, my dear,' Ida said, 'but I've never seen such beautiful hair on anybody in my whole life. How lucky you are.'

Nancy smiled.

'Would you like some tea, Mrs Shaw?'

'I would love some. And you must show me the house.'

Harry took Vincent into the sitting room.

'What is this, another cupboard?'

'Vincent—'

'I know, I know. If I don't like it I can go back to Nottingham. You do have something to drink besides tea, I take it?'

'We have some whisky, Father. Would that do?'

'It would be adequate. I feel as if I've travelled to the ends of the earth. I don't understand what anyone is saying, and the state of the damned train made me wonder whether I shouldn't have gone into some other kind of business. What a grubby little town this is.'

'Did you see Durham?' Harry asked.

'I have to admit it did have its good points, though as we only paused to change trains I didn't see many of them. You'll have to show me around.'

'We haven't time to show people around, Vincent,' Rob said. 'We're too busy working.'

'I meant the works. I've come here to help.'

'We don't need any help,' Harry said.

'Looking at the place I would say you need all the help you can get. Isn't that so, Rob?'

Rob glanced at Harry, before saying, 'Don't you have enough to do in Nottingham?'

'Oh, don't worry about that. After you left I found some very competent men. They can manage perfectly well without me for a while.'

The following Saturday Nancy stayed because Vincent had insisted on some company and Faith and her parents had been invited to dinner.

'You do know that they're Methodists,' Harry told Vincent.

'I have no objection to people not drinking and trust they have none when I do.'

If Faith's parents were offended at the wine on the table or the brandy after the meal they had enough sense not to say so and everyone seemed to get on very well, though later in the evening, Vincent came to Rob in the little back room (which they had turned into an office once Mrs Berkeley had left) and said, 'So, is Harry panting after the little teetotaller?'

Rob looked icily at him. 'I beg your pardon.'

'You can beg my pardon all you like, though I must remind you that amongst grammarians a mere "what" will suffice.

Are my eyes getting too old for the rest of me, or is my son in love with the plainest female on the planet?'

'Is he?' Rob said in surprise. 'I don't think he is, Vincent. She's hardly his style. I think he's flirting, and because she doesn't flirt it interests him, that's all.'

'Men have married for less. When I think of all the young, beautiful, accomplished women in Nottingham . . .'

'Faith's very nice.'

'You've been in Durham too long. She has no wit, no conversation, no fashion, and why is she not married? The girl is past her prayers. If Harry goes near her, I shall be sorely disappointed. This is the woman your brother was going to marry?'

'If you think I'm going to apologise for her, Vincent, you're wrong.'

'Her parents are desperate to marry her off and you and Harry are keeping company with them. Is this the extent of your social life, having dinner with people who are beneath you?'

'They're beneath you, Vincent, not me.'

'It's time you came back to Nottingham and remembered who you are.'

'Don't tell me what to do, Vince,' Rob said softly.

'I'm very angry with you. This shoddy little town has stolen my son, and it's your doing. He likes this place.'

Rob smiled. 'Yes, I think he does. I think he actually does.'

'If he stays in this godforsaken place, what am I meant to

do with my business ventures? And as for Miss Norman –
she's hardly the kind of woman that Harry could take into
Nottinghamshire society.'

Rob didn't answer.

'I wish you were younger, the pair of you, and I could beat
you both and drag you back to Nottingham. You defeat me,
Rob, indeed you do. You'll rot here, your mind will give up.
You'll end up learning to make conversation that revolves
around church teas and shop fronts. You're doing us all a
great disservice here and there is nothing I can do about it.'

'Nothing,' Rob said simply.

'It's a pity about your father. I did hope that perhaps he
would get better and you would quarrel very fiercely with
him, and that he would make your position here unbearable
and you would come home. I held on to that idea, but when
I got here and saw how truly awful it is, and understand from
Harry that you have brooked no opposition from anyone . . .
There is no way forward for you here and I think that you
know it. That knowledge will cost you everything. I hope it
isn't a complete waste, for your sake,' Vincent said.

'Your father thinks you've developed a passion for Faith,'
Rob said to Harry, later that evening when everyone had
gone to bed and they were drinking brandy in the little back
room.

Harry grinned. 'She's like that woman in Dickens' novel,

the one who sat among her wedding feast because some bastard had let her down. She sat there for the rest of her life—'

'Miss Havisham.'

'That's her. That's what Faith's going to do. She might as well be buried with your brother.'

'But you like her?'

'I've just never met anyone like her. She's strange. And I feel sorry because I think she bothers you. I wanted us all to be comfortable.'

'That was a lot to want.'

'My father's worried, eh?' Harry said, laughing. 'My God, he would be, after all the efforts he and Mother have made to marry me off to somebody suitable. Could you see Faith at a ball, not dancing and not drinking and being scandalised or lost off with the conversation, and wearing one of those awful dresses? I must admit though, I do sometimes have very warm feelings about her.'

'You have very warm feelings about every woman you meet, and more especially when you know you can't have her,' Rob said.

Vincent and Ida stayed while the better weather arrived. Rob came to be glad of Vincent's presence at the works. He helped a lot and, although he criticised and shouted and bullied, Rob was used to his working methods and had not realised until then how much he missed Vincent's good mind and bright ideas.

While he had the extra help, Rob wanted some free time to see Susannah. He thought they could go out together. In the city people picnicked on the riverbanks, shopped and walked and went dancing, but Susannah wouldn't meet him.

'You can't be seen with me,' she said.

'Why ever not?'

'Because of who you are.'

'Susannah, I'm nobody here. I'm the local lad who caused his brother's death and ran away. Nobody likes or respects me. I don't have a reputation to lose, it's gone.'

'That's not true. The people of Berry Edge respect you for what you've done since you came back.'

'They hate me.'

'You couldn't be seen with me here.'

Rob looked at her. 'Does that mean you would consider somewhere else?'

'Go away with you?'

'For a holiday, just a few days. Would you?'

'I'd like that,' Susannah said.

Susannah had gone places with men before, glamorous places with fancy hotels. She had been to London and Paris. She had never gone to the seaside with a man, and would have laughed at the idea of a tiny fishing village on the

Northumbrian coast, but that was where they went. She had never been in love before. It did occur to her that anywhere would have been as magical as it was.

They went as a married couple, which was the only respectable way they could go on holiday together. The pub was the most comfortable place Susannah had ever stayed. The bed was huge and soft, the room had a view over the bay, the food was excellent, and the weather in August was perfect.

They stayed in bed late in the mornings, walked during the day, and did silly things like running up and down beaches and buying things in the local shop. They drank beer and sat outside at night watching the sun set over the horizon, and when it grew late a man in the bar played a mouth organ and the locals gathered to drink and tell tales. Susannah was entranced by Rob's company. They had never before had enough time together to do normal things like eating meals, talking to other people, walking outside, just being together without the knowledge that he would be leaving in a few hours and she would not see him again for a whole week. Susannah never wanted to go back to Durham for as long as she lived.

He told her that he loved her several times a day. Men had done that before, in quiet dining rooms and sumptuous bedrooms; but no one had ever asked her to marry him and this time she could not blame it on shock or drunkenness.

She wished that anybody but Rob had asked her, because

then it would not have mattered. But he did matter to her so much now that she had become frightened. She felt crowded, panicked, as though if she was not careful she would do or say the wrong thing and feel again as she had felt when Sam had left her, as though the world was about to end.

It was late morning on the third day of their holiday, and they were lying on an almost deserted beach. True, another couple were walking on the sands in the distance, and a boy was throwing a stick for his dog, but there was nobody anywhere near. It was a perfect summer day. The waves could barely manage a splash as they broke, and the sky was cloudless.

In the sunlight Susannah, lying on her back on a rug, looked up at him as he leaned over.

'I want you to marry me,' he said.

'Don't be silly,' Susannah said briskly. 'We're on holiday. It's not really like this.'

'It could be.'

'No, it couldn't.'

'I know. I've been married.'

She sat up, and as she did so he moved back.

'Rob, most people's marriages aren't like that. You were lucky. It couldn't happen twice.'

'Why not?'

'Because it doesn't. Be grateful and leave it.'

'Be grateful for something that's gone?'

'Things are never entirely gone, there's a part of them that lingers.'

'Well, it isn't enough. I want you.'

'You have me.'

'I want you to marry me.'

'We've been through this.'

'Please, Susannah, say you will.'

'No!'

'Why not?'

He got hold of her so Susannah was obliged to look at him and say something.

'Men like you don't marry whores,' she said. 'It would ruin you. Can you imagine going to a party and meeting a business acquaintance and him remembering going to bed with me?'

'I don't care.'

'You would. You would resent him and me and my past life. You know very well by now that you cannot break the rules of the society which allows you to live in it. You did it once and look what happened. You can't marry me, Rob, you know very well that you can't. I think the sun has got to you.'

'You've got to me.'

'That's only because you think I'm Sarah.'

He hadn't been looking at her for several seconds but he did after that.

'I don't think anything of the kind.'

'Yes, you do. I'm dark like she was and pretty and independently minded, and you confuse the two. You want to

Elizabeth Gill

because it makes your life tolerable. And if you should marry me, you would realise straight away that I'm really nothing like Sarah and this so-called love which you have for me would not survive that realisation; and then do you know what would happen? You would despise me. I don't think I could bear that.' Rob said nothing to this. 'You know I'm right,' Susannah told him. 'I'm a substitute, quite a good one up to now, but we don't live together so that illusion isn't shattered. You can pretend to yourself that I'm Sarah all the time we're together. Isn't that so?'

'No!'

'It's just a reflection that you see, Rob, it's just the missing of Sarah.'

'How could it be when I haven't felt like this about anybody else?'

'You didn't go to bed with anybody else, did you?'

'You think I don't love you.'

'Yes.'

'And you don't love me? Go on, say it. I know what you think and feel about men, you don't have to pretend to me all the time.'

'I don't pretend to you.'

'Yes, you do. I'm just money to you.'

'That's not true.' Susannah would have got hold of him but he was getting up. 'Rob . . .' Susannah watched him walk away up the beach and out of sight.

*

206

Later, much later when he had not come back for lunch or for dinner, Susannah went to their room. He was standing looking out over the bay.

'We ruined the day as though we had so many,' she said, shutting the door behind her. 'Please don't be angry. You didn't really think we were going to get married?' He didn't answer. 'Try to be reasonable. Am I going to lose you because I won't marry you?'

'Why worry? You've made a lot of money out of me. You'll manage.'

'You don't mean it. You can have me as much as you want—'

'You don't understand, do you?' Rob said, turning around and looking at her. 'I'm tired of the desperation of it, Susannah. I want to have time to think about other things, to do other things, to be able to leave you without feeling that heavy regret, not to long for you every night. I want to see you as my wife. At the moment I can't bear to let you out of my bed or my sight, I want you so much. It's like dying of thirst and from time to time being given half a glass of cold champagne. I can't think about anything but you and I don't think I can stand it any more. I'm going to pack my things and leave.'

'No!' Susannah ran over and got hold of him. 'No, Rob, no!'

'Don't worry, I'll give you some money,' he said.

'I don't want your money,' Susannah declared. 'No, Rob, don't. Don't go, don't.'

She clung and kissed him and pleaded and all the time her mind told her that it was much too late for this. He had run out of patience. There was even a part of her glad that he was hurt, triumphant that he was leaving, a part of her nature that had never been happy to be with him, that had waited for him to betray her in some way as other men had. When he had not done, she worried that he would come to mean so much to her that she would imagine that she could not survive without him.

But there was a good reason for her to make him stay. Her body shrieked at her to keep him there any way that she could, to agree to anything because now she needed him as never before.

He pushed her from him. Her dark side wanted him to do more, to do violence, to knock her down so that he could be condemned, so that she would be free.

She cried. It would have turned many a man back to her, but Rob was not made like that and she knew it. Crying for effect was no good. After he had gone she cried in earnest, wetly and hard, trying to hate him for her own self-protection, trying to tell herself that she was better without him, that life could be as it was before she met him, that she didn't love him, had never loved him, would not miss him, did not want him. She crawled into bed and cried until she was exhausted, until her eyes stung heavily, until there was even comfort in listening to her own sobs gradually lessen and then cease. In the quietness, in the bed, Susannah went to sleep.

Fifteen

That autumn the miners rose up; that was how his father would have described it, Rob thought, as though they were some huge kind of wave about to break across a pier so hard that they would damage its very heart.

Amongst the miners' leaders was Michael McFadden. Michael gave no indication that they had ever met before, that they had been boys together or fought. His clipped tones and cold gaze enraged Rob. So far he and Harry had agreed on conciliatory action when dealing with the men, but Rob was getting tired of it. Always they wanted more, more money, more time to themselves, better housing, schools, places of leisure, churches, even improvements in the bloody park. And he knew that his anger was misdirected. The men worked hard, they were entitled to safe conditions and decent wages and better houses. His company ran their lives for them in ways which would have made him as bitter as Michael was now; but Rob felt the responsibility, and it was huge.

Harry was more sympathetic. Rob thought in his honest moments that that was why he wanted Harry there, to be between himself and the men. Under Harry's shrewd direction the company had begun stockpiling coal some time back, because they had seen this coming. The miners had barely let Rob re-establish full time work here before they began to threaten him in all kinds of ways. They wanted better wages. The men at the steelworks did too, but the miners were the worst. Some of them did little, some of them took Friday and Monday off. Rob could not run the mines and the steelworks like that, to suit their needs. He had his orders to fill. But they lived in that little town on the moors at his direction so that he could make money. Some were idle, lazy, drank, never went to church. There was little point in the schools when many would not send their children or sent them for so few hours that it was a waste of time.

This particular morning he was for once letting Harry take the weight. He was standing by the window, leaning there and looking out over the works. Harry was handling Michael McFadden and his fellow union men. Rob was thinking about Susannah. He missed her. He longed for her. In a way he missed her doubly because he always missed Sarah. Susannah had taken some of that hurt away. He couldn't believe that he had left her, that he had walked out on what he had promised himself would be a perfect holiday. He had ruined not just the holiday but everything they had together with his stupid demands. Susannah must have thought he was losing his mind. What man would marry a woman when he could have her without? But it was not just that. When you had been married you knew what it was like to be well loved, to be the joy in another person's life, to be at the centre of everything that mattered, to go to bed together and talk over your world, to turn in the night and feel her sweet warm body there.

The holiday had made it worse, shown him what he was missing, brought back to him the delights of his marriage to Sarah. Susannah was right in some ways. He did want that back. More than that, he wanted the future back, that which always now eluded him, the looking forward, the making plans, the idea of home and children. He wanted that more badly than he had ever wanted anything in his life. And worse than that now, he would have settled for anything, he missed her so much. His body was knife-edged with want for her. It clouded everything. He would have gone back to the beginning, back to nothing but Saturday nights if he could have. His pride was all gone.

He had even, he could hardly bear to think about it, gone up the steps to the house in Durham, to beg her to have him back; but the house was closed up. Enquiries brought him nothing. He had been there several times, almost ready to kill someone in the end in order to gain entry, in order to see her. She was not there. He had thought at first in dubious mood that she must be at the fishing village, that she had not come back, and he had gone there. That was the hardest thing of all, remembering how she had cried and pleaded and hung on to his sleeve so that he wouldn't go. Every woman he saw now he thought was Susannah, any tall dark woman, any shadow. He remembered her on the beach, he remembered her in the hotel, but most of all he remembered her in the bedroom at the house in Durham which stood above the Wear. He remembered her there in all her moods and in his arms. She was gone and he couldn't find her.

'Things aren't the way they were,' Harry was saying to the men. Rob knew the argument well. He had heard Vincent saying the same thing and he knew that Harry was right. Other countries produced iron and steel more cheaply. People might say that things in England were getting better, but it was all over for England to be the best. America and Germany did these things just as well. England's days as a world power were numbered; he knew it but these men could not see it. They saw nothing but their own lives, their wages and their families, and they thought that they could hold some kind of power here when in fact prices were dropping all the time. He listened from his stance by the window as Harry explained the situation. He looked out over the works, and all he wished was that he could be like them – to go home to his wife and his tea and a child or two, and for everything to be different. They had these things, they were so much better off than he, yet they didn't know it, they didn't see it. They thought that money freed a man. They thought he had everything.

He thought about Sarah, and some part of him which he had believed was gone forever, when he married her, made its twisted way up inside him. He could no longer pretend that she was somewhere waiting for him, that they would have children and see time and grow old together and look back on the years with affection. None of that was to be. He wished that there was somebody to hate, someone to rail against, some space in his life which was not filled with the loss.

He wondered whether somewhere in Sarah's subconscious mind there had been an inkling of what was to come. During their short marriage they had been happier than Rob could ever have imagined anybody might be. That was what made it so good and so bad. To know that happiness was something few people ever did, but to have that happiness taken away from him made him wish sometimes that he had never known it. It was to fall out of heaven, to drop off the cliff edge into the darkest, deepest sea that he had ever known. He had never been so far down; to know the heights, to feel the sweetest made the rest so low and so bitter. Sometimes he did not think any of it was possible, that he would wake and be a child again and have nothing and expect nothing, and exist in that void which he had thought never to experience again. It seemed to him now that he was back there, unhappy and powerless to change that unhappiness. He wished he could hold her again, just once.

At the end he could barely hold her in his arms any more, she was like some costly ornament that would break. Finding Susannah had stopped the hurt part of the time and now she too was gone.

Behind him he could hear Michael McFadden's voice so reasonable, so secretly threatening. He cut in now.

'Do you know what's going to happen, McFadden?' he said. 'There'll come a time soon when there won't be any work—'

'Oh, I see.' Michael got to his feet, knowing, Rob thought admiringly, that he was bigger than anyone else in the room, especially bigger than Rob. 'You mean the good times are over, Mr Berkeley?'

Rob hated his intelligence, hated his slow, sarcastic, northern voice. He hated the fact that Michael would fight battles which he well knew he could not win, which he might even have wondered were worth the effort, to gain just a little over his masters.

'People are going bankrupt in this business,' Rob said. 'We need to expand to keep up with other countries, we need modern thinking, modern processes or we won't survive, and those cost a great deal of money. If I compromise, if I pay you more, then I won't have enough money to make sure that the works survives. We have to grow and we need to manage our resources carefully in order to do this. We have to find and take on new kinds of work and we need the machinery and the skills to do it. If we don't we'll get left behind. Now, I am trying to build good houses, to make things better and there's full time work again. When I can afford to, I will pay you better wages, but I don't have the money to do it right now. I can't do any more, Michael, I can't afford any more.'

'I don't believe that, and I know that you're stockpiling coal. I know that you're afraid of what will happen when that coal runs out. How will you run your precious steel-works then? And do you seriously think that hundreds of miners are going to sit at home putting their feet up while you move that coal to the mills in order to keep this place working? All we want is a decent wage.'

'You've got a decent wage, and I can't afford to pay you any more.'

When the meeting was over, Harry was still sitting at the table, frowning.

'They're going to strike any minute, I can see it.'

'It won't get them anywhere,' Rob said.

'It will if they manage to keep it up until we run out of coal.'

'We can worry about that when it happens.'

*

When Susannah had arrived home two days early, Claire sat her down and made her some tea.

'He left me,' Susannah said finally.

'Never in this world.'

Susannah got up and took the pins out of her hat and the hat from her head. 'Yes, he did. He got tired of me.'

'Susie, the man is in love. How could he get tired in three days?'

'He asked me to marry him.'

'Well, by God,' Claire said, staring at her. 'You turned him down, didn't you?'

'Yes.'

'You don't care about him?'

'No, of course not. He's just another man,' Susannah said and put both hands over her face as she began to sob. 'I couldn't do it. I couldn't do it to him, and he hates me.'

'He doesn't hate you.'

'Yes he does, and I'm going to have a baby.'

'Oh my God,' Claire said.

Harry walked into Rob's office one fine day that autumn and said abruptly, 'The house in Durham's all locked up. What's going on?'

Rob looked up. 'Don't knock, will you?'

'What's going on?' Harry said again.

'I'm working,' he said. 'Can we discuss it later?'

'You've been bad tempered ever since you went away for a break. We can't discuss anything at the house, not with my father there. What's going on?'

'I thought you didn't go there any more?'

'I don't, I just . . . Has Susannah gone?'

'I don't know. I haven't seen her.'

'You make it sound as if you don't care.'

'I don't. Now will you let me get on?'

Rob's mother came home late in the autumn. Vincent was very polite to her and she seemed to get on well with Ida. Vincent talked of going home, but when the strike began he stopped mentioning it. Twice during the summer he travelled there for a few days and came back, but Ida didn't go with him and it was obvious to Rob and Harry that he intended to stay with them during the difficult time.

Rob hoped that the men would not strike until the bad weather came, but he reckoned Michael McFadden was too clever to wait, and that autumn was the best and mildest that Rob had ever known. Since the men didn't care to work during the good weather it was obvious that they would begin then, and so they did. There was money from the union, and the men were glad of the time off, Rob could see. They could go fishing or ferreting, see to their gardens, walk in the country if it suited them, play billiards and have a drink if the weather was bad as it was eventually.

Rob was frustrated. He had now built things up so that there was work and enough for all the men to do, even though the prices were not good anywhere. He considered giving in, paying what they wanted, then he thought everybody else would go the same way, wanting more. If he paid them all more it would be difficult to keep the place going and see any profit. So he sat back and watched to see what would happen.

His mother had not been back a week when she took him aside and said, 'I'm worried about Faith, she's so pale and thin. Do you think she's all right?'

It was unlike his mother to confide in him. Rob hadn't seen Faith, she was avoiding them. Now sometimes even when her parents came to dinner she made excuses that she was busy at the chapel and in the town, and could not come. When he did make an effort to see her, he was shocked by her appearance. She had indeed lost weight and her eyes had no spark at all. He had gone over to the house and found her sewing by the window in the living room. She smiled wanly when she saw him. Rob knew nothing about such things and tried hard to take an interest, only saying when he could be silent no longer, 'Faith, do you feel all right? You look ill.'

'I'm just a little tired.'

Rob's heart squeezed. That was what Sarah had said at the beginning of her illness. She was always just tired.

'Don't you think you ought to see a doctor?'

'I'm perfectly well. How is Harry?' she asked bravely.

'Worrying about the strike.'

'Aren't we all? What do you think the people will do when they have nothing left?'

'It won't go that far.'

'Why not? Won't you let it?'

'Of course I won't. Don't cast me as the villain, Faith. I'm only trying to do what's best.'

'I doubt that's how the miners see it,' Faith said.

'How was she?' Harry asked simply when he got back.

They were in the garden – it was cold out there, with a few stars – because the house seemed to be full of people, what with Vincent's loud voice and Ida's chatter and his mother joining in. His mother seemed happier than he had seen her since before John died. She liked the company and Ida was persuading her to go out and buy new clothes even though she was in mourning, encouraging her out of black. They seemed somehow to have much in common. Vincent was forever going across the road to play chess with Faith's father. Rob was amazed that the two men and three women got on so well.

'You should go,' Rob told him.

'She doesn't want me there.'

'She doesn't look well to me.'

'If she could get out of here—'

'She doesn't want to leave.'

'Maybe we should drag her out, kicking and screaming.'

'I wish there was a way.'

Rob's mother came into the garden. 'How is Faith?' she said.

'Not good.'

'If she had a husband and a child or two she'd be different,' his mother said, to his surprise. 'Your father and I have thought all along, and so have Faith's parents, you ought to marry her.' His mother paused and then said, 'You're very like John now, I'm not sure you know how much.' She went back into the house again.

Alice McFadden died in the middle of the strike and Nancy went over to help Michael with the funeral arrangements. It was the first time that she could remember having seen dust in the house and the first time that she had actually enjoyed being there.

'What are you going to do now, they'll take the house off you.'

'I'll have to go and lodge with somebody.'

'On strike pay? And what about the furniture?'

'I'll have to get rid of it. If you want any, Nancy, just take it.'

'It's better than what I have . . .' Nancy said tentatively.

'Have it, then, and sell yours.'

'You might want it.'

'What for?'

'Well, I mean, isn't there some lass . . . ?'

'No,' he said.

Nancy saw to the funeral tea. A lot of striking miners and their families came. Nancy thought disrespectfully that some of them came for the sandwiches.

'Are you still working at Berkeley's house, Nancy?' one of the miners' leaders, Tom Cowan, asked.

'And if I am?' Nancy said, looking squarely at him.

'Should you be? I wouldn't let any lass of mine anywhere near that bastard. For tuppence I'd shoot him. I've got a handgun my uncle brought back from America. We'd be well off with Berkeley dead.' Tom Cowan wrinkled his nose and parted his lips.

'If you spit on the rug, Tom, I'll rub your nose in it,' Nancy said, and there was silence.

Tom Cowan looked at Michael. 'You should teach your Nancy her manners.'

'This strike's nowt to do with Nancy,' Michael said. 'She does her job, she has two bairns to provide for. She works hard and asks for nowt, so you can all mind your own business.'

The funeral tea wasn't quite the same after that. Nancy didn't eat at the time but afterwards, when everything was washed up and put away and she had returned various plates and such to kind neighbours, she sat down by the sitting room fire with a cup of tea and a pease pudding sandwich and watched Michael playing on the rug with the children. You would have thought there was nothing the matter to look at him, she thought, no strike, no death. His face was clear of worry, his eyes were full of fun. She wondered what it would have been like if Sean had been that way.

Later he took her home, with Clarrie asleep against his shoulder and William walking by his side. For the first time, when he left her to go back home Nancy wished that he wasn't going.

'Will you be all right in the house on your own?' she said.

Michael smiled. 'I'll manage,' he said.

'Thank you.'

'For what?'

'For sorting Tom Cowan out.'

'He's a useless bastard,' Michael said. 'He needs to talk. He treats their Mary like our Sean treated you. He's muck. He likes being out on strike so that he doesn't have to get up of a morning, and he can't mind his own business.'

'Things are going to get worse, aren't they? What will I do when you and Rob really start fighting?'

Michael looked at her. 'You like him, don't you?'

'I think he's doing his best.'

'There's not much more he can do then, is there?'

Nancy touched him. She wasn't given to touching people, but it was only his arm.

'You will be all right, won't you?'

'You just asked me that. Losing my mother was like losing my dad and Sean. It was how much it didn't matter that hurt.'

Nancy watched him as he went off down the rows, and thought that in a way it was better for him without his mother. She had cared for cleaning and Michael's wage and that was about all.

It was difficult for Nancy because she saw both sides. Around here the pitmen propped up the corner ends, while the weather stayed fine, when they hadn't much money, and at the Berkeley household things went on as usual, just as though nothing had happened. Harry, Rob and Vincent went to work.

At first there was plenty of coal, but as time went on the coal that had been stockpiled further away at the pitheads had to be moved so that the mills would work. When Rob tried to move the coal from the Diamond pit, which was the nearest to the town, the miners pelted those responsible with stones and other missiles until they retreated. Vincent was inclined to call the police. Rob had to stop him.

Back at the Berkeley house Nancy bathed a cut under Rob's eye.

'You were lucky,' she said. 'Just a bit higher and you could have been in serious trouble.'

'I am in serious trouble, Nancy. You should be at home. I'll take you back.'

'Indeed you will not. You're not safe down the rows.'

As she spoke there was a blinding crash and a brick came through the kitchen window. Rob grabbed Nancy and pulled her well out of the way back into the safety of the corner where nothing could touch them. He held her there against him, tight in his arms, his hand on the back of her head against her hair, pressing her near as though he thought she might be frightened. Nancy wasn't, she was too disconcerted. She hadn't been that close to a man since Sean had died. She thought she could feel his heartbeat. They stood listening to the noise, as other bricks followed through other windows. Luckily, Nancy thought, Mrs Berkeley and Mr and Mrs Shaw were at the Normans' so there was only Harry to be considered. She could hear him shout from the sitting room, 'Are you all right in there?'

'We're fine,' Rob shouted back.

'I'll help clear up,' Nancy said, moving away from him.

'No, you won't. We'll do it. Stay there.'

Nancy stayed in the kitchen while Rob and Harry cleared up around her and in the other rooms. It was blowing a gale, and a cool dark night, and they spent a lot of time boarding up the windows as best they could without going outside. It was a strange feeling being trapped there.

'Where are the children?' Rob asked her.

'They're with Vera.'

'You should stay, Nancy. It might not even be safe on the streets for you. People know that you work here. Their mood isn't good. Will Vera understand?'

'I'm sure she will.'

They sat over the fire. The others didn't come back so they must have known what the problem was and not dared cross the street.

'I should have had the sense to send you home before now,' Rob said, 'days ago.'

'I didn't want to do that,' Nancy said stoutly.

'Would you like a drink?' Harry offered.

'A drop of whisky would be nice.'

'I couldn't agree more.'

In the morning when the streets were clear Vincent took Nancy home. He left her at the end of the row, but when she reached her yard, people had been busy there too. Her windows were smashed, the door was kicked in and the furniture which had been Alice McFadden's, some of it quite good, was broken. The crockery was in pieces on the floor, even the few toys which the children had. Their clothes had been torn, the food in the kitchen had been thrown around. Some of it was stuck to the walls and the floor. There was not a single thing left untouched. As Nancy stood there she heard a noise behind her, but it was only Vera. The tears were big in her eyes.

'Michael came and took the bairns,' she said. 'He's expecting you. I'll come with you.'

'No, really, I'll be fine,' Nancy said, but Vera went with her anyhow.

She was conscious of being watched but nobody did

anything, though she thought she heard whispers like 'blackleg'. The children ran down the yard to meet her. Vera left her. Nancy went into the house with them. Michael was in the kitchen.

'I'm sorry,' he said, 'there was nothing I could do.'

He had got rid of most of the furniture in his house, thinking that he would not be there long. All he had were the basics.

Michael had fed the children. They played happily enough by the fire as rain began to pour down the windows.

'You've got to stop this,' Nancy said. 'Somebody will get badly hurt.'

'How can I stop it? I'm only one person.'

There was not much food in the house.

'I'll have to go to the shops.'

'No, you can't,' he said quickly.

'Somebody will have to go.'

'I'll go.'

'You can't go shopping.'

'I'll have to. We can't both go, somebody has to be here for the bairns.'

Nancy made him a list and he went but after last night – after the broken windows, the darkness, the fear of not knowing what would happen next – and the morning, discovering her own house, Nancy could not be easy until he came back. He was not long, she knew he was aware that she was frightened.

It was a very long day. Not being able to go out made you want to, Nancy discovered, and she thought of what she would have been doing at the house. She missed it already.

There was only one bed left in Michael's house. She put the children to sleep there and she and Michael sat in chairs. She wasn't tired, she was too worried for that.

The next day he went out and Nancy knew what was happening. She knew that Rob had to move the coal and that they weren't going to let him. The works would come to a halt and then nobody would be making a wage, the whole of Berry Edge would be stopped. She waited by the window all the long day for Michael to come back, and when he didn't she tried to keep the children content. It was not easy, they were already fretting at having to stay inside with so little to do. Nancy had exhausted her ideas.

In the middle of the afternoon, Vera came over and took the children and Nancy went up to the works to see what was happening. She was so worried. It was frightening. The short autumn day was dark, the good weather was finished, it was cold and unfriendly.

Rob had no idea who had alerted the police; he had known it would only make things worse. He had seen similar problems in other places. He tried to get the police to leave, but all the time the situation grew worse. Somebody set his house on fire. The miners laughed and cursed him, watching as the flames danced behind what had been boarded-up windows. Luckily there was no one in the house at the time. Vincent and Harry were out with him, and Ida and his mother had gone to the Normans'. In a very short time the house was well alight, and the police and firemen had appeared, trying to keep people away from the blaze.

There was more to worry about. Hundreds of miners had gathered at the Diamond pit and they were not a happy crowd, shouting obscenities and jeering. As before, they began to throw not just what they found but what they had obviously brought with them for the purpose, big pieces of brick mostly, small sharp stones that hurt just as much, fired hard. The night was cold, dry and clear. Every sound, every movement seemed amplified until the din was deafening, the great showers of stone frightening.

No one could get near the big trucks of coal, nobody could reach the railway. Michael and the other leaders had positioned their men well, and there were so many of them that even with the police there was no way that Rob and the officials could reach what they needed.

It was the height of frustration for him. Berry Edge would come to a halt if he could not succeed here. He thought of the capital that he had put in, of the time and effort. He and Harry had sold most of their business ventures to prop up this giant ailing steelworks. Rob had even asked Vincent to buy his share of the house he loved so much, the abbey that had been his home. Vincent had refused. Instead, he had, much against his judgement he said, loaned them money. It would all come to nothing if he failed here. Berry Edge would go down and he and Harry would be bankrupt.

He glanced at his brother-in-law dodging bricks and wished for the thousandth time that he had not let Harry come with him in the first place, and that he had not let him put his money into it, even though without that money the steelworks would have closed. Harry was caught here now whether he wanted to go on or not.

It seemed at last that they were making progress, that they were moving forward, gaining ground with the help of the police. A yard or two and then a yard or two more, the missiles lessening as time went on, until finally the pitmen had no more and began shouting abuse and then coming forwards and fighting.

Rob's heart misgave. This was worse than he had thought, hand to hand fighting like a war. He could not win like this, had not thought the men so against him as to go this far. He could see Michael quite close and the policemen carrying or dragging people off, some of them injured, some of them resisting, shouting.

Harry was close beside him as though in protection, and Vincent was at hand. Rob prayed that neither of them would get hurt. They had been through difficult times before but nothing like this. Michael was very close now, and he thought that if they got any nearer they would be fighting each other. He couldn't bear to think what that would be like.

And then suddenly somebody dragged at him. Something from somewhere effectively stopped him. He thought it was strange. Nobody was that close yet, he was not fighting. Yet he couldn't move. He couldn't do anything, the impact against him was so huge that although he felt nothing there was an enormous numbing, like running into a huge wall. It not only stopped him, it held him there like great hands for long, long moments. Then it drew him down towards it like a lover and the ground came up to meet him.

Everywhere, Nancy saw, there were people about, and as soon as she left the rows she could smell smoke. As she began to get nearer to Rob's house, she could see the flames, and the fire brigade and policemen, and people gathered to see the place burn. It was burning well. The flames were coming out of every window, and the smoke was thick and black, and went everywhere and smelled hot and dirty. Nancy couldn't believe that she had been there so recently, that the house had been neat and clean until people started breaking the windows.

She kept her shawl well around her head so that she wouldn't be recognised, but nobody was watching. The fire fascinated them. Some were even pleased. The men joked and stamped their feet in the cold just far enough back from the police, but she was afraid that fighting would start because they began to shout and jeer and move around. She went on as quickly as she could through the crowds.

At the pithead of the Diamond pit where the coal was due to be moved towards the mills the men were gathered, and not just a few of them, to stop the coal being shifted. The police were there too, Nancy could see them.

She couldn't see Michael at first, but she picked him out because of his height and because he was right in the middle of things. The miners were throwing anything they could find, and the police were trying to keep the miners and the people moving the coal well apart. To Nancy's dismay, Rob was there too and Harry, and even Vincent. There was a lot of shouting through the cold, still night. Nancy kept well back. There were few women about; most had retreated to their homes. It was awful. She thought of Rob holding her against him so that she would not be frightened or hurt in the kitchen at his house, and she thought of Michael holding each of her children with one hand, seeing her home. She was horrified at how quickly things had changed.

The police were being hit by stones and bricks now, and were beginning to try to arrest the miners. In the middle of it all, Nancy clearly heard a bang. It was the same sound that you could hear when you went walking in the countryside around Berry Edge. Her dad always said that you would think men would give animals Sunday off, but they never did. When she was little and went walking with her dad, you could hear the sounds above the clear Sunday skies. It seemed to Nancy such a desecration to take life on the Sabbath.

It was a shot. After it, though there was slight confusion, it seemed to her that the general noise ceased within seconds and that where the Berry Edge works rose in the cold evening sky you could hear silence.

Everything stopped, the men were stilled, only Nancy moved because she heard somebody cry out. It was her instinct that took her there, it was like a mother's instinct somehow because she knew that cry for grief and despair, every mother knew it.

It seemed that people were moving, but they were moving slowly and quietly back whereas she was moving quickly forward, pushing her way through to where she could see Michael standing tall and still. When she reached him she knew that it had been Michael who had cried out. He must have tried to go forward, because two policemen were holding him back, and the look on his face was horror.

Harry Shaw and his father were crouched down as though they were miners, and Rob was lying on the cold ground, blood oozing over the white shirt which Nancy had ironed a day or two ago. Nancy didn't know who to go to first. She wanted to beat the policemen off Michael and shriek that he was not capable of hurting anyone, that he was kind and good and loving, but she knew that she could do nothing. She pushed through and got down beside Rob.

'No,' she said, 'no.'

He looked narrowly at her and smiled before he closed his eyes.

Sixteen

Faith went to the hospital with Harry and Vincent. At the time it seemed the right thing to do – she didn't know why exactly, when she got there she couldn't do anything. She waited in a cold grey corridor in the quietness and thought about what it had been like when John died and of how badly she had treated Rob.

In one way she had been glad to get away from Berry Edge. The streets were not safe, the Berkeley house had burned all that evening and well into the night, and the cries and shouts from outside frightened her so much that she couldn't rest in any way.

Rob's mother and Harry's mother were at her house being looked after by her father and mother. Nobody had gone to bed, she guessed. Rob's mother had not even offered to go to the hospital, like somebody who had been through too much and couldn't manage another problem like this.

As she waited, Harry came out of the room where Rob

lay in a hospital bed. She got up. Vincent was sitting with her. Nobody said anything.

'What's happening?' she said. 'Is Rob going to be all right?'

'The bullet went through his lung and into his shoulder blade but they've got it out. He's conscious but he's got some fever. I want you to go in there and pretend to be Sarah.'

Faith stared at him. 'Who?'

'I want you to . . .' Harry stopped, and then he looked up and his eyes were drenched. 'He thinks she's there but he can't find her.'

'Who on earth is Sarah?'

'My sister. She was his wife.'

'I didn't know.'

'He didn't want you to know.'

'Why not?'

'He didn't want anybody here to know. He wanted to keep that part of his life separate, after Sarah died.'

Faith could not imagine Rob married. More than that, she could not imagine him having gone through the kind of pain she had experienced with John.

'She died nearly three years ago. Please, Faith, I think it would help.'

'What makes you think he won't recognise me?'

'He doesn't recognise anybody. Do it for me, please.'

'Is he going to be all right?'

'I don't know. I don't think anybody knows yet.'

Faith opened the door of the room and walked softly inside. He was not alone, a nurse was there, but she smiled and drew back away from the bed when she saw Faith. Faith went across and stood by the bed. She thought he was unconscious because he didn't seem to know that she was there and he was quite still. He looked like John lying there. Faith took hold of his hand. He stirred slightly and said, 'Sarah?'

'Yes.'

He said nothing else, but he didn't let go of her hand. Faith stood there for a long time and then tried sitting on the chair by the bed, but it was too awkward so she sat on the very edge of the bed. From time to time he seemed to think that she had left him and tightened his grip on her fingers and said her name, and she reassured him. As the daylight began to come through the window in dark grey shadows, he looked at her and said, 'I love you, Sarah.'

'I love you too,' Faith said.

It was very dark by the time Nancy reached Michael's house. People had been at work there. They had boarded up the doors and windows, there was no way she could get back in. As she stood there, Vera came out of the house with the two children.

'I daren't take you in, Nancy, I'm sorry,' she said.

Nancy was half inclined to go back to Faith's house. They

would take her in, she knew; more than likely they would let her stay, give her money, help her, except that she couldn't. Rob had not seemed like the enemy until now. But now he had taken everything from her. Now he could be dead and Michael and ten other men, as far as she could judge, had been arrested and taken away. Nancy wanted desperately to weep over Michael. She didn't know what was going to happen to him. She hadn't realised that she had come to depend on him so much, that they had become close. She couldn't think what she would do without him now. She missed him already, and it was then that Nancy realised how much she loved Michael and acknowledged to herself that he had quite possibly loved her since the moment they met. She picked up Clarrie into her arms and took William by the hand and began to walk up the hill in the direction of the station.

She found a room in Durham. One room was all she could afford and even then she didn't like the look of it. She tried to find work but it would have meant leaving the children and she had no one reliable to leave them with any more. She missed Vera, her company and her understanding.

Nancy could not believe that it was Christmas. She had never spent a Christmas cold, hungry and frightened. She had no friends here, the weather was dark and wet and foggy and the back streets of Durham were slimy with dirt. The river was leaden.

There was work to be had but she dared not leave the children in that tiny room alone. She could not take in any kind of work other than needlework, so in the end that was what she did. Nancy was no better than anyone else at such things and it was pitifully paid. They could barely exist. The children stayed in bed most of the time.

She thought about the year before, going for a walk with Michael and how fine the day had been. Alice had been alive then and the children had been happy.

Michael was sentenced to six months in Durham gaol along with ten other men, but Tom Cowan, the man everybody thought had shot Rob, was nowhere to be found. He had left his wife and four children.

Rob, she discovered from gossip, began to get better slowly. The strike was finished after he was badly hurt, the men did not go on. Vincent and Harry Shaw ran the works in Berry Edge and there was no more talk of disruption.

It felt as though the winter would never end. Sometimes Nancy walked along Old Elvet towards the prison, thinking that somehow if she did so, Michael would know that she was near. She had the awful feeling that he might think Rob was dead – there was nobody to tell him otherwise – but she could not see him or contact him because he was allowed no letters or visitors.

One night in March when the weather was just as bitter as ever and the children were asleep, she could not resist going out just for a few minutes. Their room seemed as much of a prison as wherever Michael might be.

She stood in the middle of Elvet Bridge, she didn't go to the far side where Elvet began. Further along the dark streets there were what she thought of as evening people, prostitutes, gamblers and drunkards. She lingered for only a little but was reluctant to go back to the tiny room where the children slept, where there was no comfort of any sort, nothing but the night to be endured. As she leaned over the bridge somebody touched her on the shoulder. Nancy jumped and turned around. A man was standing behind her, a middle aged, quite well dressed man, smiling.

'How much?' he said.

Nancy pushed back against the cold stone of the bridge and shook her head.

'Pretty lass like you,' he said. 'I'll pay you well.' The coins in his hand glinted under the lamplight. Nancy's only thought was flight, but he got hold of her and began to drag her across the bridge and into the shadows beyond where the steps led down to the river. Nancy protested, cried out. There was no one to see, no one to take any notice. Then suddenly her assailant was attacked. He let go, seemingly as surprised as she was. A small young woman with an umbrella rained blows upon his head.

'That'll learn you,' she said, and watched in some satisfaction as he ran off. Then she turned to Nancy. 'Are you all right, pet?'

'Yes, now. Thank you.'

'The place isn't safe these days. Oh, I've buggered my brolly. You shouldn't be here, you know. Lasses come here to be picked up.'

'He offered me money to begin with.'

'Much?' her rescuer said hopefully.

'I can't remember now.'

'I'm not surprised. Do you want to come back and have a cup of tea?'

'I can't. I've got two bairns, asleep.'

The young woman looked at her.

'Bring them,' she said. 'Don't worry, I'm not a snatcher or from a mucky house, at least not so's you'd notice.'

She said her name was Claire. Nancy knew that she had to trust somebody. They went back to the dingy room. Claire looked around.

'It's no place for bairns,' she said. She picked up Clarrie and left Nancy to bring William, and then they walked back through the town to a part where the houses were neat and well kept. When they got inside she shouted, 'Susannah? We got visitors.'

From the front of the house a woman emerged. She was the most beautiful woman that Nancy had ever seen, with honey-coloured skin and dark hair and eyes, tall and not slender, gently rounded. She carried a tiny baby in her arms.

'Some bastard tried to accost her on Elvet Bridge. I'll need a new umbrella.'

Susannah smiled. 'She's always doing that, hitting men and having to buy umbrellas. We never have one when it rains, too busy using them as weapons. Are you all right?'

Claire led the way upstairs shortly afterwards and put the children into a clean bed in a spotless room. When they went back downstairs, the kettle was over the fire and Susannah was sitting with her baby held in against her shoulder.

Nancy couldn't help being pleased. They gave her tea and sandwiches and scones and listened intently when she told them what had happened. There was a long rather strange silence when she had finished.

'They say that Mr Berkeley's a lot better,' Susannah said.

'I heard that, and going to Nottingham for Easter. And Miss Norman's going with him.'

Claire made a noise of disgust. 'I thought she was an old maid, thirty at least and had lost her looks,' she said.

'Yes, she isn't young any more and she certainly couldn't be thought of as beautiful, but she's very nice,' Nancy said.

'Nice? Is that what men want?'

'Claire—' Susannah said.

'Do you know Mr Shaw?' Nancy said.

Claire looked at Susannah and when Susannah said nothing she said, 'Aye, I know Harry Shaw. I was what he did on Saturday nights for a while.'

Nancy suddenly felt very uncomfortable and, although she didn't want to look at the beautiful dark woman on her other side, she couldn't help it. Susannah smiled.

'So now you know. We're whores,' she said.

'But you . . . but you . . .'

'He would have done it to you and left you,' Claire said, 'maybe without a penny, and if you do intend something like that there are plenty of lasses just along the street from there who'd do it cheap. That's not the way, not unless you want to end up dead or diseased or hungry. Mind you, I wouldn't recommend it as an occupation. There must be summat else you can do.'

'I've got the bairns. I don't know what to do.'

'What about this Michael? When will he be out? Can't he keep you?'

'He got six months and I have nothing.'

'Have you ever worked?'

'Just housekeeping.'

'You can stay with us, Nancy,' Susannah said

'We don't do it no more,' Claire said. 'Made our money. We're ladies of leisure now and we could do with somebody to look after us. You'd be good with the bairn, having two of your own.'

So Nancy stayed. It was a curious way to live, without men. Nancy was happy here. The house had big fires in every room and comfortable beds upstairs. The furniture was good. Nancy knew, because she polished it. When she went shopping there was plenty of money for good food, so the cooking was a pleasure. Nobody came in from work complaining, difficult, wanting anything. During their free evenings, they sat around the fire with the children and drank French wine and ate and laughed a lot and talked. There were secrets, Nancy suspected, but they were not day to day ones. For one thing Susannah never spoke about her child, the tiny baby whom Nancy grew to love, and Claire rarely talked about anything other than gossip and important things like whether there was enough food in the house.

The baby was called Victoria after the old queen and was a much easier baby than either of hers had been. Nancy wondered whether this was just because she had experience of children; Victoria was happier with her than she was with either Susannah or Claire though Susannah doted on her baby.

'You'll spoil her, picking her up all the time,' Nancy recommended as Susannah took her from her cot every time she cried.

'I can't help it. I love her so much.'

She would sit for a long time feeding the baby, humming in a soft voice, staring into space. Nancy remembered doing the same thing herself, though Susannah had a better time than she had in spite of everything. Her life had been filled with the fear of Sean.

One afternoon, when Susannah was asleep by the front room fire and Nancy was cuddling the baby in the kitchen, Claire came in from doing the shopping. She had had the two children with her. They went off upstairs to play.

'She's lovely, isn't she?' Claire said. 'She was a surprise.

Susannah had a miscarriage years ago and then nothing. I wished she would miscarry this time an' all, the tears we had. She went through a lot for this little speck.'

'She's bonny like her mother.'

'She looks like him. He was the bee's knees,' Claire said.

'Does he know?'

Claire shook her head. 'Him being a gentleman and all that. And he was really canny. Asked her to marry him, he didn't even know she was expecting. She in her wisdom turned him down. And do you know why? Because she's bloody well daft about him. It took a man to be that nice to her to break her bloody heart. When I think of all the bastards we've known. He was like strawberry jam, you'd save him for Sundays if you could.'

'Why wouldn't she marry him?'

'He was too high up. Can you think what it would be like? Could you see yourself up there, doing the ladylike thing and pretending that you knew what you should do, how to talk to your maid and lift the right knife and know about poetry? It isn't just that he's a gentleman or that he's rich really, it's . . . the people he likes, the people he goes about with, they're people who've had real schooling. You don't know what they know and you could let them down all the time, and people would laugh at them through you, and that's harder than having people laugh directly at you, don't you think?'

'He has no other children then?'

'No. I said to her that he would want to know Vicky was

his, she's such a lovely baby, he would like to know and he wouldn't try to take her, at least I don't think he would. We went away for a while. I wouldn't have come back if it had been me, would you?'

They seemed to think that because he was big he would be trouble, Michael thought, so they knocked him about a lot to start with. You kept your eyes lowered and called everybody sir and there was no way past things. There was never quiet, there were too many people around for there to be any peace, there was no privacy and no rest and he was tortured by thoughts of Nancy, of what had happened to her and to the children and most especially of what had happened to Rob. Michael's mind gave him Rob dead nightly. It gave him slowly every second of what had happened, of Harry crying and Vincent staring and Rob realising what had happened when he was hurt, stopping there amongst the bricks and stones and people, the surprised look in his eyes, falling towards the ground and then lying there, the blood beginning to seep slowly through his shirt. Michael convinced himself that Rob was dead and that he had caused it until he heard reports from Berry Edge that Rob was alive.

He had seen nothing, convinced himself that it was Tom Cowan who had tried to murder Rob. Surely he was the only man with a gun and had threatened to do it, but Michael did not remember even seeing Tom as close as he would need to be to shoot Rob. Michael blamed himself. He had done this, he had resented and hated Rob and stirred up the feelings of the other miners because he was so bitter that Rob had never come home, that this place which he was supposed to have loved mattered so little to him that he let it decay and rot until the people had lost hope. Michael had wanted Rob to pay for that neglect.

His mind gave him Nancy alone and hungry on the streets of Berry Edge with nobody to take her in. Harry Shaw would look after her, surely to God he would, but then Harry was so concerned for Rob that everything else might go from his mind. Harry didn't see Nancy make her way through the crowd towards Rob. He didn't seem to notice her down on her knees, the stricken look in her eyes. All her concern was for Rob. Michael tried not to think about that during the long hours of the night and he prayed every day to a God he could not envisage for Nancy's safety.

He tried hard to convince himself that Rob was all right. It was the only way that he could hate him. If Rob was permanently damaged in some way because of what had happened, Michael felt that the guilt would better all his other feelings. He didn't want Rob hurt in such a way, he had just wanted to better him for all the neglect over the years. He wanted Rob to know what living at Berry Edge had been like during those years. For Rob to come back and succeed in so many ways seemed the ultimate offence to Michael, and it did not make up for the time that had gone before. Mixed up in this also was the constant picture in his mind of Rob leaving. He was jealous of that, that Rob could feel himself able to leave whereas Michael felt obliged to stay and look after his ungrateful family. Sean and his mother were dead; he no longer saw any of his sisters, they had married, had families and forgotten about him. They too had moved away. Rob had gone and made his life good and then come back and attempted to do the same thing in Berry Edge, and Michael could not forgive him. As long as Rob was not badly hurt he could be hated. The hatred grew and got easier the more they knocked him around and humiliated him and worked him, made sure that he didn't eat, that he had little rest.

At first he slept on a plank bed, two planks of wood without a mattress, and then a hard bed. If you did anything wrong, like speaking, because you were not allowed to talk, they put you on bread and water for days. Not that that was any particular hardship, the food was so bad that it was inedible anyway.

If your work wasn't up to standard you got no food at all. Mostly it was weaving and sewing, and Michael found it difficult, so very often he wasn't allowed to eat.

If you answered back they clouted you round the head, and if you forgot your number they hit you. The clothes and boots were much too small, the cells were dark and some of the prison orderlies were brutal. If they took a dislike to you they knocked you about. You learned to speak without moving your lips but Michael soon learned not to speak at all.

In the beginning he thought he would be there forever. Then after the endless days of routine he stopped caring about what happened. It didn't matter particularly, that was what pits did to you. You knew how to withstand hardship, and his past experience of his father and mother and Sean had made him resilient. He kept telling himself that it would soon be over. He did as he was told, he gave them no excuse to hurt him badly and every night when he couldn't sleep he brought his one luxury to mind.

He thought of the previous Christmas when he and Nancy had gone up and sat on the fell beyond Berry Edge. He thought of how beautiful she was. He tried not to think that Nancy was never going to love him because of their Sean, he just thought of how beautiful she had been that day and of what a lovely day they had had.

There was one thing about the good things that happened to you. You had them permanently, you had them forever. That perfect time with her was his alone, and he thought that it was possibly one of the few times she had ever been happy with a man. That was another reason he could hate Rob, because he knew how Nancy liked and admired him. It wasn't fair to hate Rob for that; in a way it was almost too easy and too low, because Rob was also one of his perfect memories.

They had been children together in those cold childhood

evenings playing within distance of the railway line, and rather than go home to their respective awful existences they would stay there while the dusk deepened and the cold took over.

Regardless of thin shirts and bare legs they would stay. He thought of the fires they had built, the rhubarb they had stolen and cooked in an old pan, of the walls they had climbed and the orchards they had raided and the fields they had run through. He thought of their secret meeting places, the old henhouse, the loft above the carriage house at Rob's. He didn't want to take it a step further and think of what had happened, how Rob's brother had died, how Rob had come to him and begged him to leave; how he had not thought that he could, because Sean would have knocked their mother and sisters around and kept them short of everything they needed, and also because he loved Berry Edge so much. He didn't want to leave it. It would be an act of betrayal that he could never take back, but he knew also that Rob had no alternative but to go ahead with that act of betrayal. His parents had turned from him, Berry Edge had condemned him. He had to go.

It seemed so awful to Michael to know that Rob himself was turning him out of Berry Edge. He could not go back now. Strange to think that if Rob had not come home, Michael would probably still be there. He would never have a job there again, and in a way it seemed connected to Rob's leaving, as though it was only a matter of time before everybody was flung from their paradise, as though nobody was deserving of the beauty of the fell above Berry Edge where the wind and snow cut you, where the heather was a mass of purple velvet in August, where God himself could have been pleased that there was on earth a place so finely tuned to nature that each breath of wind was prayer.

Michael would close his eyes and pretend that he was alone and that he could hear Nancy's voice calling down the yard to the children to come inside for tea. It was that perfect moment when the children were playing in the back lane and the kettle was boiling, the teapot was warmed and the table was laid, and night was about to fall slowly, gently, softly like a bedcover, embracing all of Berry Edge, Nancy and her house, the children and himself. They would soon be inside, the children rosy-cheeked from the cold, and Nancy would be cutting egg and bacon pie. She would be pouring tea and offering cake and smiling. She was always smiling when he went to sleep. It was the only comfort that he had.

Seventeen

Faith didn't realise that she had fallen asleep. All through the night Rob had tossed and turned and sweated and beseeched Sarah not to leave him. Faith began to understand that he had loved his wife as much as she had loved John. She could not convince him that she was still there, he begged and pleaded with her not to go. Finally, when daylight broke, he went to sleep, cool and peaceful.

She didn't know what time it was, only that it felt late. For the first time in her life she awoke to find herself lying on a bed with a man, almost the man she had wanted to find herself lying on a bed with. He was awake and smiling, and he looked across the pillows at her and said hoarsely, 'Hello, Faith.'

Faith sat up abruptly and glanced around the room and then back at him.

'How do you feel?' she said.

'It hurts like hell,' he said. And it did, she could see by the dullness of his eyes.

'I'll go and get somebody.'

'Tell me what happened first.'

Faith did as simply as she could.

'Is Michael all right?'

'As far as I know. Let me go and get the nurse.'

'Will you come back? I had this dream . . .'

'I'll come back,' Faith said.

When they let her in, a long time later that morning, he looked better, his eyes were clearer. Faith was embarrassed and didn't go too close. He even smiled.

'Were you here all night?' he said. 'You must be exhausted.'

'I'm not tired at all,' Faith said, and she wasn't. He put out a hand.

'Come closer.'

'I shouldn't.'

'You didn't mind before.'

'You were asleep before.' She went across. 'I'm not supposed to sit on the bed.'

'You were lying there when I woke up.'

'I had drifted off just for a little while.'

She had to sit on the bed to take hold of his hand. Eventually he went back to sleep. Then she left him and Vincent took her home. Her mother insisted that she went to bed. Rob's mother visited the hospital that day and, for the first few days, until the doctors decided that Rob would make a complete recovery, Harry stayed there. No one could persuade him to leave. The first thing Rob asked when she and Harry were there together was, 'The police didn't take Michael, did they?'

'Don't worry about that,' Harry said.

'He didn't do it.'

'Nobody thinks he did.'

As Harry and Faith left later he said to her from the other side of Rob's door, 'They should hang the bastard, it was all his fault.'

'What will he get, Harry?'

'A few months if we're lucky,' Harry said.

By Christmas Rob was at home; at least, at Faith's home, his own house across the way was a blackened shell. Vincent had tried to insist that they should rent a house but nobody wanted to, they were clinging together almost like children. Vincent and Harry went to work every day and Berry Edge went back to its usual self. It was amazing how soon it did.

Every afternoon when Harry got in from work at half past five he would run up the stairs and burst into Rob's bedroom and Faith would be reminded of how Harry had cried. It was as though he could not bear to be away for too long in case something awful happened to Rob, even though Rob began to get better right from the start.

One such January evening she was sitting in the room sewing. She was there most of the time; she had had awful visions of having to go to Rob's grave as well as John's, and it was not exactly a comfortable thought. Rob was really getting better, she thought, questioning Harry minutely about things. Firstly it had been Cowan's wife.

'I want you to get somebody round to Cowan's.'

'Whatever the hell for?'

'Because Tom Cowan's wife has four children.'

'He tried to kill you, for God's sake.'

'We don't know that for certain, and even if he did it was hardly her fault. You haven't had her evicted, have you?'

'What do you think I am?'

'Have you given her any money?'

'Of course I haven't.'

'Do it then.'

Straight away too he wanted Nancy safe.

'Have you found Nancy?'

'No.'

'Get somebody else on to it.'

Now it was the works. He wanted to know everything that was happening, and nothing that Harry and Vincent were doing was right. Only the fact that Rob was not better saved him from a dose of Harry's temper.

One night, when Harry had said nothing but shut the door rather firmly as he went downstairs, Faith went over to the bed and straightened Rob's pillows. 'Ought you to do that?'

'What?'

'Come down on him like he doesn't know what he's doing?'

'Did I?'

'You do it every night.'

'Do I? My father used to do that to me. I didn't realise.'

'Shall I read to you?'

'Please.'

She sat down by the fire and read. Rob rarely listened. He sometimes fell asleep, but often he would just lie staring into the fire. She thought that he was probably thinking about Sarah. He wasn't aware that he had thought she was Sarah and he never spoke about his wife, but she thought by the softness in his eyes that he was thinking about her. Faith was surprised to find that she was jealous. She had never thought she would have a good feeling for Rob again, but she did now. She liked being there with him as much as she could. One day, the doctor took her aside on the landing and said, 'You need some rest and fresh air. Go for a walk.'

'But Rob—'

'Robert looks a lot better than you do, miss.'

It was Saturday. That afternoon Harry was not at work, and when she said she was going out he offered her his company. They went out of the town and up on to the fell. It was a cold bright day.

'Did you know that my mother and father are talking about taking Rob home for Easter?' Harry said.

'Yes, they did mention it.'

'I thought you might like to go too.'

'What about you?'

'Somebody has to see to the works, we can't all go. I think Rob could do with the company.'

'You mean you need somebody to keep an eye on him because you won't be there.'

'Something like that, yes. I'm afraid to let him out of my sight. I feel as if I should have done something.'

'You did. I hear you gave money to Tom Cowan's wife.'

'I sent somebody. I just hope he's dead,' Harry said savagely.

'You shouldn't wish people dead, Harry, it's not a healthy pastime.'

'And endanger my immortal soul, do you mean?' Harry said, with a slow smile. 'I'd go to Hell over it.'

'Rob wouldn't like that.'

'I wish Rob was better.'

'He is better.'

'No, I mean properly better. The day he's declared better I'm going to take him outside and make him wish himself in Nottingham. He never talks to me any more, he just gives bloody orders. I can't stop thinking about what happened. He needs to get away from here for both our sakes.'

That afternoon, when the women were making tea in the kitchen and Vincent and Harry were alone in the sitting room, Harry said to his father, 'I want you to invite Faith formally to Nottingham for Easter.'

'Whatever for?'

'Because I've already asked her and I want Rob to think that he should go with her. He won't go otherwise, you know he won't, fretting about the bloody works, and she won't go unless you ask her properly.'

'That doesn't seem a very good idea to me.'

'Why not?'

'Because his mother and her parents seem determined he will marry her.'

'He won't,' said Harry.

'Why won't he?'

'Because there's another woman.'

'I thought as much. What is she like?'

'I'm not going to tell you anything about her. Just ask my mother to invite Faith to stay.'

Ida shook her head over it that night as they got into bed.

'It is not a good idea, Vincent.'

'That's exactly what I said.'

'I have nothing against Faith, but I don't think I want her in my house taking over Sarah's role. She's a nice girl but she isn't for him, he can do much better than that.'

'Harry has, I gather, already asked her.'

'Harry has? He's not even going to be there.'

'He seems to think that there's somebody else.'

Ida looked hard at Vincent.

'Then where is she?' she said.

*

Faith's first glimpse of the Abbey was in the afternoon just before the spring sun went down. There was a long drive leading up to the golden stone house. There were huge lawns to the front and a sweeping drive. The old part of the house from which it took its name was high and open and had big arched windows and a great long front. When the carriage drew to a halt at the front door Faith couldn't have said a word. She had had no idea that Vincent Shaw and his family lived at this scale. She had never been in such a house. She was only glad that her mother had persuaded her to have made, very quickly, a great many new clothes so that she could look her best. Her mother had obviously realised, as Faith had not, that she would need them.

There was, Faith saw from the beginning, something special in the way that they lived. Perhaps it was prosperity that she had never seen before. There were no cold draughty corners, no dark shadows and, even though there were pictures of Sarah, she was talked about openly here but did not get in the way, as though they had done their grieving and come through.

The house was comfortable as Faith had not known comfort, and it had a happy atmosphere which put her at her ease straight away. She was given a maid to herself, a girl called Jenny who enthused over her new clothes, told Faith what lovely hair she had and spent a great deal of time dressing it and seeing to Faith's clothes before she went down to dinner. Faith had never before seen herself as elegant, but she did now. Her mother had chosen most of her clothes, she had no particular interest in such things, but the dress was green and cream and it flattered her. She saw also something she had not seen in her own eyes before: warmth and excitement. Even though there were no dinner guests that first evening, Faith enjoyed herself. The dining room was so big it had two great fires, and the crockery and silver winked in the candlelight. Vincent grumbled about having to eat like that.

'I can't see what the hell I'm eating,' he protested.

Faith was used to Vincent by now. She had been shocked at his language at first, but she secretly rather liked him because he made her want to laugh sometimes when she shouldn't.

'We should have eaten in the small dining room. It's like a bloody barn in here.'

'I like it,' Ida said. 'It's our first night back and I wanted it to be special. Just eat your dinner, Vincent, and try to be mannerly.'

Vincent encouraged Faith to drink wine. He seemed to think this was an essential part of her education, and Faith was in no mood to tell him that she wasn't supposed to. It was pink and slightly fizzy and seemed innocuous, though she refused the red which the men drank. After that there was a light lemon pudding. She could have had chocolate mousse and then cheese as well if she had had any room.

Faith played the piano later. Her fingers had never touched

the keys of a really good grand piano and nobody made her feel selfconscious by sitting around listening intently, but afterwards Ida came to her and said, 'That instrument hasn't been touched since Sarah died. I'm so glad you play, and you do it so well.' She kissed Faith and hurried away to see about the coffee. Faith saw Rob and Vincent sitting by the fire, talking softly together, so she just carried on playing until the coffee was brought in. Vincent smoked a cigar and poured brandy into his coffee, a habit his wife said she deplored. They offered Faith brandy, something she felt sure nobody else in the world would have done, but the pink wine had been sufficient. She shook her head and thanked Vincent and sat down in a comfortable chair by the fire with her coffee and smiled at them.

She wasn't late in going to bed, she was worn out from the anxiety about the journey, the journey itself and all kinds of new things. Jenny was waiting for her. Faith said she must not wait up if it made her too late, but the girl smiled and said that it was all right. Faith had never been helped to bed before and the bed itself was like sinking into a cloud. In the lightness Faith went to sleep.

Rob wanted to teach her to ride a horse, and in the tiredness of that late evening Faith had agreed. She was not however quite so sure the following morning down at the stables. As Faith hesitated he said encouragingly, 'Don't worry, it's not a horse, it's a slug.' Though she felt rather precarious balanced on the horse, she decided that he had been right. She soon felt quite safe, and it was a new delight to see the world from a horse's back. A golden sun appeared above the dew-white fields.

It was Sunday and a number of people had been invited to the midday meal. Faith enjoyed the new company, and a walk in the afternoon when she saw Ida's Japanese garden. The next day the men went to work though Rob was only going to look, he assured her, and she was rather disappointed until Ida suggested they should go into Nottingham and do some shopping. She took Faith out to lunch and later to a tearoom. Ida knew a great many people. Faith suspected that Ida hadn't spent such a day since her daughter had died, though she didn't say so. Faith's mother had provided her with a great deal of money, which Faith said she would not need but which her mother had insisted on her taking. She found herself even that first day buying things which she had never before wanted and which now seemed essential, a pretty scarf which went with her coat and some sweets for Jenny because she had been so kind.

That evening when the men came home to dinner Faith felt so happy that she could burst. Ida was talking about invitations which she had received and how long they would stay, and whether there would be time to go and stay with some old friends who had a house just outside London.

'We came back here to do some work,' Vincent said.

'Nonsense,' his wife declared, 'we've all done quite enough work. We're entitled to some time to ourselves.'

Faith wasn't going to argue with her hostess. Once again the dinner was perfect, beef in a wine sauce, an almond pudding, port for those who wanted it. Faith didn't. The white wine she had consumed made her exhilarated. She wanted to go out and look at the stars, which were very clear that night. Outside on the gravel drive, Faith had never felt like this before, the stars looked so big and bright and the sky behind them almost navy. She heard footsteps crunching the gravel. It was Rob.

'Are you enjoying yourself?' he asked.

'I'm so glad I came,' Faith said. 'I don't understand now why I was so reluctant. It's wonderful here, Vincent and Ida are so kind and generous and I may even learn to ride a real horse.'

'We won't leave you to the mercies of The Slug once you feel confident,' Rob said smiling

'Did Sarah ride?'

'Yes.'

'And very well, I expect.'

'She was brought up with horses and that's different. I think you did very well today. It isn't easy, but you liked riding, didn't you?'

'It was fun. How was work?'

'A year is a long time to be away. It makes you feel either that you aren't necessary, or frustrated that you weren't there to do it better.'

'And which did you feel?'

'Both in some degree. It's like being torn in half between here and Berry Edge.'

'I thought you would have learned to hate Berry Edge.'

'I neither love nor hate it any more, I just wanted to try and put things right there.'

'I think you've done that.'

'Do you? I wish I could be sure.'

He said nothing more, but Faith knew that he was thinking about John and how she felt.

'Rob, I don't understand why you didn't tell me about Sarah. If I had known that you had understood what I went through it would have made things different.'

'I wanted you to forgive me because you wanted to forgive me, not because you felt sorry for me.'

'I have forgiven you.'

'Have you?'

'Have you forgiven yourself?'

'No, it's an endless debt, like a well. I never reach the bottom; each time I think I've conquered it, it springs back up again.'

'Nobody could have done any more, Rob.'

'My father's dead and my mother doesn't care for me.'

'She never did. You can't help that. She adored John and your father and adoration isn't something that goes round well. You're the apple of Ida's eye. Be thankful for that.'

'I've been lucky there.'

'Yes, you have, and with Vincent and living here, it's so beautiful. The stars are much brighter in the country. They look so near and low. I didn't realise you lived as richly as this. I didn't think. Going back to Berry Edge must have been awful for you, and your father's house must have seemed so small.'

Rob laughed. 'Harry had never seen a bedroom without a fire in the winter. I thought he was going to turn around and come straight back here.'

'Harry's not like that,' she said.

'No, I know. His loyalty will be the undoing of him.'

'He's certainly loyal to you. The times he tried to persuade me to be kinder to you!'

'You are kinder to me.'

'When I think now that you almost had to die before . . .'

'I didn't almost die, Faith.'

'You were off your head. You thought I was Sarah. And Harry told me lies, he told me that you were all right.'

'I was all right.'

'You weren't,' Faith said, faltering.

'I'm fine. I'm here. Look, there's the North Star, there's the Great Bear.'

Faith looked.

'I'm going to take you to London.'

'Really? Oh, I've always wanted to go. Are you sure?'

'I'm sure. I just need a few days here. I'm going to show you the town.'

*

Their house in Berkeley Square was huge and elegant with great bay windows and long, echoing rooms. Faith soon realised that it was one of the most prestigious places to live, the best address in London. Vincent grumbled because he hated it all but Ida insisted on going to help Faith along socially.

Faith went walking in Hyde Park, riding in Rotten Row, both at the correct hour, dressed to suit, as though she had lived that way all her life. In Nottingham she had done the kind of frivolous things which she would once have thought ridiculous, played croquet and gone with Ida to fashionable shops like George Huttons' fur warehouse in Pelham Street, taken tea with the right people and had dinner with the best families.

In London Rob took her to the opera and the theatre, and again she met people and had invitations to dine, and it was so exciting. Women went into restaurants there, a new idea for Faith. It was another world after Berry Edge, and Faith had the feeling that she would never want to go home.

Rob did little work, they amused themselves. The days turned into weeks and she saw the way that the people here who were his real friends treated Rob, the respect and liking there was for him. She knew now something of his achievements, and she was pleased for him.

London went to her head, moving in interesting society, meeting people, spending money on clothes. Faith saw herself in the mirror in her bedroom one June evening and stopped, she was so surprised at the woman who looked back at her, so fashionable, so well dressed. She could not believe that she was the same woman who wore old dresses and poured the tea for Chapel meetings.

She went off downstairs. The weather was good, there was tea in the garden. Rob and Vincent were sitting under the trees. As she arrived, Rob smiled at her, and she was so reminded of John that she tripped over the edge of the lawn and almost fell.

Later Vincent went across the garden to where his wife was pulling weeds from the flowerbeds. They had gardeners, but Ida liked being involved and did most of the garden designing herself. It was not the garden she mentioned to him now.

'Don't you think it's time Faith went home?'

'She seems perfectly happy here.'

'That's what's bothering me. I have no objection to having her here, but she's not good enough for him and you know it.'

'Harry assures me there's no problem.'

'Harry isn't here,' Ida pointed out. 'I don't believe this story about another woman. Where on earth in the north would Robert find a suitable girl? He wouldn't, Vincent. You haven't gone and left them alone, have you? Faith may not be in the first flush of youth, but she's turning into an extremely pretty woman, and he thinks he owes her a great deal because of John. I want you to talk to him.'

'Don't you think that would exacerbate the problem?'

'If he asks her to marry him she's hardly likely to say no, is she? He's the biggest catch she's ever seen in her life, she's unlikely to refuse. And he'd regret it, Vincent, very much, because if he loves her then I'm the Queen of Sheba.'

That evening Vincent went outside to smoke a cigar.

'You're not smoking that horrible, dirty thing in my house,' his wife had said. 'Why you have to take up new bad habits at your age, I don't know.'

'It's precisely because I'm this age that I have to take up new bad habits. Just be thankful it isn't young actresses.'

'No young actress would look at you, Vincent,' she assured him.

Rob followed him into the garden.

'Now, Vince,' he said.

Vincent shuddered over the northern greeting.

'Missing the place, are you?' he offered.

'Not especially. Harry can manage.'

'And Faith, is she homesick?'

'I doubt it.'

'Her parents will be wondering how much longer she's staying here,' Vincent said.

'She's never been away from home before. There's no reason for her to rush back.'

'Three months is hardly rushing.'

'Are you tired of her company, Vincent?'

'No, she's a very nice girl when she stops talking about God, but she does rather lack social graces.'

'That's not very fair,' Rob said. 'We're all the product of our upbringing. God only knows what yours was like.'

Vincent ignored this jibe.

'Are you fond of her?'

'Yes. Much more so since we've spent time together.'

'And your affections are free?'

'What is this, Vincent?'

'Harry assured me that there was no question of your becoming involved with Faith because there was another woman.'

'I like the way you and Harry discuss me. I don't think that side of my life is any of your business, Vincent.'

'It would be if you married Faith and expected to bring her home.'

'You could hardly refuse me since I own a good part of the Abbey.'

'I don't need to be reminded in such a vulgar fashion.'

'I don't need to be told who I can and can't marry. I'm not your son, Vincent.'

'Alas. I'd have brought you up with better manners.'

Rob said nothing to that. Vincent went on more softly.

'I have nothing against the woman except that I doubt you love her, and if she loves you it's only for your brother's sake. Don't marry her out of guilt, Robert, you'll only regret it.'

Rob still said nothing.

'Is there another woman?'

'No!'

'But there was.'

'Nobody you would have wanted me to bring home,' Rob said bitterly. 'If you think Faith's an unsuitable match, you should have seen *her.*'

'We must all be relieved for your good sense, then.'

'It had nothing to do with my good sense. She wouldn't have me.'

'Lord,' Vincent said, 'I just wish for once that you or Harry would get something right. Between the pair of you, you can't find a decent woman.'

Rob didn't stay to hear any more.

Faith could not be accused of being insensitive to atmosphere, Rob thought that evening, when they went into the garden after dinner, escaping Ida's eagle eye.

'I think I've outstayed my welcome,' she said.

'It's nothing to do with you,' Rob lied. 'Vincent and I are always quarrelling about work. You mustn't take any notice.'

'I think I ought to go,' she said, smiling. 'You've all been very kind to me.'

Rob thought that evening that Faith had turned into a remarkably pretty woman. All she had needed was good clothes, a little freedom and some town polish.

'I don't want you to go. I like having you here with me.'

She smiled and Rob leaned over and kissed her. He had had no idea that he was going to. He had thought that he had conquered the need for Susannah Seaton or anyone else. He had put her from his mind savagely. Faith moved back away from him.

'You mustn't do that,' she said.

'I'm sorry, I didn't mean to.'

'You seem like John to me, you know that you do, and you're nothing like him really at all. You're very important and respected and—'

'Faith—'

'No, it's true. You can have anybody you want.'

Rob smiled at that. He didn't seem to be able to have anybody he wanted.

'I belong in Berry Edge,' Faith said. 'It's been very nice here but Vincent and Ida are polite because they think I'm dull and—'

'No.' Rob caught hold of her. She tried to back away from him, but he kissed her properly this time. He did not forget that the last person to do so had been his brother so many years ago. She was sweet in her half-hearted resistance. When she drew back harder he let her go. Faith fled.

He caught up with her before she reached the door.

'Wait!' he said, taking her arm.

'Why did you do that?' she said. 'You must have met women younger and prettier and easier to deal with than me, and I don't believe for a second that you have any regard for me.' She was almost in tears. 'You're not going to tell me that you love me, are you?'

'Faith—'

'Harry told me all about your wife, how beautiful she was, how accomplished, educated and admired. You could pretend to be John for a little while. Do you think I could pretend to be Sarah?'

'I don't want you to pretend to be Sarah.'

'Then at least one of us can be honest,' Faith said, and pulled open the heavy oak door and ran inside.

Rob reached her before she got to the stairs.

'I'm sorry,' he said. 'I didn't do it on purpose. It's just that we've spent so much time together recently, and it's been very nice having you around me and ... I've got used to you. I don't want you to go, I don't want to be without you. Stay just a little while, just a little longer.'

As soon as they had gone, as soon as Harry was left with Rob's mother and Faith's parents and the works all to himself, he realised that he had made two serious errors. They began to talk about Faith and Rob warmly and kindly. The word 'wedding' seemed to hang in the air like rainclouds. His mother and her mother got together over the teacups and discussed times and places and people and grandchildren and it was to Harry as though Rob had known, even before anything was said, that this was what he was meant to do now. That this would make up for everything that had gone wrong, and that he could finally bear it.

Had Faith not been there almost every minute of every day since Rob had been hurt? Had not Harry himself sent her to Rob on that fateful night and persuaded her to take the part of his wife? Perhaps things had been decided then in some way and there was no other road to go ahead, and perhaps Rob had known long before they set off on the journey to Nottingham that he would woo and win her. He would do it easily, Harry thought, closing his eyes over his own shortsightedness. The ghost of Sarah would not stop Rob, and he had had Susannah's answer long since. Love didn't matter now, it was duty that presented itself. He could imagine Rob trying with Faith, talking gently to her, spending time with her. They had been together such a lot lately; sometimes there had been laughter from Rob's bedroom and the sound of voices in harmony. He thought of Rob kissing Faith. She had not been kissed in so long. She would marry him, thinking he was John, she would marry him because she would see him as rich and clever. No wonder Faith's mother smiled so much. And Mrs Berkeley could go on for the rest of her life comforted that Faith had finally married her almost forgiven son.

The second mistake was even harder to bear, and this one did not become immediately apparent. It was like a dripping tap. It took days to get to him. It took Harry weeks to admit to himself that he missed Faith, to think of how much time Faith and Rob had spent together without him, and more time than that before he lay sleepless in bed and wanted

Faith with a longing such as he had never felt for another person in his life. And even then he tried to talk himself out of it.

How could he love Faith? It was stupid and impossible. He came to the conclusion that it was only because he could not physically have her; but then he could not physically have any respectable woman without a wedding, and he had not felt like this about them before. Faith was not even of his social class, if you thought particularly about it. She had no connections, little money.

It took Harry all his determination not to go to London and somehow stop Rob from asking Faith to be his wife. Only the knowledge that it would do no good held him back. Rob was probably the only man Faith could marry now, because he was almost John. Harry had to make himself stay there and work hard and keep things together without any help, and put up with the cosy chats over the fire in the evening.

To Faith, it was all a repetition of the happiest time of her life. Rob had become John to her, and although she was older it seemed that she was eighteen again; everything in her life was in front of her, and behind her were the long sunny days of her childhood with him. It was the perfect part of her life come back.

She had tried to resist, she had tried to refuse, knowing

that Ida and Vincent were very much against the idea, but Rob pressed her, held her, kissed her. It was all too much for Faith. She knew that Rob's mother and her parents hoped and longed for such a thing to happen. When Rob held her in his arms, it was ghostlike somehow from all the years before, and compensation for all those nights without John. She didn't have to be alone any more. The dullness of her life in Berry Edge was gone. She could have a future with Rob, be his wife and have children. It was interesting and exciting, and he was so liked and admired that Faith became caught up in it.

When Rob asked her to marry him, he kissed her very slowly and gently on the mouth. Faith couldn't stop him, she didn't remember how. All the years, all the emptiness fled. She could feel his fingertips on her neck lightly, he wasn't touching her but for that and his mouth. Faith closed her eyes and lifted her face so that he could reach her better, and his fingers closed around her chin. She couldn't think about anything but the feel of his fingers and the warmth of his lips. She drew closer and he put one hand on her waist and pulled her against him; and there the memories stopped, because John had never done such a thing. Under a hard, searching kiss, her love for him began.

Eighteen

Nancy saw Michael before he saw her, and but for his height would not have recognised him. He obviously did not expect to be met. His shoulders were hunched, he didn't look up, he was very thin and had about him such an air of defeat that Nancy hesitated even from just across the road. He had never looked less like Sean, but she could not be grateful for that. And when she crossed the street and saw his white tired face and dull narrowed eyes she hesitated again, and then he saw her and his whole face lit.

'Nancy!' he said. 'I didn't think you'd come, not for a minute.'

He looked as though he would have liked to hug her. Because he didn't move, she went to him and put her arms around him and she could feel the sudden gladness on him, the delight and she was pleased. She had missed him so much, thought about him so often.

'I was worried about you,' he said.

He had his face buried down against her shoulder just for a few seconds, and then he looked into her face and smiled.

'How are the bairns? Where are they?'

'They're fine. They're back at the house.'

'Where are you living and how?'

Nancy didn't know what to say to him. She released him and he let go, and they began walking very slowly along the road towards Elvet Bridge.

'You look very well,' he said.

'We're fine. We had to leave Berry Edge.'

'I thought you would, but then I thought maybe . . . maybe Rob had looked after you.'

Nancy glanced at him to hear Rob's first name on his lips. 'He couldn't do that.'

Michael stopped. 'Is he all right, Nancy?'

'He's fine. He's gone away back to the south. Miss Norman's gone an' all.'

'Miss Norman?'

'Aye. She spent a lot of time around him after— after things went wrong.'

'I don't think they'd make much of a couple,' Michael said. 'She says her prayers too often.'

'Everybody says their prayers more often than you,' Nancy said.

'I'm glad he's all right. I never meant for it to go that far.'

'It wasn't just you. He was bad for a long while. I don't think he's better yet but he will be—'

'You can't keep a good man down, is that it?' Michael said, and looked like his old self, Nancy thought.

'I don't know about good. I've cursed him into Hell and out of it since we had to leave. Caught between you and him, I didn't know where I was.'

'How are you getting on? How have you managed?'

'I want to talk to you about it before we go back.'

'Why?'

They reached the bridge, and when they got to the far side they went down the steps and began to walk along the towpath a little way. Nancy didn't know how to start.

'You haven't got married, have you?' Michael said in a queer hard voice.

'Married?' Nancy wanted to laugh, but didn't when she looked into his white face and saw that his eyes had darkened almost to black. 'Who on earth would I marry, and whatever for?' She wanted to add, 'when I have you', but she couldn't.

'What, then?'

'It's just that . . . I had a hard time at first. I tried sewing and it wouldn't make enough to keep us in this horrible room . . . and then I met some people. Susannah and Claire.'

'Susannah?'

'Susannah Seaton. Do you know her?'

'Everybody does. She's the most beautiful woman in the county. I thought she'd left. Is that how you've managed?'

'And if I had, what would you say?'

'I'd say that I should've had more sense and taken better care of you.'

'I'm living with them, keeping house for them. They took us in, but I didn't want to go back there with you and for you to think ill of us.'

'You mean I can go there?'

'Yes, if you want.'

'How could I think ill of people who were willing to have me when I have nothing?'

'That's what I hoped you would say,' Nancy said.

They walked slowly back to the house. There Michael had a bath, Nancy gave him new clothes which she had bought for him, and he had a meal with them. Apart from the way that the clothes were big on him, Michael looked good, Nancy thought, though he was obviously pale and tired.

'You didn't say he was like that, Nancy,' Claire said when they washed up together in the kitchen.

'Like what?'

Claire glanced sideways at her. 'Is he yours then?'

'I'm not sure,' Nancy said, breathless at the idea. 'I hope so.'

'Be sure,' Claire said, 'otherwise somebody might grab him.'

That night, after the children had insisted on being put to bed by Michael, he stood in the sitting room looking out. Nancy went to him there.

'It's very strange not being in gaol. I feel almost as though there's too much space around me, like I'm going to fall over because there's nothing to hold on to. I'm grateful for the help, Nancy, I really am. I'll go out and find some work tomorrow.'

'Grateful?'

'Yes, I didn't expect it. I know how you feel about me.'

'Do you?'

'I know what our Sean did and I know how much like him I am.'

'You're nothing like him,' Nancy said.

'Yes, I am. Only I've learned to be different lately.'

He was like Sean to Nancy. He was like she had thought Sean might be, like she thought Sean was before they were married. A little distressing voice told her that Sean had been like this when she knew him as she knew Michael now, and he had made her hate him, except that Sean had never been really kind or generous. He had never liked the children, he had never looked at her as Michael did. He had wanted her, had married her out of lust, because he craved her body, because she had been young and pretty.

'Will you come for a walk with me?' he asked. 'I want to feel really free.'

Susannah and Claire were both in to listen for the children, so Nancy and Michael walked along the towpath, away from the town, towards Pelaw Woods. Nancy waited for him to stop and kiss her but he didn't. It was the only thing that marred the day.

*

When Rob and Faith came home that summer Faith was almost a different person. Harry was disappointed with this beautiful, elegant woman. Rob had dressed her in expensive, fashionable clothes, had her hair done in the latest style, and most of all she was happy as Harry had never seen her. He wished to have back the dowdy little chapelgoer who had cared so much. All Faith could talk about was what they had done in London, the concerts, the parties, the people she had got to know until Harry itched to slap her. Rob had put a diamond ring on to Faith's finger. It sparkled in the summer evening.

She was a woman in love, Harry could see, and it made him miserable. He wanted her to be happy but he wanted her to be happy with him. She shone for Rob, she looked at him all the time, hung around him, put her fingers about his arm, laughed up into his face. She didn't go once to the graveyard after she came home and neither did she go to Chapel. Harry was jealous. Her lovely green eyes were brilliant.

Rob went back to work and he complained about everything that had been done in his absence.

'You've done nothing for months. I've had it all to do,' Harry fumed.

'I thought I could leave you to get it right.'

'You're turning into your father,' Harry said, and went away to his own office so that he wouldn't hit Rob.

Half an hour later Rob walked in.

'Leisure doesn't suit me,' he said. 'I wanted to come back a month ago.'

'Did you?' Harry said eagerly.

'I knew you'd make a mess of things while I was gone.'

Harry clipped him lightly round the ear. 'How are you feeling?'

'I'm fine.'

'Faith looks wonderful.'

'Doesn't she? I knew she could.'

The wedding was planned for August. Harry wondered if Rob would remember that last year he had gone away with Susannah.

'Have you heard anything about Michael?'

'No.'

'He must be long out by now. Didn't he come back?'

'He'd hardly think we'd give him a job, would he?' Harry said, and when Rob didn't answer he said, 'Come on, Rob. You can't take him on, you can't afford to. The men would laugh at you.'

'This is his home. He's lived here all his life, and Nancy, she belongs here too.'

'Well I don't know where either of them is, so there's nothing we can do about it.'

Claire had been out to do the shopping. The two children were playing happily in the small garden at the front and

Nancy was baking bread, it was one of her favourite occupations. She was worried. The people in the area knew that Michael had been branded a troublemaker and no pit manager would take him on. During the weeks since he had been out of gaol he had tried everywhere, and when that failed he had looked for other jobs, but the only thing he could get was the worst-paid labouring. Nancy wanted to talk to him but she didn't dare because he was so quiet and withdrawn. He was out now after yet another job.

She took the first batch of bread from the oven. She knew that the smell was enough to entice Susannah and the children in from the garden, and by the time Claire came in they were eating bread hot from the oven, spread with plum jam.

Nancy thought when Claire came in that she didn't seem very happy. She looked hard at Susannah and then put down her basket and included both of them in her gaze as the children ran outside again with their bread and jam.

'Got some news,' she said.

'What's happened?' Susannah said.

'Robert Berkeley is back and he's going to be married.' They had long since abandoned any pretence that Victoria was not his child. Nancy was glad of that now.

'Married?' Nancy said.

Susannah stared.

'He's going to marry Miss Norman. They're just back from London. That plain, skinny, old—'

'Claire,' Susannah admonished her.

'Well, she is,' Claire said, picking up her basket and beginning to unload the groceries. 'Some fun he'll have with her.'

'He can marry whoever he likes,' Susannah said calmly.

'Yes, but why her? He could have anybody he wanted in the whole world. She's thirty. Can you imagine being as old as that and never having a man?'

'Claire . . .' Susannah said again.

'She must be like a prune by now.'

Nancy giggled. She didn't mean to, she knew that Miss Norman was very nice, but it didn't seem right that she should have Rob.

'He can't care about her,' Claire said.

'Why should he marry her if he doesn't care about her?'

'I don't know. You don't think he's got her up the whatsit, do you?'

'Well, it wouldn't be the first time for him, would it?' Susannah said.

'She wouldn't let him do that,' Nancy said.

'He's very good at getting what he wants.'

'Aren't they all?' Claire said.

'Don't you really mind, Susannah?' Nancy said later, when the children were in bed and Susannah was sitting by the window with a glass of wine.

'Mind? I could kill her.'

'You do care about him then?'

'God, yes. I was half dead until I met him. He doesn't go on like other people, you know. He treats you really nicely, and even before he cared about me he still treated me like I mattered to him. He does that. He doesn't know how to be nasty to people and they get the wrong impression, they think he minds them but he doesn't really. He likes things to be right for the sake of it, he likes to put things together so that they work, like solving puzzles, just because. You don't get many people like that, you especially don't get many men like that, they're too greedy. And he knows, he knows that he doesn't manage things whereas other men, they pretend that they do, they pretend to themselves as though they had to get everything right. Going to bed with a man is a sure way of finding out what he's really like. He asked me to marry him.'

'I know. Claire told me. He can't love Miss Norman.'

'I think he feels as if he has to marry her, and when you can't have who you want you don't really care who you have. He never forgave himself for what happened to their John and she's part of that. After all, it's not very likely anybody else would have her, is it? She hasn't got a lot to offer.'

'She used to be bonny,' Nancy said, 'so everybody says before John died, before she came over all churchy and good. Maybe she'll be bonny again now.'

Michael came in when it was very late. Nancy was waiting up for him.

'I had to stay, I got offered two days' work. I'm starting again early in the morning,' he said.

Nancy said nothing. He went to get washed and changed and she gave him something to eat. When he had eaten, he went over to where she was sitting mending the children's clothes and said, 'I'm going to have to leave here, Nancy, I can't get any work.'

Nancy stopped, looked up. 'Leave? What, the area?'

'I'll never get a decent job again here, nobody'll have me. There are plenty of other coalfields. I'll send you money for the bairns.'

'I don't want you to send me money,' Nancy said. 'I want to go with you.'

He looked at her.

'I didn't think you would.'

'If you think I'm staying here without you, you're wrong. What do you think I've been waiting around for, my birthday?'

'I can't marry you, Nancy, I haven't got any money.'

'I've been married and believe me it wasn't all it's cracked up to be.'

'That was different. You should never have married our Sean.'

'Now you tell me.'

'I'll make some money and find a house and I'll send for you.'

'Oh no you don't,' she said, getting up, pushing the

mending aside, 'you go off south by yourself and some woman'll grab you. If you're going, I'm coming too.'

'Nobody's going to grab me, Nancy. I love you. I've always loved you. Don't you believe me?'

'I might if you showed me.'

'When did you change your mind about me?'

'When I didn't have you. It took me until I didn't have either Sean or you to see the difference.'

He didn't say anything for a minute or so and then, 'You're a good Catholic woman.'

'I'm not that good,' Nancy said.

Michael got hold of her. Nancy had been waiting for him to for weeks, and was afraid that she had misjudged his feelings. Part of her knew that Michael wanted to look after her properly. He wanted a house and a job and a wedding and, in a way, had wanted her for so long, so badly, that to actually take her into his arms now seemed impossible, might always be impossible. And she was frightened. Sean had treated her so badly. She had never been loved, she didn't know what to expect. It was such a big risk, especially now that she had settled here in this house with Susannah and Claire and the children, and been as happy as she could be during that time knowing that he was in prison.

Sean had never kissed her like Michael did now. Sometimes his kisses had set her body on fire, but he had never kissed her slowly and gently like this. And once they were married, once Sean had begun treating her badly, there had not been any affection of any kind. There had been no kisses or caresses and Nancy had forgotten, or never known, how good it was. Sean had mocked displays of affection or any finer feelings. She did wonder just a little whether even now, here with her, Michael needed to triumph over his brother. She saw now that in his way he was just as devious as Sean had been, or Rob or Harry. Maybe men were all alike in that way. They saw what they wanted and then they tried to take it. Michael had infinite patience, but he would take what he wanted when he judged that the time was right, and he had judged it correctly because she wanted him.

He took her to bed and there he was not like Sean had been. He was sober and kind and tender and Nancy discovered what it was like to go to bed with a man who loved her. It was quite different. Nobody was taking anything, and it was warm and easy and quite delightful. Nancy was greedy and bold for the first time in her life. She was surprised at herself. He was just pleased to be there, she could tell.

The curtains were not closed. She could see the dark shadows of the cathedral from her bed. She had lain there night after night and thought how near Michael was, and yet she couldn't see him or touch him. She couldn't see him very well now, because she had turned out the light; but she could feel him well enough, as close to her as he could be.

'I love you, Michael,' she said.

He didn't say anything, but she knew that if she had carved it up on the wall in the room he couldn't have been better pleased. He was like Sean in some ways. No doubt there would be battles, but Michael would never use against her the kind of weapons which his brother had employed, and if he hurt her it would not be with his hands, those hands which were now caressing her past her reason. She forgot Sean, she even forgot the children. All her troubles went away, all her worries ceased.

Nineteen

Harry wondered whether Rob was deceiving himself over Vincent and Ida's reaction to his forthcoming marriage. Neither of them was pleased, they had just given in because there was nothing they could do. Harry knew that his mother, while wanting Rob home again, was aghast at the idea of Faith at the beautiful Nottingham house where Sarah had reigned. Rob's mother and Faith's mother were happy sorting out the wedding, but Ida was restless.

'Do you think that Mother might like to go home?' Harry asked his father, one warm evening when they were alone in the garden at Faith's parents' house.

'Home?'

'Yes, you know, the small cottage in the country that you occasionally frequent. I think she misses the garden.'

'If we go home she'll miss the wedding,' Vincent pointed out.

'Will that be a great loss?'

Vincent sighed. 'She's very disappointed.'

'Yes, I can see that.'

'Not that Faith hasn't improved immeasurably, but she will sound her "a"s as though they were scarcely worth the trouble. I can't bear the thought of her in Nottinghamshire society permanently, she's such a parochial little soul.'

'Aren't Faith and Rob going to live here?'

'Not if I can help it.'

'Mother might prefer it if they did.'

'No, she wouldn't. She'll get used to Faith and anything would be better than losing him. You will come back with us next time, won't you?'

'If I can get away.'

'How could you prefer this place?'

Harry was about to say that he didn't because he didn't want to hurt his father, and then he smiled at himself and said, 'I don't know. I feel as if I can be myself here.'

'And who else have you been?' Vincent asked tartly.

'I've been your son, Vincent, for the last thirty years. Being the son of a supposed genius is very trying.'

'I'm proud of what you've done here,' Vincent admitted. 'I want you at home, but I like seeing you here in your awful little office. You've done so much.'

'Are you feeling all right, Father?'

Vincent grinned.

*

That evening Faith and Rob went for a walk because the house was very crowded and they liked being alone. They walked across the fell. It was the way that Faith liked best and she said to him, 'John and I were going to rent one of the terraced houses that overlook the park. Do you remember?'

'Were you? I don't remember anything about it. It would be a bit cramped, wouldn't it?'

She smiled. 'We had very modest aspirations. Have you thought about it at all?'

'I thought we'd just go on as we are, unless that's a problem.'

'There's hardly any room,' Faith said.

Rob frowned.

'The place is huge,' he said.

Faith stopped. They had reached the highest point around there. She could see the works and part of the town.

'You're talking about the house in Nottingham, aren't you?' she said.

'Where else?'

'You want us to live with Ida and Vincent?'

'Would you object to that?'

'*They* might,' she pointed out.

'No, they wouldn't. I do partly own it.'

'But you lived there with Sarah.'

'That doesn't have to be a problem. We'd get used to it. It's far too big for them on their own, and Vincent would never sell. Ida is too kind a woman to resent you, Faith.'

'No, no, I didn't mean that she would, it's just that . . . I thought we could live here.'

'I never intended to live here.'

'Berry Edge is your home.'

'No, my home is in Nottingham.'

'It's my home.'

'Faith, your home is going to be with me.'

'What about my parents and your mother and—'

'I would have thought you'd be glad to get away from them. Harry wants to stay here. I can just come up from time to time for a few weeks and help out. Harry will buy or rent a decent-sized house and we can stay with him when we come.'

'I have friends here and commitments and . . .'

'And John's grave?'

'I haven't been to John's grave, and it's very hurtful of you to say that.'

They went back to the house and found the others sitting in the garden. Faith told her mother and father that Rob didn't want to live in Berry Edge, and could see by their faces that they were displeased and disappointed. So was Rob's mother. Ida and Vincent said nothing other than that she was very welcome to live with them, but Rob's mother said, 'I never heard anything like it. The Berkeleys have lived here since the works began. Who's to run the place?'

'I am,' Harry said.

'Why can't you go back to Nottingham with your parents, and Rob and Faith can stay here?'

'Because that's not what either of us wants,' Rob said.

'What about what *I* want?' Faith put in.

'You'll be my wife,' Rob said.

'What does that mean?'

'It means that we'll live where my work is and essentially my work will be in Nottingham.'

Faith wanted to cry, so she got up and ran into the house. He followed her there, all the way up to her bedroom which he shouldn't have done. The windows were open and from them she could see the countryside.

'I can't leave here, I don't know how to,' she said.

'I thought you liked the house and the country and the people, and you certainly liked London. Didn't you?'

'Yes, but only to visit. I wouldn't want to live there.'

'You'll soon make friends. There'll be plenty to do. You can ride there, and go into Nottingham with Ida and—'

'You're going to insist, aren't you?' Faith said, turning and looking at him.

'Only if you make me.'

'That's the same thing. It's not a side to you that I noticed before.'

'What?'

'Making me obey you.'

'I'm not making you obey me, Faith, I have to live where my work is, that's all.'

'Your work has been here.'

'Just lately, yes, but it was never my intention to stay here.'

'You hate it?'

'I don't hate it any more. I did but I don't now. We can come back here from time to time. I often go to London too and you can come with me and stay at the house there. Surely you understand?'

'If I must then I will,' Faith said.

Berry Edge seemed after that to get more and more precious each day. She went to John's grave and to the Chapel, and to see the people whom she knew, but everything was different now and they treated her differently. The people of Berry Edge would never like Rob, and since she was to marry him they included her in their dislike and so excluded her from their lives. She lost her contact with them, she was not asked to help with the Chapel. She was not asked into their homes, and when they discovered that she was going away to Nottinghamshire to live in some country mansion, the gap widened even further. Faith in some way began to long to be gone because she had no place here.

She saw Vera Ridley one hot day, and though she knew Vera very little she also knew that Vera had been Nancy's good friend. When Vera would have crossed over the road to avoid her, Faith went to her and asked for news of Nancy.

'She's living in Durham, Miss.'

'Then you have heard from her. How is she?'

'She's all right as far as I know.'

'I would very much like to see her. Do you know where she's staying in Durham?'

'I couldn't say, Miss, I've never been. Near one of the bridges, I think. Don't know which one though. She wrote to me once. North Street, I think.'

'North Road?'

'No, Miss, it was a street, I'm sure.'

'It couldn't be South Street, could it?'

'I don't remember, Miss,' Vera said, and left hurriedly.

'Do you hear anything from Nancy?' Faith asked Harry that evening when he got home from work.

'Nancy? No, why?'

'I just wondered. I met Vera Ridley, her friend, and she says that Nancy is living in Durham. She gave me what could be an address.'

'If you find out, let me know. Rob worries about Nancy.'

It wasn't that Faith deliberately went into Durham to see Nancy, it was just that she decided she wanted to do a bit of shopping. It was while she was there and walking down the winding hill which was Silver Street towards the river that she remembered what Vera had said. She crossed the bridge and made her way up the hill, and then knocked on the nearest door. She knocked on four doors. She didn't know why particularly she wanted to see Nancy, just that she knew Rob was concerned, she wanted to make sure that Nancy was getting by all right.

At the fourth house a small, pretty woman opened the door. Faith enquired tentatively and the woman said, 'You're a friend of Nancy's? That's nice. Come in.'

Inside the house was quite big and elegantly furnished. The woman led the way into the kitchen. Nancy was sitting with a baby on her lap. Faith beamed at her and said, 'Hello, Nancy, how are you?'

She wasn't surprised that Nancy didn't seem overwhelmed to see her. She pushed the baby at the other woman and got hastily to her feet.

'What a lovely baby,' Faith said. 'It's not – it's not yours?'

'Goodness me, no, Miss,' Nancy said.

'What a beautiful baby you have,' Faith told the other woman.

'She is, isn't she?' the woman said and took the baby and left, much to Faith's disappointment.

'How are the children?' Faith asked.

'Oh, very well. Fine.'

'They're not here?'

'No, they – they've gone for a walk.'

As if to call it a lie there were sounds in the hall. The children burst in, and following them was Michael McFadden. Faith was surprised to see him.

'Good afternoon,' she said.

'Hello,' Michael said.

Michael confused Faith, she didn't know quite why. He took up a lot of room in the kitchen and she didn't know what to say. She didn't know why she had come now. She felt like apologising for intruding on them.

'How's Mr Berkeley?' Michael said.

'He's very well. We're – we're to be married. We're going to Nottingham to live.'

'Yes, so I hear. Congratulations.'

'I mustn't stay, I really mustn't. I just wanted to make sure that Nancy was well.'

Nobody protested that she was leaving. Nancy saw her into the hall. At that moment the front door opened, and what Faith thought afterwards was surely the most beautiful woman in the world stepped into the house. She wore thin white clothes because the day was so hot, and her skin was golden. Her hair was black and her eyes were almost black with thick, long lashes. She was tall and, although her dress was modest, Faith did not doubt that her body was exquisite. She looked perfectly cool, she smiled from white, even teeth and when she took off her gloves her fingers were long and slender and looked after with pretty nails. They had no rings on them nor needed any.

'Good afternoon,' she said.

'Good afternoon.'

'Susannah, this is Miss Norman. Faith, this is Susannah Seaton.'

Faith would have had to have lived a lot further from Durham than Berry Edge not to have heard of Susannah, though she knew that respectable women were urged to believe that women like Susannah did not exist or were not seen to exist. No respectable woman would have done anything other than crossed the street and ignored her, but Faith couldn't, because she realised now that this was Susannah Seaton's house. So she put out her hand and said how very nice it was to meet her, and Susannah said the same.

'You must stay and have some tea with us,' she said.

'Miss Norman has to go,' Nancy said.

'Yes, yes, I really must.'

'Must you? Well then, another time.'

From upstairs came the unmistakable sound of a baby screaming for its mother. Even Faith recognised it. The baby knew that its mother had entered the house, perhaps even, if babies did such things, recognised her voice or smelled her presence.

'You must excuse me,' Susannah said, 'it was very nice to meet you,' and she went off upstairs.

Nancy saw Faith out of the house. She walked slowly down the hill and across the bridge. She had never met a prostitute before and had never thought to meet one. She never imagined that a prostitute could look like that. Susannah Seaton brought the sun and the moon down, she was so beautiful. What man could resist her? And she had a child. Faith longed for a child. She wondered what it was like to have a child and to bring it up without a father.

That evening when Rob and Harry were playing billiards, Faith went into the room.

'I saw Nancy today,' she said.

Rob stopped. He had been about to attempt to pocket the blue.

'You found her?' he said.

'She's living in Durham, and I saw Michael too, and the children. They're living in South Street with – with some people.' Faith didn't like to say Susannah's name. She thought it might prejudice Rob about helping Nancy and Michael.

They all knew what that meant. If Michael was at home during the week, it meant that he had nothing to do.

'Isn't there some way that you could get Michael work?'

'Don't be silly, Faith,' Harry said, 'Michael McFadden almost got Rob killed.'

'It wasn't his fault, surely. He was just doing what he thought was right, you can't blame him for that.'

'I can blame him.'

'What is he to do?'

'I have no idea, Faith, and I can't say that I really care.'

'What about Nancy? They belong here just like Rob and I do. Why should they move away because of what happened?'

'Because they lost,' Harry said.

Faith stared at him. 'You make it sound like some kind of game. Michael has just as much right to live here as you do. More, in fact, because you're a stranger.'

'How long do you have to live here before you cease to be a stranger.' Harry demanded, glaring at her. 'Twenty years? Thirty?'

'You have to be born here,' Faith said, 'and they were, and you've made it impossible for them to come back. They can't stay here now. I thought you came here to make things better.'

'Things are better,' Harry argued.

'Not for Nancy and Michael they're not! Or for Nora Cowan and her family, or for a lot of people who have had to leave because of what happened. It's no use you pretending that everything is all right, because it isn't. There are a lot of people who wish you'd never come here in the first place.'

'And are you one of them?' Harry asked stiffly.

'I was today. I was ashamed,' Faith said, shaking. 'Nancy did nothing, but you put her out.'

'We did not!'

'She left because she had nowhere to go because of her loyalty to you. How do you think she felt when she had to leave because of you, and now she can't come back because of Michael? You don't care about the women and they're the ones who were hurt most.'

'Enough, both of you,' Rob said and then looked at Harry.

'I think Faith's right. I think we ought to give Michael a chance. What do you think, Harry?'

That evening Faith got Rob alone and kissed him all over his face.

'I knew you would,' she said.

'Don't.'

'Don't what?' Faith drew back. It was late at night in the garden. They had to go outside to be alone. 'You aren't cross with me, are you, for going there and then for going on and on about it?'

'I'm very proud of you.'

'Are you sure?'

'Yes. You were right.'

'Was I? I love you to tell me that I'm right. Kiss me.' Rob did. Faith put herself into his arms until she was pressed against him. 'I love you, Rob, I love you. I never thought I was going to love anybody again. You make me so happy and you're kind. If it weren't for you Harry would turn into a stone, he's so stupid.'

Two days later a man turned up at the house in South Street asking for Michael. When Nancy ushered him into the downstairs sitting room, Michael recognised him as a miner he had known some years since, a deputy called George Hobson.

'Why Geordie,' he said, getting up, 'it's been a long time.'

'Hello, Mick, how are you? Is that your missus? What a bonny lass.'

'Thanks. I didn't know you were around.'

'I've come to manage the Diamond.'

'Manage it?'

'I went back to school and then I went on and took the tests, you know, and I'm a manager now. Mr Berkeley has given me the Diamond.'

'That was lucky. Jobs are hard to come by.'

'I know. You should get yourself some schooling, Michael, it's the best way.'

'Aye, well.'

'In the meanwhile, do you want a job?'

Michael stared at him. 'What, hewing?'

'Well, you're a bit big for owt else.'

'Don't you know what happened? He'd never have me back.'

'Told me different. Says he wants you.'

'After what happened?'

'Says he'll take on all comers.'

'The bastard was always like that,' Michael said, remembering Rob as a small boy. 'I can't do it, man.'

'Why not?'

'It's charity.'

'Hewing down the Diamond? I don't think so, Michael, the Diamond's a bitch and you're good.'

Michael hesitated.

'He isn't asking you to bloody tea, man, he's offering you a job. You'd be daft to turn him down.'

'He's rubbing my nose in it.'

'Mebbe he is, but there's them that'll call him soft for doing it.'

'Well, it won't be me. He showed me what he was made of.'

'You'll come in then?'

'Aye, I'll do it. When?'

'Monday, early shift.' Geordie got to the door and then hesitated. 'There's a house in it an' all of course, one of them new ones, just close enough to the Miners' Arms,' he said with a grin. 'I'll see you there Saturday night if you fancy a game of dominoes.'

When Geordie had gone Michael went into the kitchen. Nancy was peeling potatoes for tea. He sneaked up behind her and grabbed her around the waist so that she shrieked.

'Michael! I nearly cut my finger off,' and she turned around, brandishing a knife.

'Will you marry me, sweetheart?'

'What are you talking about, you great lump?'

'I've got a job.'

Nancy shrieked with pleased surprise. 'Where?'

'At the Diamond.'

Nancy stared at him. 'How did that happen?'

'His lordship requested it,' Michael said dryly.

'Even he wouldn't do that.'

'He did.'

'My God, Michael, you'll never be able to cross him again. However will you stand it?'

'And a new house,' Michael said.

'We can get married at our own church,' Nancy said and then her face fell.

'What?'

'Well, they'll know, won't they, that he took you back. They won't like him or you the better for that, and when everything went wrong they turned on me because of him.'

'I won't let anybody hurt you, sweetheart. I'll be there this time. We're going home and nobody's going to stop us. They'll accept it in time. In the meanwhile we've got a house and a job and I've got the offer of a domino game on Saturday night.'

Harry came into the garden later that day, where Rob was sitting with his arm around Faith. It was early evening and the day had been perfectly fine. Now the peace and the quiet were what he needed. He looked up as Harry disturbed him.

'Michael McFadden's here. He wants to see you. Shall I put him in the sitting room?'

'No, send him out here. You don't mind, do you, Faith?'

She smiled at him, kissed him twice on the nose and then left. Michael came into the garden, cap in hand.

'Hello, Mickey,' Rob said.

Michael said nothing. He didn't even look at Rob at first.

'Have a seat,' Rob offered.

'No, thanks.' He looked at Rob then. It was a straight, dark look that made Rob want to get up, or at least move around in his chair, but he didn't.

'I don't think you know how badly I feel about you. You've given me a job. You've made me feel guilty. We're never going to be friends.'

Rob sat back further. 'It has nothing to do with feelings. And it isn't for you, Michael, it's for Nancy. Since I came back here you've made very plain what you think of me. I'm not going to be around here much longer so you don't have to worry about it.'

'And if I make trouble?'

'I wouldn't,' Rob said softly.

'I wish that just once I could get you into the Station Hotel before I've had a drink.'

Rob said nothing to that, but smiled. 'What's the new house like?' he said.

'It's a bloody castle. Nancy and me, we're getting wed.'

'Nancy's a picture. I'm going back to Nottingham where I belong, but I'll be back from time to time so don't go getting any funny ideas.'

'Are you leaving Shaw here in charge?'

'Any objections?'

'He's all right for a southerner,' Michael said.

Twenty

Everything was going well, Faith thought, when she had the final fitting for her dress. It flattered her in every respect. She had thought that she would never see herself as a bride, and looking at her mother in the mirror she knew that she was thinking the same thing. Her mother was pleased but mostly relieved. She was marrying the most eligible man in the area and her parents could not have been more delighted.

They were not pleased that Faith was going to Nottingham to live. The idea of living at the abbey frightened her, but most of all she thought of how she and John had planned to have a small terraced house, and the important thing was that they would have been able to live there alone. The house in Nottingham was huge with dozens of servants, and she would have to watch what she said and how she behaved. She would rarely have Rob to herself. Also, Ida and Vincent intimidated her. They didn't mean to, she knew, but they were so knowledgeable and educated. They were well read and worldly. They didn't go to church, they didn't understand how people in Berry Edge lived. Faith liked them but she didn't want to live with them, most especially because they had been Sarah's parents. She could never live up to Sarah Shaw, she knew very well, and it made her heart thump. She didn't want to live up to her, she didn't want to go anywhere, she wanted a modest house in Berry Edge and for Rob to be there with her and manage the foundry.

Harry was looking for a house. He asked Faith to go with him. He was tired of lodging with her parents even though they were very nice, he said. He wanted his own place.

'It doesn't have to be a big house,' Harry said, 'just somewhere I can go and be on my own and you and Rob can come and stay.'

Faith was pleased to be asked to go with him because they hadn't been getting on very well lately, arguing over everything they discussed. He said that he would let her know when he found something suitable and it was only a few days later that he said, 'I think I've found somewhere. Will you come and see it?'

Faith said that she would.

The house was perfect, she thought. It was near the top of the bank so it was not far from the works and the station, being further along from the terraced houses where she and John would have lived. It was a bigger house than those, but by Harry's standards very modest. It had a garden to back and front and a carriage house and stable, a well and even a paddock, and the usual assortment of buildings outside, the hen house and the wash house. It looked out over the park and in the distance you could just see the fell. The rooms were nicely proportioned, and on the outside it had a stone piece that was completely decoration, between the ground and first storey windows, on which were carvings of fruit and flowers which Faith thought very pretty. It also had on the first floor a garden room, a wooden structure in which plants could be grown and people could sit. The view from there was what Faith thought of as the best view in the world.

'Do you like it?' Harry asked.

'It's the prettiest house I ever saw,' Faith said. 'I wish we could have it. I wish we weren't going. Couldn't you talk to him?'

'There's nothing you can do about it, Faith. You must have known that you would probably be living in Nottingham.'

'I didn't think. I always think that Rob belongs here. I don't want to leave.'

'It isn't for good.'

'I don't understand why you are staying here and Rob is going. It ought to be the other way round.'

'Thank you, Faith.'

'I didn't mean it like that, it just seems all wrong.'

'How can I put this? I'm content here. Rob isn't.'

'Is he content anywhere?'

'Not that I've noticed.'

*

Nancy had mixed feelings about moving back to Berry Edge, but they went. Once she was there and saw how nice her new house was, she was pleased. They were to be married in a fortnight, the same day that Faith and Rob were to be married. Michael was so happy to be there that Nancy hid her misgivings. The very first day that she was in Berry Edge, Vera arrived with a big rice cake and some ginger wine and an offer of help in putting up the curtains. Vera talked about Rob and Faith.

'I never thought he'd marry somebody like her, nobody did. Nobody can understand why he's marrying her except that he feels he has to after what happened to that brother of his. They're moving away, you know. A lot of the men say "good riddance to bad rubbish" but my Shane says if it wasn't for Mr Berkeley there would be no works by now. Mind you, he only says it to the right people, there's plenty won't have Mr Berkeley's name mentioned. You like him, don't you?'

'I hardly dare say it,' Nancy admitted, standing back to admire her new net curtains in the front room.

'It's a lovely house,' Vera said.

'Don't tell Michael, but I liked the other one better. I've missed you.'

'I've missed you an' all,' Vera said. 'Put the kettle on and let's try this cake.'

They were glad of the sit down and the cake was pronounced good.

'I tried to tell Miss Norman where you were in Durham because she wanted to come and see you, but I couldn't remember the address.'

'She found us anyway,' Nancy said. 'I wish she hadn't, it really upset things, but I think that's why we're back here so we should be glad.'

'What you do mean "it upset things"?'

'Oh, the people we lodged with in South Street,' Nancy said obscurely.

'Here, isn't that where that woman lives?'

'What woman?'

'You know, the one the men all fancy. The dear one. She's back here, my Shane says. Saw her in Durham, says she's a real bonny piece. Huh, I know what I'd do with her, pinching other women's men, taking money like that for what other women do for nothing. I think it's disgusting.'

'As a matter of fact she's very nice,' Nancy said clearly.

'You know her?'

'I've seen her.'

'How could you think a low person like that is nice?'

'It isn't her fault.'

'Oh, isn't it? I would think there's many a lass cried her eyes out because that Seaton woman had her husband.'

'Not round here, nobody could afford her,' Nancy said.

'Only men with a lot of money, like that Mr Shaw. He's like that, he has fancy women.'

'How do you know that?'

'Everybody knows. Him and Mr Berkeley. Mr Berkeley has a woman in Durham.'

'Where did you hear that?'

'You told me.'

'I did not.'

'Maybe it was Theresa then.'

'She didn't say that?'

'Well, somebody did.'

'How would Theresa know?'

'She worked at the house, she would know a lot. He used to go every Saturday night to Durham and sometimes not come back. You wouldn't have known that likely because you weren't there at weekends. Posh men are like that, they can't keep their hands off. And they don't need to, not when they've got deep pockets.'

Nancy was wishing that Michael and the children would come home. He had taken them out of the way so that she could get on and he thought that she wanted some time alone with Vera. If only he knew, Nancy thought.

'You don't think it was her, do you?'

'What?'

'You know, that Seaton woman. Her and Mr Berkeley. She's got a bairn, I hear. Disgusting, isn't it?'

'Let's put the bedroom curtains up, Vera. I can't sleep for the light so we have to get them up before we go to bed.'

'Righto,' Vera said and she put the dirty cups and plates in the sink.

They finished putting up curtains in the bedrooms and Vera went home when Michael came back. The neighbours had helped him in with the furniture earlier that day, and they had done a lot, so when the children were in bed Michael said, 'You don't mind if I go to the pub, do you? I promised Geordie I would look in.'

Since he had come out of prison Michael had not once gone to a pub. Nancy looked anxiously at him and he came over and kissed her.

'There's no need for you to worry, sweetheart, I won't ever come back here drunk and knock you around. I won't go with other women or gamble away the little we've got or any other of the awful things the McFaddens are famous for. I'm going to play a game of dominoes and have a couple of pints, which is all I can afford, and then I'm coming home to go to bed with you.'

'Michael . . .'

'What?'

'Vera mentioned something to me about Mr Berkeley and Susannah. I think some people know.'

'It's an old rumour. She hasn't seen him since long before the baby was born, isn't that what you said?'

'Since last summer.'

'Well then, there's nowt to talk about, is there? Stop worrying about things, Nancy, and just be glad. I won't be late.'

Nancy prowled the house when he had gone, so pleased that he was happy, the children sleeping upstairs, the house quiet. Things were better now in Berry Edge than they had been for a long time, she thought, and she would be part of that. Michael would have a good job, and she would have the kind of marriage which she had intended to have in the first place. A small part of Nancy still thought about how Sean had come back from the pub and the awful things he had done to her, so when Michael was later than she had thought he might be, she began to feel sick. Just as the sickness turned into a pain, the back door opened and there he stood, looking the picture of Sean. Then he smiled and wasn't.

'Am I late? You look worried.'

'No.'

He shut the back door and came over. He was wearing his good suit and he really did look nice, Nancy thought.

'What are you looking at?' he asked her.

'The best looking man in Berry Edge.'

'Get away with you,' Michael said.

The sickness went as though somebody had stolen it.

'You look a bit white, Nancy. Are you sure you're all right?'

Nancy hesitated. She had been putting off telling him for days now, because although she knew that he loved her, there was a tiny part of her which was still afraid.

'I think I'm expecting actually,' Nancy confessed. 'I'm not sure, mind you, but—' She got no further. He grabbed her and kissed her and wanted to make her a cup of tea and accused her of not telling him sooner.

'I said I don't know. You are pleased though, if it is?'

'Pleased? Nancy, I love you. You're the bonniest lass in the whole world, and the kindest. I've never been as happy in my life as I have been since I came out of gaol. I've got you and the bairns and a house and a job – and I beat Geordie at dominoes.'

Nancy threw her arms around him and whispered in his ear. 'If you carry me up the stairs I'll give you something nice.'

'Will you? What's that?'

'Me,' Nancy said.

Twenty-one

Rob and Faith were a week away from their wedding and Faith could tell that his mother and her mother were excited. They had had new outfits made, ridiculous hats with feathers and pretty dresses. The food was ordered, the chapel was cleaned, the guests had all answered and most were coming. Faith could not believe that in less than a week she would be married. She was cross because the weather was bad, but perhaps even that would change. Everything else was fine.

Three days before the wedding Faith went into Durham for a last few things. It had rained earlier, but had cleared, and she hoped that it would settle in time for Saturday. She lingered in the shops but it was funny how, now that she could have anything, she wanted nothing. Nothing held her interest but the man who was at work in Berry Edge. She could not see enough of him, he could not kiss her enough or hold her enough. She longed for the very sight of him, even though they had been parted for only a few hours.

She lingered, leaning over the bridge looking at the castle and cathedral, missing them already because she would be leaving for Nottingham straight after the wedding. It was her one regret.

In the middle of the afternoon she made her way up the narrow street towards the cathedral. A woman was coming the other way with a pram. Faith recognised her immediately. She lived with Susannah Seaton. The pram was new, bright and shiny. She wouldn't have stopped but Faith smiled and said, 'Good afternoon.' The pavement was narrow and the pram was cumbersome. Faith looked at the baby, thinking of how beautiful the child had seemed, as she would with a mother like Susannah Seaton. The woman would even then have brushed past and gone on, except that Faith was in the way. Faith was about to make a complimentary remark about the baby, because she loved babies, and had of late spent many happy hours thinking of the children that she and Rob would have, and then she looked at the baby. Something happened inside her head, and she knew that she was his child. There was just something about her that was completely him.

She let the pram past, she even smiled and said goodbye, but she knew. She felt as though she was going to faint, her head was dizzy and her feet didn't know where to go. She went up the bank towards the green which had the cathedral on one side, the castle on another and houses on the other two sides, and she went into the cathedral and sat down there in the cool quiet, and tried to think. She could not believe what her heart was telling her.

It could not be true, such a thing could not happen to destroy the only real happiness that she had felt in ten years, and yet there was a part of her which knew with a clearsightedness that it was.

Faith went home. She walked back to the station, she stared out of the train window, she went slowly back to the house where soon Harry and Rob and Vincent would finish their work and come home to eat. Presents had arrived, the house was festive, it had an air of excitement about it as though it would burst with joy. Her mother was so pleased, her father was smiling at her, and Rob's mother. Faith thought he had finally managed it, he had managed to please his mother. He had got something right, his mother spoke softly to him, smiled on him. Faith did not think that she had ever seen Mrs Berkeley look like this since before John died and everything went wrong.

Rob came home. He looked different to Faith now. He no longer looked to her like the young man she had loved. He was somehow all at once profoundly not John, and Faith wondered how on earth she had ever thought she loved him. He looked like the man she had thought he was before he came home, the careless, uncaring, selfish person he had always been who went around thoughtlessly destroying other people's lives. He was the person who was John's brother.

Dinnertime came and went. The talk was all of the wedding. Faith must have eaten something, but didn't remember doing so. After dinner, because it was pouring with rain, the older people sat around the fire and Rob and Harry went into the billiard room. Faith followed them there.

'I want to talk to you,' she said.

'Just a minute.' He executed a perfect shot, which had to cannon off the cushion to sink a red ball, and Harry laughed and called him names.

'I want to talk to you,' she said.

'In a minute. I could do this.'

'On your own.'

He wasn't even listening. He was lining up the next shot and Harry was laughing. They were neither of them paying any attention and why should they, she thought? Their world had come together. They were rich and successful. They had everything.

'I want to talk to you about Susannah Seaton.'

That stopped them; their laughter was silenced, and whatever shot it was that Rob was boasting about to Harry, he didn't make it. He stopped, looked up.

'What?' he said.

They left the room. He closed the door. In the hall he looked at her, but Faith went into the dining room, which was now cleared and empty, although the table and chairs took up a great deal of space. It was not a room which got the sunlight and was not a room which she had ever liked, and with the summer rain excluding what light there was from the window it was quite gloomy in there. It could have done with a lamp or two, though none were lit because after dinner nobody went in there.

'I want you to tell me all about her,' Faith said softly.

'Why?'

'Just tell me about Susannah Seaton and you.'

Rob stopped leaning against the door and moved further into the room. 'For a short while after I came back to Berry Edge she was my mistress.'

Faith looked at him. 'At the time I used to hear stories about Harry. I believed them about him, but I didn't think that you would do such a thing.'

'Why not?'

'Because I saw you differently.'

'You saw me as John.'

'Yes. Yes, I did. Perhaps that was how I wanted to see you. I should understand now that I've been about a little in the world, because I know that in places like London it's quite common for men like you, men who call themselves gentlemen, to sleep with prostitutes.'

'I never did,' Rob said.

'But you did. Not there, but here, where most people already disliked you. Didn't it seem reckless?'

'I loved her.'

'You loved Susannah Seaton, knowing that she gave herself to other men for money?'

'It wasn't anything to do with that. I didn't care what she did, at least I did but . . . she gave them up.'

'And that made it right?'

'No, I didn't say it was right. This was last spring and summer. I haven't seen her since then. I'm not so bad a person, I wouldn't do that to you or to her. It's done and finished. It's over a year.'

'But you weren't going to tell me, were you?'

'About something that happened before us? No, why should I?'

'I think,' Faith said slowly, 'that if that had been all, though God knows it's enough that you should pay a woman to go to bed with you, if that had been all I think I might have forgiven you—'

'Forgiven me?' He was staring at her.

'But there's a child, isn't there?'

He went on staring at her, his eyes darkening. 'A child? No, it can't be anything to do with me. She would have told me. She wouldn't risk that happening.'

'I've seen the baby. It looks just like you.'

'No.'

'Yes, it does.'

'Susannah wouldn't do that to me.'

'You can go there and see for yourself. The whole world can see. It's obvious.'

Rob said nothing. His head went down and he leaned back against the door again.

'You don't think I'm going to marry you now, do you?' Faith said, her voice shaking badly. 'You should be relieved. You didn't want to marry me.'

'I did.'

'Don't pretend either to yourself or to me that you have any honour, because you don't, you never did have. You didn't want me because what you wanted was Susannah Seaton. You preferred a whore to me, a woman who has been with countless other men. You preferred that to me.'

'No.'

'You disgusting liar. The only reason that you offered to marry me was because you felt guilty.'

'No.'

'Yes, it was, Rob! You feel guilty over John. You always will, and as far as I'm concerned you always should. You destroyed him with your stupidity. You spoil everything that way, just like you've done this time. I thought you were different but you aren't, you're still the stupid boy that you always were, and you ruin everything because you don't think about anything but what you want. You've taken everything away from me, even yourself. You couldn't bring yourself to be honest and say that you had never cared for me. You would have married me while you love another woman.'

The room was quite dark now. Faith wanted to get out because her throat was full of tears, but he was leaning against the door like he had forgotten how to move.

There was a knock on the door, and when Harry pushed it open Rob moved away. As soon as Harry came in Faith ran past him into the hall. She was already crying. Her mother came out of the sitting room.

'Faith?' she said.

Harry closed the door.

'Did you know that Susannah was back?' Rob said.

'No.'

'Don't you ever go into Durham?'

'No, I don't.'

'Why not? Are you a reformed character or something?'

'Something like that.'

'There's a child, Harry.'

'Oh God, is there? How the hell does Faith know? Is it a boy or a girl?'

'I didn't ask.'

'Well, that's typical of you. That's what you do in important meetings, stare out of the window like bloody Henny-Penny, waiting for the sky to fall. I won't get my best suit pressed for Saturday then, eh?'

Rob made for the door. Harry got hold of his arm. 'Just a minute. You can't go off to Durham and beat the truth out of Susannah. It won't help at all.'

Rob looked at him. 'Do you know what this means, Harry? It means that I was right, that Susannah never did care about me or she wouldn't have let this happen to hurt Faith so much. She would know that I was trying to repair things that can't be repaired. She must hate me. I was just another stupid man paying for things I was not entitled to.'

'That's not true,' Harry said.

Rob pulled away, left the house. Faith's father was first into the room.

'Where is he?'

'He's gone.'

'That's what he always does, runs away.'

Vincent came in. 'Where's Rob?'

'I don't know.'

'Is this true? Is there a woman with a child? What is he, a bloody imbecile?'

Harry left the house. He went back to the office for a while, but Rob did not go there or to the house. When it was late on the summer's evening Harry walked the streets, trying to decide whether to go to Durham.

The streets of Berry Edge were not as they had been. It was not yet a prosperous place to live, but it would be. There were still many houses where nobody wanted to live, but not nearly as many as there had been, and a lot of them were still being altered. Rob had been so excited about it and it was clean now, the streets were almost rubbish free and the works itself went night and day in the old 'time's money' code that industry had.

The shops were full of goods because there was money

and the children played games in the street. The rain was well stopped and the sun was creating a brilliant sheen on the roads and pavements. The houses had that just-washed look which made them more handsome than they were. Here and there people greeted him – not all of them, some hated him because he was the boss, but most of them accepted him now. He walked the streets until well after they were deserted, until the children had gone to bed, the women to their houses and the men to the pubs or to work. The only noise was the midweek clamour of beer-happy workmen.

Harry couldn't go back to the house. He went past it on his way up the hill, he went through the park and then out to the top and walked right along the road, past the terraced houses and further on to where his own house was. He found the key in his pocket, unlocked the door and went inside. There wasn't much furniture in the house. He was planning to move in within a few days but he hadn't had time to buy things. There weren't any glasses. He found a bottle of Scotch in the kitchen and emptied some into a thin fluted china cup. He stood around even though there were hard chairs, and when he had swallowed half a cup and refilled it he wandered up to the garden room which Faith had so much liked. He stood there while the summer evening turned into night.

He had not wanted Faith to marry Rob, and now she was not going to. He wished that he had been more generous. He remembered her crying and the stricken look on her face.

She had found out that Rob was not his brother because, from what Harry could gather, John Berkeley would never in a million years have gone with a prostitute, much less got her pregnant. Harry wondered what the baby was like. If Faith deplored Rob's conduct what would she think of a man like himself? Rob was a saint by comparison. Rob had been Faith's last chance because he was the one man in the world who seemed like the only man that she had ever loved. Harry doubted that she was capable of loving again.

He drank the rest of his Scotch as the day disappeared and the sky came down to meet the fell in darkness, and he thought about himself. He wondered whether he had fallen in love almost on purpose with a woman he could not possibly have so that he would not have to marry her, so that he could be forever free in that solitary way to which he had become accustomed. At least it was a comforting thought, and he wouldn't go mad if he thought like that. He might go mad otherwise. Sometimes he wished that he had never come to Berry Edge, never met Faith Norman, never discovered the pain of unrequited love. He had heard that it was the only kind that lasted, which made things about as difficult as they could be.

It was late evening by the time the doorbell went. Susannah was lying on the bed with Victoria, who had just fallen asleep. The doorbell rang again, and she hastened down the stairs for fear that the baby should hear it and awaken suddenly, crying. Claire had gone out.

She threw back the bolts and opened the door. Evening light spilled into the house, and there on the doorstep stood the man she had told herself she never wanted to see again. When she saw who it was she tried to shut the door, but Rob was too quick for her and too big, so she stood back until he had closed the door and they were enveloped in the gloom of the hall.

'Why didn't you tell me about the child?'

Susannah took a deep breath. 'The child is nothing to do with you.'

'That's not what I hear.'

'Nothing in my life is anything to do with you. You walked out and left me, don't you remember?'

'Faith found out and now she won't marry me.'

'Faith did? Oh I understand. She came to see Nancy, she discovered that Nancy was living here.'

'So Nancy knew all about the baby?'

'Are you going to accuse her of disloyalty too?'

'Nancy doesn't owe me anything.'

'I'm glad you think so.'

'Can I see my child?'

'She's not yours.'

'What is she called?'

'Victoria.'

'May I see her?'

'No.'

'Why not?'

'Because . . .'

'You hate me.'

'I don't hate you, Rob.'

'Yes, you do. What other reason could you have for keeping the knowledge from me when you knew it might cost me so dearly?'

'I didn't think about that. You didn't love Faith.'

'It wasn't meant to be love. I was trying to save myself from Hell,' Rob said, smiling just a little. 'Isn't that what always motivates people? You know in your heart that that's where you'll end up because God lets bits of it seep through until you get accustomed to the idea or make some sort of huge effort to atone. You can see the full horror of what you've got waiting. Couldn't I see her just for a moment?'

'She's asleep.'

'Don't children look best when they're asleep?'

Susannah led the way upstairs and into her bedroom where Victoria lay, not in her cot – she wouldn't rest in there – but in the big double bed. It was a new bed, Susannah comforted herself, no man had ever been there, but that thought did not prevent her from remembering how she had discovered what love really meant in this room. It seemed so strange, because it was the same room where she had taken men to her for money, in distaste, in dislike. She didn't work now. This room was hers and Victoria's, and she had sworn to herself that she would never let a man over the threshold.

It even looked different than he would remember it, all pale blue and cream, so feminine. The thin summer curtains were drawn back, the windows were open to the warmth and from there the view was the same as it had been for eight hundred years, the river and the outline of the cathedral and the castle across the water. But he was not noticing any of it.

Victoria was so tiny, her dark hair against the sheet, her eyes closed, the lashes long and luxuriant. Susannah held her breath, convinced either that he would pick up the baby and run out of the room, or that Victoria would awake and instantly scream, but neither happened. Susannah watched him as he sat down carefully on the bed. He looked out of place.

Susannah had pretended to herself before now that he was never here, that she had not fallen in love with him, that he had not opened her heart with his readiness to begin again. His gaze was fixed on the child.

'She doesn't look like me at all,' he said, not sounding disappointed, 'she looks just like you. Perhaps she isn't mine.'

'There was no one else,' Susannah reminded him.

'You weren't going to tell me, were you?' he said.

'I thought you might try and take her.'

'Take her?'

'You might have, though not after you decided to marry Miss Norman. It would hardly have benefited you. You were going to Nottingham to live. You would have been married, having your own children. She's all I have.'

'You could have prevented my marriage.'

'Perhaps I didn't wish to prevent it.'

The room was so quiet after that that Susannah could hear the river beyond the windows. He got up. It was even worse then, it was all those times come together, all those mornings when he had left her; and that was when she remembered the nights.

'I think that you had better go,' she said.

When he had gone Susannah's heart beat so hard that it hurt. In her mind she had tried to turn him into things that he was not just to survive, but surviving did not seem quite as important as being glad that he was none of those things, even though he had gone.

She knew that there was nowhere in their small civilised world where they could have hidden together, and that she would never be forgiven by this man's world for what she had done. His achievements, his successes, his talent and ability would count for nothing with the wrong woman at his side, and she knew that he could not have stood that, having lost so many things. His work was all he had now.

Susannah was angry. Most of all she was angry with Faith for not seeing how things really were, but then perhaps Faith had done just that. Perhaps she had seen that he would never belong to her when morally he belonged to the prostitute who lived up the street from the bridge in Durham.

Twenty-two

Harry was still sitting in the garden room, even though he could no longer see anything. When the banging began, he stumbled downstairs in the darkness and opened the door.

'I thought you weren't here,' Rob said. 'Then I thought maybe you were asleep.'

'Just at present Faith's parents' house holds little attraction and sleep . . . is for the innocent alone.'

'Are you drunk?'

'I could be if you helped.'

'Have you got any whisky?'

'How long have you known me, Rob? We don't have any glasses.'

'A bottle will do.'

'I'll get you a cup.'

They went back upstairs to the garden room. There were no chairs in there, but you could sit on the floor. Because the windows were way down, not quite to the floor, like a conservatory, you could look out over what you fondly imagined was the view of Berry Edge. When you had had a few, as Harry presently explained, you could see anything you wanted.

'Did you see Susannah?'

'Yes, and the baby. She is mine.'

'Is she beautiful?'

'She looks just like Susannah. She's so small though, so very, very little.'

'Was Claire there?'

'No.'

'Claire was good fun,' Harry said.

'How was Faith when you left?'

'Crying. You know, I always think of her crying into the coats that first night. Do you remember that? She stood in the hall and cried into the coats.'

'I wish I could cry into some bloody coats,' Rob said. 'I'd feel a lot bloody better.'

'You wouldn't.'

'How do you know?'

'I don't. One thing about my parents, however awful I thought they were as parents, they didn't make me cry. If I did for some reason, they always came to me.'

'Christ, did they?'

'Always. Ida was a big apologiser. Women are very good apologisers, don't you find?'

'Well, I don't see Vincent being much good at apologies.'

'No, but he makes up for it in other ways. He called you "a bloody imbecile" after you left, but I think he was relieved and my mother will be ecstatic that you and Faith aren't getting married and it's quite ir— ironic. Do I mean "ironic"?'

'I don't know what the hell you mean,' Rob said. 'Why is it ironic?'

'Because of Faith. Because I love her.'

'You love Faith?'

'I do, yes.'

'Well, don't go telling anybody anything, for God's sake.'

'I'm telling you now.'

'Christ, Harry, you pick your moments.'

'I didn't want to spoil anything.'

'There's nothing to spoil now.'

'I know. Do you want some more whisky?'

'I do, but do you?'

'I do definitely. We should never have come here.'

'For once in your life you're right. We shouldn't. We should have listened to Vincent.'

'I'm sick of listening to the old bastard, he's always there.'

'He's all right though, Harry, really.'

Harry poured out more cupfuls of whisky. 'What are you going to do now?' he said.

'I'm going to Nottingham and then to London. That was what I intended to do.'

'I can't come with you, not if you want the works keeping right.'

'I don't need you to come with me. I need you here. You will look after the place.'

'I'll look after it,' Harry said.

Faith cried until she felt sick. Rob did not come back and neither did Harry. It seemed so cow-hearted of them both, Faith thought, to just go like that. There was nobody there to be shouted at, nobody to blame. Her mother put her to bed, though Faith thought she could detect a small amount of resentment on her mother's part. She had failed to marry again. She had run out of Berkeley brothers, and there was nobody else. Whatever was she to do now?

Faith was so exhausted that she slept. When she awoke in the early morning, it was with the disbelief that anything so cruel could have happened to her. She hated Rob as she had not hated him before, and most of all she didn't want to show her face in Berry Edge for the next ten years.

When she finally ventured downstairs her mother was wrapping presents to be sent back.

'I'm sorry,' Faith said.

Her mother looked up.

'It wasn't your fault,' she said. 'How people will talk. How shocking, and how dreadful for Rob's mother to know what he has done and to know that everyone else will soon know.'

'It won't be very nice for us either,' Faith pointed out.

'Your father has gone to see the minister and the other

arrangements are to be cancelled. Rob's mother is already packing to leave to go to Ashington. I doubt she will come back. Mr and Mrs Shaw are taking the first train back to Nottingham.'

It was as her mother said. Suddenly the house was empty and it was rather to Faith as it had been before Rob came home, there was just her mother and her father and herself, except that now there was nothing to do, nowhere to go. She had no life there any more, having given it up to be Rob's wife.

Faith took her pretty clothes and put them in the attic, and tried to resume her life. Going out was difficult, she knew that people were talking about her. Her parents didn't mention Rob's name, and since Harry had his own house she didn't see him.

Faith went to Chapel but people were polite and distant. She wore her old dresses to get them to see her in the same way they had before, but she was not deceived herself, so how could they be? She had one wild idea when a visiting minister came from London, and talked to the young people about a Methodist college in London which trained people to be teachers, but they were surprised when Faith made enquiries. She was too old. She had amazed herself by thinking that she might leave Berry Edge. When Rob had wanted her to go, she had wanted nothing more than to stay, but now she would have given almost anything to leave this place where she was branded, for good and all, an old maid.

For the first time in her life Faith felt trapped in Berry Edge, with the future empty before her.

She went to John's grave and there she felt nothing. She realised then that she could not resume her life as it had been. Rob had cured her of wanting his brother. She remembered only too clearly the feel of his mouth and hands and his body against her. When she longed for someone it was Rob, not the long-dead brother, and she came to acknowledge that it was the lack of someone as much as the lack of a particular person that she felt. She knew now that she ought to have married, that if anyone else had taken time and trouble over her, had guided her away from John, she would have been married by now with her own house and children. Rob had taught her that.

There was nowhere here she wanted to be. Faith could have screamed. She walked the short distance home and wondered how she could ever have borne Sundays here. What did she do? How did she fill those endless Sunday hours? Time went by so slowly. She went to Chapel twice just as she used to do with her parents, and there was the big meal to get through, but even so there were huge long gaps which had not been there before and there was nothing to fill them with. She sewed, she read, she even invaded the kitchen, much to the surprise of the maids, and offered to help there and had to leave, having embarrassed both herself and them. She would have gone into the garden but that was not allowed either; their gardener was the kind of man who had to be talked nicely to before he would let anybody pick a bunch of flowers, much less tolerate interference of any kind, or even suggestions except from her mother.

Faith avoided Durham because of Susannah and she avoided the streets of Berry Edge because people were talking about her. She escaped to the fell and there, thinking of how she and Rob had gone walking several times that summer, she sat down and cried.

Harry had moved into his house straight away in spite of the lack of furniture. He had no intention of going back to face the house down the bank. He went to work on Saturday and was glad of it, and on the way back he called in at Michael and Nancy's house because he had bought them a present. The wedding had been early, the party afterwards was still going on though many people had left.

Nancy unwrapped the present. It was a dining room clock, a handsome mahogany one inlaid with walnut, and after they had thanked him they gave him a drink. Nancy said, 'I hear the other wedding didn't happen.'

'That's right,' Harry said.

'Poor Miss Norman.'

'Where's Rob?' Michael managed to ask him in a quiet moment.

'Nottingham.'

'He'll find somebody else,' Michael said comfortingly.

'Yes.' Harry sighed. 'We could eventually be treated to a permanent state of Miss Castleton and *Furry Leaves*. I dread to think what he might do now.'

'Who's Miss Castleton?'

'She's a very young, rather pretty lady at the top of Nottingham society. Her father owns a hosiery factory. She plays the piano and she does like Rob's money.'

'Does he like her?'

'He likes parts of her,' Harry said.

That autumn Susannah began to run out of money. She had been badly advised on what investments she had made, the income from them was tiny and she had spent too much trying to put Rob from her mind with shopping and luxury. When they had stopped taking men into the house she had bought all kinds of new things as though everything could be changed, and now she would lose the beautiful house because she could no longer afford to pay the rent on it.

They had to move very reluctantly in the middle of the autumn into a much smaller house with no view and try to think of other ways of making money. No one would employ them, they were too well known and they had no skills.

'I don't know what kind of work we could do,' Claire said. 'I can't add up. We don't sew. What are we going to do, go back on the game? I'm getting so old they'll start asking for me cheap next.'

'I hate this poky little house,' Susannah said. 'All I can see is the house across the street, and I can hear next door shouting at each other.'

'Maybe Robert Berkeley's coming back for Christmas. You could ask him for money for his bairn.'

'I wouldn't.'

'You might have to.'

After a while the people of Berry Edge accepted Faith back among them. Sometimes she awoke in the night and knew for certain that none of it had happened, that she had never gone shopping in Bond Street or been invited to the big houses, four storeys high, near Marble Arch. She persuaded herself that she had not seen Harrods in Knightsbridge, not gone to dinner parties where six courses of delicious food was the norm, or been to parties, receptions, balls and dinners in London, or cantered her horse beside the shining Serpentine. She thought of the opera – the most fashionable entertainment, where people wore formal dress; she thought of the liveried footmen and starched nursemaids in the houses where she had been, the West End plays, the musical comedies, the luxury fruit and confectionery, the hairdressers, the new hats, everything she had been so delighted with. She could not believe now that she had ever left the dismal scene of Berry Edge. Her finger was bare, the diamond had gone, and she heard nothing from Rob nor wanted to. It had been a glorious dream but it was over, and she must accept that because it would never happen again.

The first time that she saw Harry was not even difficult. She had told herself that he was on many committees and involved in almost every part of Berry Edge life, and there was no way to avoid him, so when she was handing out tea after a meeting in the church hall and he walked into the room, Faith looked up and tried to act normally.

She had not seen him for weeks. She thought then that there was something jaunty about Harry, something that brought a new dimension to Berry Edge. It was not just Rob who had brought changes. Harry stood out here, it was possible that he did so deliberately, as manager of the works and the collieries and everything of importance.

He was tall and slender and bright-eyed and well dressed, and the women who sat on the committees and ran a great many things in Berry Edge liked him very much. How could they not, Faith thought. He always remembered their names after first meeting them, and he remembered details about their lives and their families. He gave them attention and they warmed to him.

Harry was not a Berry Edge man. He had brought flirtation to a fine art. He must have known well that these were modest women who kept their homes and families clean and neat, that they would never have seen inside a pub, that they knew he had been rather wild but was not any longer. How he managed to give off this dual role perplexed Faith. He ought to have been beyond the pale but was not because he ran the works with authority, lived alone without scandal and was seen to be in all the correct places when he should have been. And they respected him for it. He treated them as they wished a man would treat them, and he did it without giving offence. He praised the cake he ate, he held a cup and saucer though Faith was convinced he drank barely half of his tea, and he talked to everybody in the hall.

It was therefore a long time before he reached her. He didn't need to come near for a cup of tea, willing hands always provided what he needed, and so it was late and she was washing up by the time Harry had talked to everyone, smiled at everyone, pleased a great many people and learned whatever he had intended to learn by being there that evening, Faith felt sure.

She was not taken in by him as they were. She knew that he was like Rob, that he preferred whisky and bad women to anything else on earth. When he finally came in search of her alone there with her hands covered in soapsuds, having refused the offers of help until other people went back to tea and gossip, she was quite ready to be coldly polite.

'Hello, Faith, how are you?' he said genially.

Faith turned a little, though she didn't look at him. 'I'm very well, thank you.'

'You have no help.'

'I'm quite able.'

To her consternation he picked up a teacloth and began to dry the dishes. Faith stared. 'When did you learn to be useful?' she said.

'Since I've been living alone.'

'Don't you have a maid?'

'Yes.'

'If anybody sees you . . .'

'They won't,' he said comfortably, 'they're all busy.'

'How was your cake?'

'Perfectly abominable, it had seeds in it. As though one were a budgerigar.'

'Mrs Leslie made it.'

'Indeed. Remind me not to accept her invitations to tea.'

'Has she made them?'

'She has,' he said solemnly and then pulled a face.

'You're dreadful,' Faith said.

'I know, but I can't talk like this to anyone else in the whole area, so you will have to forgive me.'

'You haven't learned to be serious here, have you?'

'I've learned a great many things. I'm a pillar of society. I notice that you don't come and see me, though, and that you don't send me invitations to tea at your house.'

'I don't think my mother could stomach it,' Faith said, as she finished washing the dishes and concentrated on drying her hands.

Harry looked at her.

'Guilt by association? Hardly fair,' he said. He looked at the cake stand and cloth in his hands and put both down with an air of sudden distaste.

'Has Rob gone back to Nottingham?' Faith asked, surprising herself as well as him with the question.

'Yes, for the time being. Then he's going on to London. He didn't intend to stay here. If it hadn't been for his father's illness he wouldn't have come back at all.'

'That was the problem,' Faith said. 'Rob always stood out, he was never of Berry Edge even though he was born here. He didn't fit in, he thought differently from other people. He would never have talked to people in there like you just did.'

'It's easier for me.'

'Why is it?'

'Because nobody thinks I murdered my brother. Somewhat fortunately, I often think, I have no brother. Perhaps one is always inclined to help him lose his footing so that he will not be there to be the preferred child. Families are such vexatious things, doomed to be a disappointment.'

'I'm a great disappointment to my parents,' Faith said, smiling a little in remembrance. 'I now have two wedding dresses in my wardrobe, neither of which will ever be worn, almost a collection.'

'Put them in a trunk in the attic and forget about them.'

'I would but my mother won't hear of it. I think she almost enjoys the way that I see them daily.'

'While you search for the dullest of your dresses,' Harry said, looking woefully at her.

'This is the dullest one,' she said, indicating the grey dress.

'I don't think it's as bad as the blue one you wore the first time I saw you.'

'How could you possibly remember?'

'How could I help it? I'd never seen such a shocking garment on such a pretty woman.'

Faith looked disapprovingly at him. 'I'm not Mrs Leslie, you know.'

'Indeed, I do know. Aren't you going to invite me to tea?'

'Certainly not. You'd only complain about the food as you always do, and my mother would be offended since she does some of the baking herself.'

'On the contrary, your mother cooks very well for someone who thinks that the height of culinary sophistication is individual custard tarts.'

Faith started to laugh. 'You're very rude about my mother. You're a snob.'

'A man who chooses to live in Berry Edge cannot be called a snob, Faith. He could barely be called discerning. There now, you're laughing.'

'I'm not laughing, Harry Shaw.'

'Yes, you are. Look at you.'

Faith was indeed, she had to quell the laughter as one of the committee ladies came in, frowning at the noise. The committee lady collected Harry and went off with him. Faith went on with the clearing up.

By the time Vincent and Ida went home that autumn, Rob had left Nottingham and gone to London. He hadn't done that deliberately, at least he didn't think so, but other than work there was nothing for him there so he did what was necessary in Nottingham and then left.

He had expected to be alone in London for Christmas. He was asked everywhere just as usual, and he knew that there were plenty of girls' mothers who were relieved that he had somehow got rid of the drab little northern woman and was eligible again. Rob missed Faith, that was the stupid part; he did wish they had got married. It would have been so much easier than this, and they would have grown to love one another, he thought. He drank a lot of whisky late at night and couldn't sleep, and then couldn't get up and couldn't work and couldn't eat. He did do all of those things, but it was not easy.

He thought that Ida and Vincent might have had enough tact not to come to London before Christmas, but they didn't. When he got back from work on the Tuesday before Christmas, he came face to face with Vincent in the hall. Vincent looked straight at him.

'Well, Robert, and how are you? You look like Hell warmed slightly.'

'Don't worry, Vincent, you're not responsible,' Rob said and brushed past him.

He lingered in his room beyond dinnertime, and there was a soft knocking on the door. When he called out Ida ventured inside.

'I've missed you,' she said.

Rob went over and kissed her and said, 'I'm sorry, Ida.'

'I'm not. I never did think it a good match, though I do wish occasionally that you would do the right thing. Why isn't Harry coming to London for Christmas? I begged him.'

'Too much work, I expect. He'll come for New Year.'

'It's some woman,' Ida said. 'You know what he's like.'

'We've caused you a lot of grief.'

She smiled at him. 'Fortunately I know the difference between grief and dismay. You and Harry have upset and dismayed me, but I love you both very much. Couldn't you persuade him to come home just for a little while? I miss him so dreadfully, and I won't go back to Durham. I want to spend some time in my own homes, not other people's. Come downstairs and have some dinner, my darling, you look as though you haven't eaten in a week.'

Vincent was civil all the way through dinner. Afterwards, drinking his brandy by the fire, he said to Rob, 'Do you hear anything from Harry?'

'No, don't you?'

'I shudder to think what dreadful thing either of you will do next that I shall have to countenance. My God, Robert, illegitimate children? Why cannot you learn to be respectable? You let us all down.'

'Did I, Vincent? Do accept my apology.' And Rob walked out of the room.

In his own room – with the whisky bottle – Rob sat down by the fire and allowed himself the rare luxury of thinking about Susannah and the baby. He didn't understand how a man could miss a child he had seen for only a few seconds. The missing of Victoria was a space inside that was getting bigger and bigger, and there was nothing he could do except bathe it nightly in alcohol.

In the mornings he would think that if he could just get through the day he would not need whisky, and in the evenings he would think if he could just manage without a drink then he would sleep, and wake refreshed and energetic, and the pattern would halt. But it didn't because he couldn't get through any of it, and it repeated itself again and again except that it got harder all the time. Just before Christmas the days had been short and dark and wet which made it worse somehow.

He didn't want to go to work, he didn't want to go out, he didn't want to go anywhere, he didn't want to do anything. Most especially, he didn't want to eat, because it took the whisky so much longer to do its job through all that food.

Nightly his failures danced before his eyes. His bed was empty and so were his arms, and the London house tortured him with memories of Sarah. Worst of all was knowing that Susannah was in Durham. To know that she was there, and that she would not have him or let him go to her, was unbearable.

Twenty-three

Faith saw Harry a dozen times before Christmas. He was at the Chapel Christmas service – she suspected that he had gone to all the Christmas services, thinking it part of his job – and at the works dinner, at lunches that the various societies and committees in Berry Edge saw fit to celebrate Christmas. He was even at the few Christmas parties she was invited to. Every time he treated her as though he was pleased to see her, even though they didn't manage any private conversation.

Faith thought often of the Shaws, of their country mansion, of their smart London house, of their rich successful friends and many influential acquaintances.

She wondered how Harry saw the little north-country nobody she now was. She knew from visiting the Shaws and seeing how highly they regarded themselves that they were proud people. Their son, however easily he might pretend to fit in here, only did so for the sake of his works, his achievements, to prove that he could be successful here where the Berkeleys had failed. Harry would leave in time, just as Rob had done. Rob was as much a Shaw as Harry in his way. Harry would become bored in Berry Edge eventually, when he had mastered the work completely, and where there was no high class entertainment, no luxury, no people like himself.

That Christmas Faith went to John's grave and put greenery there and tidied it, but only out of habit and guilt. The feelings were not there. Rob had broken her heart anew.

Harry went home after Christmas, mostly because his father had written in his usual high-handed way and demanded his presence. Harry heard the message through the clumsiness and went back to London.

It was strange and it hurt, but London didn't feel like home any more. It was true that he had lived most of his life in Nottingham but he had always hankered for London, because his infancy and the first part of his childhood had been spent there. He had happy memories of the parks, of his nanny, of the various little girls he knew, families of them dressed alike out with their governesses, the more modest house which the Shaws had then in a less fashionable address when Ida's parents were still alive and had the big house, though he and Sarah were allowed the run of it.

Christmas was endless days of outings and toys, parties and pantomimes.

He went home and pretended to be happy. At least it wasn't Nottingham and he was glad that he had gone for Rob's sake. Christmas was always a difficult time for them and Rob was particularly low. Even though he said nothing, Harry knew him too well to think otherwise.

On New Year's Eve they went out with a number of friends, had supper, gambled, got drunk and, somewhere before the evening was out, ended up in a brothel. Harry hadn't really noticed where he was going, just went along with the others until he stood there in the hall, glanced across at Rob, and then without a word both walked out.

'I've had enough of women for one year,' Harry said.

'Me too.'

Ida had invited several people for New Year's dinner in the middle of the day which was a shame, Rob thought, when he could think of anything. Ida insisted that they should both be there, although neither of them was in any fit state to eat or make conversation. Vincent seemed determined to make things worse. At the end of the meal, when the men were sitting around drinking brandy – except for Rob and Harry who couldn't entertain the idea – Vincent turned to Rob and said, 'I was wondering whether you could spare Harry from the steelworks, whether he could go back to Nottingham for a while. They're talking about building a bridge—'

'I'm not interested in bridges,' Harry cut in.

'I just—'

'I know what you just, Father,' Harry said, regarding him severely.

'You seem so wasted up there, considering your talents.'

'I'm perfectly happy where I am. Nobody else can do my work except Rob, and he isn't there. I'm good at it, and I'm going to stay there and do it.'

'Fine, that's fine,' Vincent said, putting up both hands. 'And how is the lovely Miss Norman? Do you see her?'

'Sometimes,' Harry said.

'I imagine that her company is most illuminating.'

'It can be.'

'Does she interest you?'

Harry said nothing to that.

'What interests you most about her? Is it her beauty, her intelligence, or her fine hazel eyes?'

'Vincent . . .' Rob said.

'Do tell me, Harry, what you like most about her?' his father said, and the table was silenced, everyone listening.

'I think it's the way that she pours her tea into her saucer before she drinks it. It's the best way if your tea's very hot,' Harry said.

Vincent looked around at his company.

'You do remember Miss Norman, I take it,' he said. 'She

was Robert's intended bride, a badly-dressed north-country girl with a thick accent, no schooling and piety that would offend a priest. She's plain, charmless and commonplace.'

Harry excused himself and left. As soon as he could get away Rob followed him.

Harry was standing in front of the fire in the library smoking a cigar. Rob closed the door. Harry threw the half-smoked cigar into the flames.

'I always imagined that when this happened she'd be eighteen and brilliantly lovely and funny and witty and . . . and adore me and I could bring her home to Vincent and Ida and . . . Faith is as old as me and she's embittered. I don't think she likes me at all.'

'I wish you'd told me.'

Harry looked at him. 'You couldn't control the guilt that you felt about John. Marriage to Faith would have done that, possibly.'

'But if you loved her—'

'I didn't want to love her, it was the last thing I intended. You saw how my father reacted. They didn't want you to marry her but me . . . I think he'd never speak to me again, banish me—'

'He wouldn't. He has too much to lose by it.'

'I've been so badly raised that I think even I'd be ashamed of her. What values have been instilled into me that I care so much for a woman's age and appearance, as though a wife was a prize for coming first in something? God, I hate that.

I miss her. When I'm away all I remember is that first night when we met and you quarrelled with her and she stood in that bloody freezing hall at your house and cried into the coats. I always think when I'm not there that that's what she's doing. There's nobody to look after her. I want her in that house on the hill. I want her in my bed and at my table and by my side. I want children who look like her and who have to wear long coats and thick boots half the year because the weather there is so awful. I want children who have those lovely singing Berry Edge accents, and I can't because she doesn't like me.'

'You could come home for a while, and I'll go there and run the works.'

'I don't know how to come home any more. When I'm here or in Nottingham, I'm wretched for Berry Edge. I feel like I'm having my guts pulled out.'

'I used to feel like that.'

'But not now?'

'I don't feel like that about anywhere now, they're all just places I can use and leave. I don't want that again. I don't want to be tied to any place because of family or memories or anything that matters ever again. I think your parents know or at least suspect how you feel about Faith. Vince suspected you of liking Faith ages since.'

'It's probably his worst nightmare,' Harry said.

*

Their guests left in the middle of the afternoon, just before the winter's day gave in to evening. Harry searched out his father, who was sitting alone before the drawing room fire. Vincent immediately looked up.

'You're going back, aren't you?' he said.

'Tomorrow.'

'You can't wait.'

'No.'

Vincent shook his head. 'I don't remember when you were children, you and Sarah, ever being aware that I was to lose you both so surely. I didn't think that it was going to hurt like this. Childhood problems are nothing compared to the pain of this. I thought that you would both settle near us and have a family and that there would be grandchildren and that things would go on and that . . . I thought we would run the businesses together. I made such plans. Now Sarah is dead and you . . . you don't really want Faith Norman, Harry, you'll never be able to take her anywhere.'

'Rob did.'

'That was different. You're a Shaw. She would not be accepted as your wife, she's too plain and too old and too opinionated. Men like you are obliged to marry pretty simpletons so that other men can envy them their supposed good fortune. All successful men need a mirror so that they can see themselves.'

'Mother wasn't a pretty simpleton.'

'Your mother came from an aristocratic background so

it didn't matter. Faith has neither background nor anything else that would make her acceptable in the society to which you belong.'

'I don't want to belong to it. I don't care about it.'

'You will care about it when you're older, and you would care very much if your wife was snubbed. She would care, too, I think. You and Robert are a great disappointment to me. I thought that no matter what your general behaviour was like, you would have enough sense to marry suitable women. I didn't expect to be caught up in the middle of scandals and muddles. You're thirty, for God's sake. Why don't you just bed her and be done? That's what you usually do with women.'

Harry couldn't think of anything to say.

'That's the trouble, isn't it?' Vincent said. 'You want her. You don't love her, Harry, you just want her on a bed or over a sofa. She won't let you, is that it? She's hanging out because you have money and position and all those things which she can't have. She would never be acceptable to your mother or me.'

Harry still couldn't think of anything to say. He had a picture of Faith in her grey dress in the kitchen in the Chapel hut, up to her wrists in soapy water as a lady would never be.

'I love her,' he said.

'Very well then, take her, marry her, do whatever you like. Just don't come back here. And when you grow tired of her, your dull little north-country woman, when you wish that you had married a beautiful, charming, educated girl whom you could have been proud of, just remember what I said. You can leave any time you like – and take Robert Berkeley with you. I'm bored with his bloody north-country face!'

'He'll get over it, Harry,' Rob said as they stood by the fire in the library.

'I won't,' Harry said.

Somebody had broken into the house and taken Susannah's precious store of jewellery, even though she and Claire thought it well hidden.

'Thieves know where to look,' Claire said dismally. 'That was the rainy day money. Now what, now that it's pouring? We won't remind ourselves of how rich the man was, shall we? We'll just content ourselves with having to go on the street. Susie, can you not go to Berry Edge and see him? He's back, you know, he came back at New Year. You could always offer him a good time.'

Susannah smiled. 'He's just come back from London. I imagine he's had plenty of good times.'

'Would you rather do it for somebody else, because that's what we're getting to? By the end of the week we'll have nothing to eat.'

'There are plenty of men.'

'I don't want any of them in my bed and neither do you.'

'It's the only thing we're any good at.'

'I wish I'd listened to my mother now,' Claire said, trying to smile, 'and learned something useful.'

By the end of the week, unable to think of a way out of the problem, Susannah resolved to go to Berry Edge and talk to Rob. She didn't know where he was staying but she knew that Harry had a house just off the main part of the town, and if he was not there then at least Harry would know where he was.

She went in the late afternoon under cover of darkness. She was too beautiful for people not to notice her and remember who she was, but even in darkness, in the mid-evening streets of Berry Edge, most respectable women were indoors. There were men standing around or going into or coming out of pubs. They shouted and whistled at her. Susannah quickened her pace but somebody caught her by the arm.

'Now then, pet,' he said as she turned around, 'you're not from round here. Oh, look what a bonny one.' His friend came nearer, laughing, and Susannah remembered that awful night in Newcastle. 'Give us a kiss then, pet,' the first man said, and when Susannah tried to hit him he said, 'Why, what a little bitch, Walter,' and grabbed her.

The problem didn't last. She was aware of a voice behind them saying, 'Get your mucky hands off her,' and the man was whisked away.

She was confronted with Michael McFadden, large enough to shut out the rest of Berry Edge.

'Susannah!' he said in astonishment. 'What are you doing here?'

'Michael,' Susannah said in relief.

'You shouldn't be on the streets here, it isn't safe for women at night.' He put an arm around her. 'Howay home with me. Nancy'll put the kettle on.'

Michael had the good sense to go out and leave Susannah and Nancy, having made it clear that if there was a problem he and Nancy would do whatever was necessary. Nancy had hugged Susannah, asked after Claire and Victoria and sat Susannah on an easy chair by the kitchen fire.

'I hear he's back,' she said.

'Aye. Came back with Mr Shaw the day after New Year. You've got to admire his face after what happened.'

'What is he doing back here?'

'Working. I daresay it won't be for long. Mr Shaw's got the place going fine.'

'I need to see him, Nancy. My investments haven't worked out and somebody broke in and stole everything. I won't go on the street again, not after what happened. I feel so awful going to him. I tried to stop him from seeing Victoria. He can be quite intimidating when he's in one of those moods.'

'He's not going to see you on the street, is he? Look, you can stay here—'

'Nancy, I couldn't.'

'Yes, you could. You did all kinds for me when things went

wrong. When Michael comes back I'll send him for Claire and the baby. We've got three good bedrooms—'

'Nancy, you have two children and a baby due any day. I won't put on you.'

'You're not putting on me. Just for a little while.'

'Your neighbours will talk.'

'It'll be nothing new.'

'You don't mind, do you?' Nancy said to Michael when they went to bed. 'Susannah's not the kind to outstay her welcome.'

'How could I mind after what they did for us?'

'You'll get some stick at work,' Nancy said.

Harry didn't know how to approach Faith, so he just waited for Sunday. When he thought it was her usual time, he went to the graveyard, but she was not there. It was mid-afternoon. He waited around there for a while, and when she didn't appear he went to the house and banged on the front door.

Faith opened the door herself.

'Why, Harry, how nice to see you. Do sit down,' she said, ushering him into the sitting room where a big fire burned. 'Did you have a good holiday?'

'It was monstrous,' Harry said, 'and I have to tell you that I brought Rob back with me.'

'He does own the works,' she said.

'I own some of it,' Harry pointed out.

He didn't know what to say. He had never proposed marriage before and had no idea how to go about it, especially as she looked at him from clear green eyes. He was convinced that no matter what he said she would turn him down. His hands were sweaty and his shirt collar felt too tight. He wanted to go home.

'I don't think Rob will be here long. He's very restless.'

'I'm afraid my parents aren't at home, but I can give you some tea—'

'Please don't. I always know when I'm back in Berry Edge because people start offering me tea all the time.'

'We don't have anything stronger,' Faith said solemnly.

'That's a pity. I could have done with a stiff Scotch.'

'Why?'

Harry looked down, then back at her again. 'Faith . . . I don't know how to do this because I've never done it before and I hope I'm not going to have to do it again. Faith, I love you and I want you to be my wife. Will you marry me?'

She stared. Harry didn't blame her. It wasn't an elegant proposal, and he didn't pretend to himself that she cared about him.

'This isn't meant to be funny, is it?' she said.

'Not so far.'

'Whatever are you doing?'

Her voice shook. Her face began to fill with what he thought was anger.

'I can't help it,' he said. 'I love you. I've loved you since the day we met when you were wearing that awful blue dress and you cried into the coats in that freezing hall in Rob's house. I thought . . . when I was younger I thought I had loved before but it wasn't anywhere near the same kind of thing, that was just . . . want.'

'It could hardly be that,' Faith said, her voice shaking, her mouth barely managing a smile. 'You forget, I've been in your kind of society. I know how beautiful and accomplished the women are and I know now who you are. You could never marry me.'

'I could never marry anybody else,' Harry said. 'If you turn me down . . .'

'What?'

'I don't know. I can't bear to think about it.'

'You're not the kind of man that I could marry.'

'Why not?'

'We have nothing in common. No one ever had less. You're . . .'

'Yes?'

'Self-indulgent, irreligious, you drink . . .'

'I smoke cigars.'

'Yes. You would be chasing other women within six months.'

'Sooner, possibly. You see, I don't know. I thought it was

all to do with falling in love, with beauty and desire but it isn't, it isn't for me anyway. When I saw you in that hall I just wanted to make sure that nobody ever hurt you again. I haven't always felt like that. Often I'm so irritated with you I have trouble keeping my temper. You're just more interesting than any other woman I've ever met. I'm bored when you're not there. I look for you everywhere. I know you don't love me but . . . I don't know how you see your future life . . .'

'I see it as bleak.'

'Well then, you could take a chance. What have you to lose?'

'Very little,' Faith said, 'but you might.'

'I have nothing to lose that I wouldn't give up willingly for you.'

Faith didn't answer. Harry was half inclined to run from the house.

'I loved John,' she said. 'We had everything in common. He was kind and devout and I admired him because he was good. I know now that I didn't love Rob, he was just almost John for a while for me. I couldn't possibly love him. I do like you but not in the same way. You make me laugh. John was always there, you see. Sometimes as much like a brother. You don't seem like that to me. If I married you, people would say I'd done it because you're rich and clever and run the steelworks, and they would wonder what on earth you had married me for. Have you told your parents?'

'Yes.'

'I imagine they were opposed to it.'

'I want to be married and have children and live here at Berry Edge with you. It's the only thing in the whole world that I want—'

Harry stopped there. He heard the outside door, her parents' voices. Moments later, it seemed to him, when they had taken off their outdoor things, her mother opened the door of the sitting room.

'I thought someone was here,' she said, disconcerting Harry by staring at him from the same colour eyes as Faith. 'How are you, Mr Shaw? You will have some tea?'

Harry nodded and smiled. Mr Norman came in, looking curiously at him and making remarks about the weather. Harry had to suffer several minutes of weather and politics before a maid came in with the tea tray. To his surprise, there on the tray, in true nightmare fashion, were tiny custard tarts.

Faith looked at him and began to laugh. Mr Norman stared.

'Are you feeling all right, Faith?' he said. 'Excuse me, just for a moment. I have a book you may care for, Mr Shaw,' and left the room.

'How dare you laugh when I'm in purgatory about this?' Harry accused her furiously.

'Do you ever read the books he loans you? Have a custard tart and I'll pour you some tea.'

Harry was out of his seat in seconds, pulling her up with him.

'Say "yes" to me, you little wretch, right now!'

'Oh Harry, your face. When we're married I will never ever bring you tea.'

'Do you mean it?'

'You can have coffee or cocoa or even—'

'Faith!'

'I will marry you, but only because I want another wedding dress.'

'You're not going to have one. I'm not going through all that. I'll get a special licence and we'll be married as soon as possible. Do you think your mother will mind?'

'She'll be too relieved to care. I think she would have been almost as pleased if the butcher's boy had proposed.'

Harry kissed her. To his surprise she let him, even encouraged him, and then the door opened. When he let Faith go, Mrs Norman was staring at him, a smile just about to take over her lips.

'I . . . er . . . I was going to talk to Mr Norman,' Harry said swiftly, releasing Faith. 'I thought Faith would refuse me.'

'You underestimate yourself, Mr Shaw.'

'I must be the first Shaw that ever did,' Harry said, weak with thanks.

Mrs Norman beamed at him, then sat down and began to pour out the tea.

*

That evening when it was late, Harry went home and told Rob.

'I want you to be my best man.'

'I'm sorry, Harry, I don't think I'm going to be here that long.'

'Not even for a few weeks?'

'No.'

'Where are you going?'

'America.'

Harry sighed. 'That's an awfully long way to go just to avoid my wedding,' he said. He looked into the fire and then at Rob. 'This isn't a sudden idea, is it?'

'No.'

'You weren't intending to come back here at all. You only came because you thought I was upset over Vince.'

'You are.'

'Why didn't you tell me? I could have come back here alone, I'm not a child, you know! I'm not your responsibility, Rob. I'm not your brother.'

'To me you are.'

'But you're going away.'

'I'll be back. Can't leave you to the mercies of this place forever.'

'You thought Faith would refuse me?'

'I thought she might.'

'Thank you very much.'

'She's unpredictable.'

'Why America, and how long have you been planning this?'

'Quite a while. I was going to take Faith with me.'

'But you didn't tell me?'

'It wasn't worked out. I've been having meetings in London with two German businessmen. They want to set up a factory in America building motor cars.'

'Motor cars?'

'We build bicycles. Why not? Motor cars not just for the rich, for everybody.'

'You want to get away, in fact.'

'Yes.'

'More so now than ever?'

'You don't need me here and Vincent can handle everything in Nottingham. I want to do something myself.'

'Faith would have hated that, she didn't even want to go to Nottingham. You didn't tell her.'

'At the time it was only an idea, and if she had been set against it I probably wouldn't have gone any further with it. As it is, there's nothing to stop me, no reason to stay.'

'The wedding's going to be soon,' Harry said, 'with no fuss. You could stay for that.'

'How soon?'

'As soon as I can arrange it. I'm frightened she'll change her mind.'

*

Faith was not about to change her mind. She had seen the look on her parents' faces, and it was delight. She was not about to let them down again. She did not imagine for a moment that Harry would make a good husband, it was only that he had not met women like her before and that she had not, like most single women, fallen over herself to be agreeable so that he should like her. She was unusual and that was all, but it was the only opportunity left to her so she took it. She could no longer face the idea of herself as an old maid in Berry Edge for the rest of her life.

She was also honest enough with herself to say that she wanted to be married, she wanted children and she liked his kisses and his arms around her. She had become reconciled to the fact that she would never love anyone again, that John Berkeley stood alone in that respect.

Harry had money and position and brains. He was also kind and funny and attentive, at least at the moment. Faith determined to make the best of it, but she was happier right from the first. Her mother and father were less pleased when they heard that Harry wanted to be married swiftly and with as little fuss as possible, but then her mother considered the other disastrous almost-weddings and changed her mind and said that it was a good idea.

Faith went often to the pretty house on the hill which would be her home and there she found true joy. Harry had said that she could buy whatever she wanted, and since the house was extremely sparsely furnished and Harry was either too busy to go with her, or didn't mind what she bought and was generous with his money, Faith had a wonderful time furnishing the house just as she liked.

He seemed pleased with all she did. Often, when he came back from work, she was there and they would sit together by the fire. Harry would sip whisky and she would drink tea and they would talk. Faith had never considered this aspect of being married, and she liked it. Her mother did tell her that she ought not to spend time there alone with him, but she didn't insist. Faith began to come home late and reluctantly, because she had to leave him. Often Rob was there. Faith hadn't known what to say to him at first, but she learned not to mind. He didn't stay long.

Rob, even in his absence, was a useful chaperone because her mother didn't know that he wasn't there. On those evenings she would lie on the sofa in Harry's arms and be perfectly content. He didn't try to make love to her as she had thought he would. He was gentle with her. Faith had never expected to feel safe with him but she did now, so much so that she encouraged him to kiss her past what was considered proper between unmarried people. Her mouth stung and her body yielded, and even then it was Harry who drew away.

'So much for the meek little Methodist,' he said.

'I'm not meek.'

'No, you're not. Go away and make some tea.'

'I don't want any tea.'

'Obviously. Go anyway.'

Faith did with great reluctance. He followed her into the kitchen shortly afterwards and she paused, new tea caddy in hand and said, 'Did your parents write?'

'No. I told you, they won't come to the wedding.'

'I want to go to my son's wedding,' Ida said.

Vincent looked down the breakfast table at her.

'Some wedding it will be,' he said.

'I want to go.'

Vincent concentrated on reading his newspaper.

'He's our only child, Vincent.'

'He behaved extremely badly.'

'Children always do.'

'You don't like Faith, not as a wife for Rob, so how much less as a wife for Harry?'

'He's chosen her. There's nothing we can do about that. We'll be the people who lose, Vincent, not them. They have love and each other and the future and probably children. Have you thought about that?'

'I hope they do have children,' Vincent said, slamming down his paper. 'I hope they have a dozen so that they come to understand what ungrateful, unnatural little beasts children are.'

'I would like grandchildren,' Ida said. 'He won't come back, you know that, don't you? I don't want to lose him,

Vincent. Sarah is dead and Robert is lost to us, but if we go to Harry's wedding we could be friends again.'

'Robert will be there and apparently that Michael McFadden, God knows why, and his wife.'

'Nancy is a charming girl.'

'Charming girls don't marry men like that.'

'I did,' his wife said.

Nancy's baby was a boy. She had an easy labour.

'What shall we call him?' she asked Michael as he sat on the bed holding and admiring his son.

'I don't care, as long as it isn't Sean.'

'Do you want to call him Michael?'

'Now, Nancy, I'm not that bad. What would you like to call him, you went through it all?'

'What about Robert?'

'His lordship'll love that.'

'It's not because of him.'

'Isn't it? You fancy him something shocking, Nancy.'

'I do not!'

'Yes, you do,' Michael said with a grin and put the baby down carefully and kissed her.

He was glad then that Susannah and Claire were at home with Nancy when he was at work. The work at the Diamond was hard, and coming back to two small children and a new baby would have not been easy, though plenty of people did it, he knew. Susannah was good with the new baby, having had one herself not long since; Claire was a competent cook and between them all they managed everything. Although the house was rather crowded it was a pleasant atmosphere.

They had been asked to the wedding. Susannah said that she couldn't possibly go.

'I think if Faith was polite enough to ask then you ought to go,' Michael said one evening when they were alone in the kitchen. Claire was putting the children to bed and Nancy was upstairs seeing to the baby.

'I can't face Rob. What am I supposed to do?'

'What's wrong with this?'

'You can't go on keeping us all and the place is heaving with talk. What are they calling you at work? No, don't tell me, I don't think even my ears could stand it.'

Michael went over to the back door from where a vigorous knocking was coming. He pulled open the door and there stood Rob.

'Hello, Michael.'

'Hello.'

Michael regarded him carefully. Rob unsmiling and calling him by his full name was not a man in a good mood.

'I understand you have Susannah Seaton staying with you.'

'Some men have all the luck,' Michael said.

'I'd like to see her.'

Behind him Michael sensed rather than saw Susannah

glance at the inside door as though she would have bolted into the sitting room, but she didn't.

Michael opened the door wider to let Rob in, and wished he hadn't had to. His employer looked anything but pleased at the beautiful woman who was standing in front of the cooker, probably a good deal more plainly dressed than he had ever seen her before. Her hands were red because she'd done the washing that day, her hair was neatly back from her face. She wore a dark dress and a long apron, as unlike a prostitute as any woman Michael had ever seen. He hesitated.

'Alone,' Rob said.

'I'll be upstairs if you need me,' he said, and went.

Susannah felt awful. It was the first time in her life she had ever felt plain.

'What the hell are you doing here?' he said.

'Helping – helping out with the baby and everything.'

'That's not quite what I meant.'

'I had no money,' Susannah said.

'What did you do with it?'

'Invested it badly, lost it.'

'Michael doesn't have any money. Why didn't you come to me?'

'I was going to.'

'When? When you'd completely destroyed his name in Berry Edge?'

'I've only been here a short time.'

'Even a few days of you can ruin a man's reputation,' Rob said. 'Get your things and leave. How much money do you want?'

'I wouldn't take it,' she said.

'Yes, you will. You'd do anything for money,' Rob said. 'You look rather fetching in a pinny. You could cultivate the look.'

'Shut up,' Susannah said.

'A hundred pounds?' he said, throwing a small bag on to the table. 'That should get you re-established.'

'I don't want to be re-established.'

'You could always take in washing,' Rob said.

'I don't want your money,' Susannah said, unrepentant.

'If it bothers your conscience you can always call round later and drop your drawers for me,' Rob said, and slammed the door after him as he left.

When Michael came back in Susannah was weeping bitterly.

'At least you've got some money now,' he said.

'I don't want the money. I want him.'

'You heard the man.'

'Not like that.'

Michael drew back and looked at her.

'Susannah, have I got this right? The reason you won't marry him is because of what you are.'

'He wouldn't have me now anyway,' Susannah said, digging into her skirt pocket for a handkerchief and blowing her nose so hard that Michael winced.

'I was talking to Harry outside the pit today, about the wedding and things, and he says that Rob's going to America.'

'America?' She lifted a tear-shiny face.

'Yes. Something about motor cars. America would be far enough, don't you think? You could marry him there and nobody would know anything.'

'America?' Susannah said again. 'He wants to get as far away from me as he can.'

'I don't think so. If he didn't care, he wouldn't come in here like that on the bottom rung of his temper. I've known him a long time. You hurt him a lot.'

'He hurt me.'

'Why don't you go over? Go on, give it a chance. You can always come back, and whatever happens you're a hundred pounds better off than you were at teatime.'

Twenty-four

The house was empty. Harry had gone to Faith's for a meal.

'It's always the same,' he had grumbled, 'almost inedible and nothing but water to drink.'

'You like it,' Rob told him.

Harry looked aghast.

'Good Lord, I do, don't I?' he said.

Coming into the empty house after seeing Susannah was awful. She had looked so lovely, so wistfully out of place in her apron. She must have been in a bad way to come to Berry Edge, she must have been penniless. He wished that she had come straight to him. It was not fair to Michael. At the Diamond pit that week Rob had been within hearing of some coarse remarks about Michael McFadden's manhood. They were all complimentary to him, but Rob knew that it would do Michael no good to take women of low repute into his house, however innocent it was. Michael had suffered enough in Berry Edge; Rob was determined it would not happen again. Michael could not leave here, and Rob wanted to make sure that he didn't have to.

He understood why Susannah was reluctant to come to him for money, even though they had a child. She was fiercely independent and he might demand to see the little girl, he might demand all kinds of things for his money. She thought so little of him.

He reached for the whisky bottle, poured some into a glass and stretched out his legs by the fire. The wind was howling around Berry Edge, straight across the valley from the fell. He thought about leaving. It would be a relief to be away from here and from the influence of the Shaws, which had helped him so much these past ten years. He didn't need that any more, he could leave. His father and John were dead, his mother was gone and he could accept how things were and go to a new place and make a fresh start. Vincent would look after things until he came back.

He had been to John's grave that Sunday. Faith was not there. He had known that she was not, she was sitting by the fire with Harry in the house on the hill. Rob noted her absence with satisfaction.

He had won the fight with John for Faith, he had finally won it. There were no flowers, no evidence that anyone was looking after it. The past had relinquished its hold on her but in some ways, Rob thought, John had won the bigger fight. He had gained and held his parents' affection most especially in death, he had even in a way taken the works, because Rob had had to leave both his parents and the foundry. At least Rob had gained the foundry. Gained it and then lost it again to Harry because the love was gone. Harry loved this place and Faith Norman and the works as the Berkeleys were meant to love it and no longer did. Harry had restored the balance to Berry Edge and would keep it. Rob was pleased about that. He had a notion that some day Harry would have a son and all that son would want was to get away. Harry could always send him to America.

He thought about Nancy and Michael. They had a baby boy. Michael had never looked as happy before now, and from there Rob began to think about his own child and to long for her. He swallowed the last of the whisky in his glass just before somebody banged on the door.

When he opened it, there stood Susannah, looking as near to an ordinary Berry Edge woman as she could, with a shawl over her dark dress. All that was different about her was that she had discarded her apron. Rob went back into the sitting room and she followed.

'Do you want some whisky?' he offered.

'No, thank you.'

Rob looked at her. 'No men, no whisky, a dress like that. You could always go into a convent.'

'Michael says you're going away to America. Why?'

'To join the motor industry.'

'Couldn't you do that here?'

'I could but I don't want to.'

'You won't come back.'

Rob went over to the sideboard and poured more whisky into his glass. 'I have to come back, I have too many concerns here to leave them for very long. I have the feeling Vincent won't look after things as well as he should, just to make sure that I *keep* coming back. And I can't leave Harry with the works for good. He'll get bored eventually, just like he does with everything once he's bettered it. I won't let it slide like that again. I'll sell my share of the abbey to Vincent if he'll have it, and there are all kinds of other things that need seeing to from time to time.' He looked at her. 'I'd like to see my child before I go.'

'She'll be at the wedding.'

'That'll give the gossips something to talk about.'

Susannah said nothing to that.

'I still don't understand,' Rob said. 'You must have been pregnant when we went on holiday. Why didn't you tell me?'

'You walked out.'

'That was after three days. Three days of trying to persuade you to marry me.'

'It would only have made things worse.'

'How could it have done that? You didn't care enough about me to tell me.'

'I did care!'

'If you had cared we would have been married and I would have seen my daughter every day. You only come to me now because you're penniless. Look at you, you look like a washerwoman—' Rob could feel himself starting to lose his temper. He swallowed the whisky to steady it.

'I am a washerwoman!'

'All you ever wanted from me was money—'

'No!'

'Yes, it was. You've never recovered from what men did to you when you were very young. You go on and on making them pay as though the whole damned sex was to blame. You made me pay dearly for what those men did to you—'

'I did not!'

'Yes, you did! As if it was my fault. You had no real reasons for not marrying me—'

'I did!'

'Do you think that I care about my so-called reputation? Do you think I am so stupid that I couldn't do what I do anywhere? We could have left, we could have gone away, but that wasn't what you wanted '

'I was thinking about you.'

'No, you weren't! Plenty of other women have bad things happen to them, but they didn't become prostitutes. You could have gone somewhere else where people didn't know you and started again, but you didn't. You chose to stay here and take revenge.'

'I was hurt! And I had done nothing. I shouldn't have had to leave here. I wasn't to blame.' Susannah was crying, knocking the tears away with her knuckles.

'Yes, it was awful, and it wasn't right, but you could have

done it, you could have behaved differently. You didn't have to take revenge on every man you met.'

'I didn't have to become a prostitute, is that what you're saying?' Susannah said coldly, and when Rob looked at her she had stopped crying and her eyes were full of anger. 'Then I would never have met you, gentleman that you are, taking your pleasure where you chose.'

Rob couldn't defend that. He stood with an empty glass in his hand.

'You can't imagine what it's like doing such a thing for money. And it's all very well saying that I should have left. I didn't have any money to go anywhere, I didn't have any family. My friends had deserted me because they had discovered the kind of woman that I was. I couldn't even marry anyone, not anyone really respectable, not after what had happened, because he would have known that I was unchaste. The only kind of work open to women like me is cleaning other people's houses, like Nancy was obliged to. It wasn't much of a prospect and there was no money to be made. But I do have one asset that most other women don't have. I can look at myself in the mirror and like what I see, and men like it too, don't they?'

Rob still said nothing.

'And then you came along and dear me, I had never seen anything quite like you. I couldn't believe my luck. No more fat, middle-aged men, just you, so rich and so young. You gave me my freedom. Never to have to do it again, except with you.' Susannah took the money he had given her and put it on the table. 'I don't want to be bought by you any more. You had no right to walk into Michael's house like that and tell me how I should behave. You have no claim on me or my child, and just because you're rich doesn't give you rights. You aren't in any position to do that. You paid me to go to bed with you, so don't tell me how I should have behaved. You bedded me and gave me money and expected me to pretend that I liked it. You're a bastard. You're no different from anybody else.'

She left. Rob had forgotten how to move. He did eventually remember the whisky bottle. Luckily, it was almost full. He got to his chair by the fire with the bottle and his glass, and congratulated himself for getting that far.

Susannah stood outside in the street and wept.

All of Berry Edge turned out for Faith and Harry's wedding. Unbeknown to them, Rob had given everyone a holiday and had arranged for celebration feasts at the various church halls and pubs. The church was packed.

'I thought this was supposed to be a quiet wedding,' Harry accused Faith at the altar.

'It was nothing to do with me,' she said.

Faith was wearing cream. It was a compromise. She suited cream better than white anyway, her mother had said. Susannah had come with her little girl in her arms and Claire beside her, and Nancy had brought the baby and her two children. Ida and Vincent were there, though they had arrived too late for conversation before the wedding began. Faith was pleased for Harry's sake, though she could see by their faces that their disapproval had not lessened. Now that his parents were here, she would have to be polite and sociable, and she didn't know whether she could manage that. She was only glad that she and Harry were going away for a few days.

After the wedding there was a meal at the church hall which Rob had organised. Faith was glad. She kissed him and thanked him.

People were coming into the hall now. Vincent and Ida were first.

'I'm so glad you could come,' Faith said stiffly.

'You look lovely,' Ida told her.

Harry hugged his mother but only nodded at his father. Vincent kissed Faith and then took his son into his arms.

'You're in the north, Father,' Harry objected.

'I don't care. I behaved appallingly.'

'You did, but since you always do and we expect it, we'll forgive you.'

Vincent went to Rob. 'Are you really leaving?' he said.

'I was going to come and say goodbye to you, I'm not going for a few weeks yet. I have to stay here for the next few days because Faith and Harry are going to the Lake District. After that I have quite a lot to sort out both in Nottingham and in London.'

'If you want to leave here, I'll stay for the week and look after the place.'

'Thank you, Vincent, I would appreciate that.'

Susannah Seaton was coming into the hall with Claire, Nancy and Michael. She had her small daughter with her, holding her tightly by the hand. Ida left Vincent with the bride and groom and went across.

'I'm Ida Shaw, Miss Seaton. How do you do?'

Ida, Faith thought, enjoyed herself immensely. She sat beside Susannah and held Victoria for a while, and then she went to Nancy and Michael and borrowed the baby. It occurred to Faith that the moment she produced a child her mother-in-law's doubts would disappear. Ida came back to her later and gave her a wedding present, an emerald ring set with tiny diamonds.

'It was my mother's and I want you to have it,' she said. 'We shall expect you in Nottingham for Easter.'

Rob stayed well away from Susannah and the child, just as though they didn't know each other. Faith wished there was something she could do.

Faith and Harry went away to the Lake District and everyone left. Rob went back to Harry's house alone. The quietness was strange after all the people. What Rob wanted now more than anything was to be gone. Mrs Portsmouth, Harry's maid who was only there part time, packed his bags for him.

When she left, Rob tried to persuade himself that he could spend his last evening in Berry Edge drinking whisky and reading a book by Arnold Bennett. He very much wanted to do that. He looked regretfully at the sitting room fire burning away as he left the house.

He walked slowly down the bank to Michael and Nancy's house. When Rob banged on the door Michael answered it. He came straight outside and closed the door behind him.

'Is Susannah here?'

'She doesn't want to see you,' Michael said.

'I have to sort this out, Michael, I'm leaving first thing in the morning.'

'She said no.'

'Just five minutes.'

'No.'

'Are you going to keep her forever?'

'We'll think of something.'

'Will you? She'll go back to whoring again because it's all she knows. Five minutes. Please?'

Behind Michael, Susannah opened the door.

'It's all right, Michael,' she said and Michael went in.

She stood back against the wall. It was not ideal, Rob thought, it was a cold night and there were neighbours on every side. She folded her arms across her front and put her head down.

'I want you to know that I'm sorry,' Rob said. 'Men are evil creatures, it's true. If there had been some way that we could have met as equals it might have been different, but I barged into your life paying for what people were never meant to pay for. I didn't deserve your love. I'm well punished, I can't even hold my child. I meant to tell you yesterday that I've made some financial arrangements for you. I meant to tell you before, but my temper got in the way. You'll get a letter from my solicitor in a day or two. You can take any problems to him, he's very good—'

'Would you like to see her?' Susannah's head came up. She looked at him.

He followed her. The stairs led straight up from the front door so they didn't even have to disturb the others in the sitting room. In a small bedroom at the back of the house, where the other children also obviously slept, judging by the beds, Victoria was alone, asleep. Rob had sneaked looks at her that day but he had not been close when she was awake. He wished that she would wake up now just so that they could look one another in the eyes. He lingered for as long as he felt he could, and then made himself say, 'I have to go.' He left. He walked up the hill even more slowly than he had walked down it, back to Harry and Faith's house. The fire wasn't burning as brightly, but that was easily remedied. There was no whisky, he had finished it the night before, so he poured brandy generously. It smelled wonderful.

Some years ago he and Sarah, Harry, Vincent and Ida had gone to Venice. Every time he smelled brandy now he could remember sitting outside in the late evening with cups of coffee, and brandy in tall, thin glasses. It had been the happiest time of his life. That holiday had been the very highest enjoyment that God had provided for man.

It was early June. They had stayed at a friend's house, a sumptuous palazzo, five minutes' walk from the Grand Canal. It had a garden with trees which gave complete shade, and roses gone wild, in cream and red. There were statues in the garden, figures with peacocks under their arms. He and Sarah would sit out there and eat lunch.

At the far end of the house were great doors with diamond-shaped stained glass above them in blue and red and yellow where, in older times, people had arrived by water and stepped up into the hall, so high and wide. In the hall were huge chandeliers. The bedrooms had eight-foot square beds and wonderful painted ceilings, and halfway up the stairs were glass doors and a balcony so that you could step out and watch the boats passing by.

Always in Venice there was music, the sound of violins from open windows. Doves gathered in the courtyard. There was a bakery in the narrow alleyway beyond the house, and from it came the sweet smell of biscuit-baking. In the evenings there was seafood to eat and salad and white wine. He had thought that his life would always be like that. He had thought it was for good.

Then a voice behind him said, 'You drink too much.'

He turned away from the fire and there was Susannah.

'Yes, I know,' he said ruefully.

'I knocked hard on the door.'

'I didn't hear you.'

Rob looked at her, thinking that he might have to remember for the rest of his life how she looked in the neat, modest dress that she had worn for the wedding. It was brown with touches of cream and made her eyes the same colour as the liquid in his glass. He hesitated for a moment and then said, 'I love you, Susannah.'

Susannah didn't look at him but at her fingers.

'I want you to take me with you,' she said.

Rob put down his brandy. 'Are you quite sure?'

'Quite sure, yes.'

'There'll be enough money for you. You could have back the house in Durham and never have a man in your bed again if that's what you want, and I won't bother you even when I do come back.'

'I don't think you'll come back,' she said. 'I do love you and I want you and I'll marry you.'

Rob couldn't move. He still didn't believe her, he didn't dare. She went to him and kissed him, and for the first time since John had died the turmoil in Rob's head ceased. It was peace, safety, warmth, all those things which had for so many years evaded him. Nothing could hurt him now. His child was asleep a little way across Berry Edge and the woman he had wanted was close. She would stay with him, and their child would grow up in a new country away from Berry Edge, where they could be free to live as they chose.

The hotel room looked out over Lake Windermere. The maid had been in, drawn the curtains, turned down the bed and built up the fire. Faith peeped through the curtains.

'What are you looking at?' Harry said patiently.

'The lake.'

'It's dark.' He was opening champagne. The cork eased its way out of the bottle with a discreet little sound. He could tell that it was good, he could smell that wonderful honey background to the bubbles as he poured it.

'I'm imagining the fell from our house.'

'We could have stayed at home for that. Of course my father and mother would probably have insisted on being at the house, and Rob's there, and probably Susannah if I know him at all.'

'Do you think so?'

'With the house to himself, after the way he looked at her today?'

'I didn't notice,' Faith said.

She let the curtain fall and went back to the fire, where Harry gave her a glass.

'Let's have a toast,' he said. 'To the people of Berry Edge

who are kind, courageous and bonny, and to us who belong there and are lucky.'

'To them and to us,' Faith said. They clinked their glasses together and smiled into each other's eyes.

Acknowledgements

The people who helped me with this book deserve a mention. Shortly after I moved to Lanchester near Durham I decided that I wanted to write something about the area, but I didn't know much about it. My friend of long standing, Norma McDonald, took me around Consett, showed me the park and Blackhill, and the various streets and the big houses. She also introduced me to her mother and her sister and their reminiscences were very useful. Norma and I had some good times and some fun lunches.

Tommy Moore of Derwentdale History Society and his wife Norma took me to a slide show all about Consett, and Tommy gave me a morning of his valuable time, trying to get me to understand what goes on in a big steelworks. I'm not an apt pupil but Tommy was great. I would also like to thank them for loaning me two excellent books which Norma's father, Mr J. T. Carr, had written about his life in the Consett area. Mr Carr died so I had no chance to meet him but I gained from his work and knowledge. Tom and Olive, who live across the street from me, loaned me some books on Consett and told me a little about the old days. Dorothy Agar loaned me books and her precious Consett Iron Company magazines. The librarians at Crook and at Durham found me books about the area. The librarians at Lanchester were good enough to invite me to the twenty-first anniversary of the Old Court House library and cheer me up generally because they read my books. W H Smith's of the Victoria Centre in Nottingham deserve a mention because they were all over their shop hunting out various books on old Nottingham. Center Parcs at Nottingham also come into it because it was there that I had the idea, as well as the staff at Newstead Abbey, Byron's beautiful house with the Japanese garden of which I used parts for the big house in my story. Durham County Records Office provided old maps of the Consett area.

Read on for a sneak peek of

The Foundling School for Girls

Available to buy now in paperback, eBook and audio.

Prologue

Crawleyside, Weardale, County Durham, December 1855

Her mother called out to her from the door.

'I'm going now, Ruth.'

Ruth would have said goodbye and even held her mother, though her mother would not want to hold her. Her mother never wanted to hold anything or anybody; when Ruth reached the outside door of the house, her mother had already set off down the path towards Stanhope.

She had said earlier that she was going to the village, but she was always saying that and never going. Ruth's father did not like either of them to go out, other than to bring in milk from the cow, vegetables from the garden or to feed the hens.

Ruth watched her mother's skinny form until she could see it no more. She worried, because if her mother did not get back before her father came home from the quarry at the end of the day, he would shout and swear. She comforted herself that tomorrow was Christmas Day, even though he would have been paid and he would probably go to the Grey Bull. It was the pub at the bottom of the hill, and there he would spend as much of his wages as he could drink while still being able to climb up Crawleyside and fall in at the front door; it was not something to be looked forward to.

Ruth stood at the door after her slight, grey mother was out of sight. She knew that her mother had been stealing from his pockets for months. She told Ruth it was so that they could have a decent Christmas, because otherwise they would have as little as they always had. They always had to make do because he gave her mother so little to keep them and yet he complained. But Ruth was not convinced. Her mother often took money from him and so far there were no signs that this Christmas Day would be better than any other.

She let go of her breath. She decided that she would make everything right for her mother coming home. She cleaned and swept, she saw to the animals, she kept the fire going and the kettle on the boil and she kept herself busy. Yet her mother was gone such a long time.

She had gone off shortly after her father had left in the morning and she was not back by mid-afternoon. Ruth thought that perhaps she was enjoying this rare freedom and had stayed in Stanhope. Ruth could not remember the last time they had been to chapel though her mother assured her that they had gone at one time. Now her father did not want them to go, but her mother probably remembered people in the village and maybe had even spent time with them. Ruth never did. She tried not to begrudge her mother the contact just because she had no contact herself. Her mother deserved a little time, so she made sure that when her mother came home she would have nothing to do.

As the sun set very early, she locked up the hens, saw to the fire and made sure everything was right so that her mother could come home to tea. Ruth had even made a cake; she sat and waited.

The sun went down, it set, the darkness came on soon as it

always did at that time of the year. Ruth hated how the darkness covered the land as though it was suffocating it. By four it was pitch-black, and she did not like to use candles or the oil in the lamp because there was so little left.

She did build up the fire, thinking that both her parents might come back together. That they had never done so before did not deter her. They might and she would be there, and it would be Christmas and the Christ child would be born. She thought it was such a lovely idea that she dozed but when she awoke the fire was almost out and she was still alone.

She was worried now that her mother did not return. She listened and listened and nothing happened. She couldn't eat, she couldn't drink. She went into the tiny room which was hers but she didn't sleep. She had no idea what time it was, just that she should let the fire down. Had something happened to her mother? Had something happened so that her father did not come back?

She lay there awake and longed for the light of the next day. The night seemed endless. She was convinced that her mother had died.

Ruth had never liked her parents. She knew that it was sinful not to love the people who had given you life. She knew enough of the Bible to be aware that you must honour your father and mother, but she didn't know what more she could do. Her parents were unhappy. She felt as though she had caused it. Daily her mother told her that they would have had a much better time of it had she never been born. As though there was something she could do about that. Maybe she should have been able to. Maybe she should have walked out and put herself into the river if they disliked her that much.

Her mother called her hair 'that devil'. Ruth knew that her hair was a very strange colour, so red that it looked like the fire. Her mother brushed it and combed it and Ruth cursed it because it was always full of knots. Every time her mother brushed her hair, it hurt, so she hated her hair too.

There were no mirrors in the house, no looking glass, so she had no idea what she looked like, but her mother convinced her that she was the plainest girl in the world and would never get a husband. Ruth thought her chances of marrying were few since she never saw a man or a boy. Besides, if marriage was like her parents had, who on earth would want it? Though she had no idea what else life could hold. Were things worse in other places? She couldn't imagine it somehow.

Ruth thought her mother plain so if she looked like her mother she must be awful. Her mother was skinny, with sunken cheeks, and she wore the kind of pinny which came up over her shoulders and fastened at the back of her waist so that it covered her dress completely. She never took it off, except presumably when she went to bed.

Her mother cooked and baked and cleaned and knitted and did crochet work and embroidery and she taught Ruth to do all these things. The only book they had in the house was the Bible and Ruth was not allowed to read. Her mother didn't read and didn't see why women should. Her father did not approve of such things. In the evenings on Sundays he read the Bible to them, but haltingly because he didn't know many of the words. Ruth suspected he made it up from the garish pictures which illustrated the book.

They lived on what was called The Velvet Path because of the heather that covered it so smoothly in August, above Stanhope near Crawleyside. Her father worked at the quarry there. Sometimes he would bring home his pay. More often he

went into Stanhope and drank it. Her mother would wait fret-
fully by the door until he came back and fell in and then she
would extract any copper that was left from his pockets.

Her parents shouted at one another. She found things to do
when they did this. She went outside or started sewing or knitting.
She liked best the piece of land which was as sheltered as anything
got up there near their tiny cottage. It stood below the house and
she grew vegetables there. She couldn't remember a time when
she didn't grow things. It was the only pleasurable thing in her life.
Life was duty and nothing to do with pleasure, her father said very
often, so why it was that he drank she did not know. She and her
mother got no pleasure from that and there was often nothing to
eat so she presumed he did it for his own pleasure.

The house was built of stone and her father said proudly that
his ancestors had lived there for hundreds of years. She thought
he was wrong. The house was owned by Mr Forster who owned
a great number of small farms in the area, but she didn't think
any of them could be that old. Perhaps it was true, stone well-
built there lasted.

She didn't know why her father would be pleased about that.
She had thought they should try and get away to better places,
but it was a disgrace to do that, so her father said. You were
stuck in one place because God had allowed your ancestors to
build here. You would be accepted nowhere else, her father said,
because you did not belong. This was their home and they must
cling to it and look after it.

Everything seemed to fail up there. A fox killed the chickens.
Sheep suffocated in the snow. Their only cow ate something
which blew up its stomach and it died with its legs in the air.
Ruth felt as though they were doomed never to have anything
go right, and in time, she thought, you got used to that.

So her mother went down to the village, ignoring what her husband had said about not going, that he would bring back what he could. She would go down and make sure they had something to eat for their Christmas dinner.

Ruth lay in bed in the half-light with the fire almost out since the wood was low, and waited, worrying that her mother would come back to the darkness. Perhaps something might happen to her on the way. Nothing happened until her father came back, drunk and singing as ever, and then he fell in at the door.

Shutting it, she left him there. That was what her mother had always done. In the morning he would wake up and know where he was and be amazed that he had yet again climbed that hill to get back to his house. He always said the same thing. How he had got there he would never know. Ruth was so tired of hearing this.

In the mid-morning she could hear him yelling her mother's name and then he came out of the bedroom; it was the only bedroom of any size. Her room was tiny and had nothing in it but a narrow bed. He had no doubt made his way there sometime in the night. He came out shouting for her and calling for her and then he said,

'Where is she?'

'I don't know. She went out yesterday and didn't come back.'

He so obviously didn't believe her, as though her mother was under the bed or had gone outside into the frosty morning.

'Is she collecting the eggs?'

'I said, she didn't come back from Stanhope.'

'What was she doing in Stanhope?' he said, as though the place were a hellhole.

'She said she was getting some things for today.'

'What things?'

'For Christmas Day.'

'You didn't tell me.'

She wouldn't contradict him. There was no point. He would have knocked her across the room. She said nothing. He gazed all around, then he went outside and she could hear him shouting.

'May! May!' He went on shouting from time to time all the rest of the day and then he fell back into bed and slept.

The following morning, he went to the village, and presumably to the pub. When he came back in the middle of the night he shouted his wife's name over and over again and when he didn't find her he came into his daughter's room. She sat up suddenly at the intrusion, but he came over to the bed and pushed her down. She shrieked and cried and said that she was not May, she was Ruth, but he didn't hear her. She didn't think he could hear anything.

She screamed and fought but he was a big man and she was very slight. This could not be happening to her. He had never done such a thing before and she was almost fourteen. In all those years, he had never touched her except to knock her down when he was angry and drunk, and that didn't happen so very often. He pushed open her legs and put himself into her. Her body recoiled at the pain and the intrusion and it got worse, and hurt more and more as he went on, despite her screams. Ruth thought she had died and gone to hell. She screamed and wept and tried with all her might to push him away. She was horrified but he took no notice and held her down.

Whatever he was doing to her, it was disgusting and awful, and went on and on until she thought that it would never stop. Then he grunted and shoved and shoved and then stopped suddenly and after a few seconds – though it felt like forever – he took his disgusting thing out of her, did more grunting and then left her as suddenly as he had come to her.

Ruth could not believe it. She went on disbelieving it, trying to convince herself that she had had the most awful dream of her life, but the bed was bloody and she was in a lot of pain. The pain did not go away, inside and outside, and she could do nothing more than lie there, fearing he might come back and in his drunken state maybe do it to her again. But as she lay there in the darkness, waiting and not daring to move, she could hear him snoring. He went on snoring. When daylight eventually arrived in a thick snowstorm which blotted everything out, she got up as usual and lit the fire. When she had sufficient hot water, she put a hot cloth between her legs and washed herself. It stung and she was in a lot of pain, but it did help. Then she stripped her bed and got rid of the bloody sheet.

One

Ten Years Earlier

Jay Gilbraith remembered nothing before the streets. He did not know who had given him his name. There must have been a mother at some time. Maybe she had died. Maybe she had weaned him, and taught him not to piss or crap in his pants, because he didn't, and he ate food and drank water, but that was all. No matter how often he struck at his memory, he could find nothing.

Nobody had taken him in. Why would they when he was just a ragged child and there were so many? They slept where they could, ate what they could find on the ground or steal. Often he had to fight for bread and he learned to sleep anywhere, no matter what the weather. You had to learn to look after yourself. He stole a knife from an ironmonger and learned to use it.

There were men who had you, literally, and used you badly, so you had to learn to hide; he had become very good at such things. He was quick, and though he was tall, he was light and could use his fists and dodge and weave. He could outwit other heavier or stupider boys or men and they were almost all these things. And some of them drank and others sat about too much. As he learned to own the streets, they did not better him.

He didn't remember when he first met Wesley Hallam. It seemed to him as if they had been together always. They were about the same age, he thought, and Hallam too was a street child. It was good to have a friend. There were lots of people about, but nobody knew you and nobody stopped to help you. The crowd was always moving on, always had somewhere to go, but you had nowhere to go, you were stuck here because you had not the strength, the maturity or the money to go anywhere. The rain came down and soaked you, the road came up and chilled you, but there was sunshine, which dried out your clothes and your body, and there was always a wind off the river. He didn't know whether to love or hate the wind that came off the Tyne, just that it was always there like a faithful though poor friend.

It would softly touch his shoulders while he slept, on long summer nights when darkness barely arrived, in May and June and July. It whispered to him that the snow would not fall too hard upon him because there was too much salt where the river flowed to the sea, and it was not that far away. It was somehow too far away for him to move nearer. When it was cold, he slept under the bridge near the water so that the rain and wind were tempered.

Hallam was always around and he needed a friend too, so although they didn't talk much, they stayed close. Jay soon saw why Hallam was a good friend to have because two men jumped him down a dark alley. They put a rope around his neck and tried to throttle him and he was gagging, falling to the ground, and all of a sudden one was taken away and then the other.

By the time he had loosened and got rid of the rope and could breathe, the two men were lying on the ground, one of them moaning, the other turning over and over, clutching at his stomach.

Hallam turned around and walked away. Jay followed him. Hallam had a big gash on his face where somebody had knifed him. It hadn't improved his looks.

At first they stole anything they could reach, anything they could manage, and the more they stole the quicker they were to run away. They never got caught no matter what it was; they knew the streets around them so well and could outrun any shopkeeper. It made them laugh to outwit folk. In the end, Jay found a broken-down house which was empty, and he gave people who had nothing a place to shelter, and he went out and found food for them. There they lived, sheltered from the rain.

Most of them were very old and ready to lie down and die, or very young and could not steal well. Jay became so adept at it that he taught them to steal. Then he went into a church and stole a Bible and began to teach himself to read with help from an old woman, Morag McInver, who slept in the house he had provided. Hallam told him he was mad but went along with it, being helpful although he would have denied it.

Jay gave Mrs McInver clothes and blankets and all the food she could take, bread sopped in milk when her few teeth gave out. She helped both of them to read and write. She died in the winter, as so many people did.

'Now what?' Hallam said.

'I want to buy a house so that I can let other people come inside.'

'Bloody hell, are you Jesus?' Hallam said and then they laughed.

'Have you got any money?' Jay asked him.

'You want it?'

'Aye, give it up.' Hallam did.

By then Morag had given them both a basic education. Lads like them were born knowing how to add up. They knew how important it was and learned before they could speak. So with the money in their pockets, and bartering what they had, they began to steal anything that was worth money. They were able to feed the people in the house. They grew better and more wily and started to prosper. It was strange how suddenly they were able to buy new clothes and decent food. Eventually they bought a tumbledown house in a backstreet and put it right and put tenants into it who could pay. Then they bought another and they began to put money into buying and selling and building.

Jay liked the building best of all. He could then attract people who would pay because he employed good workmen to do what he could not do himself. Specialists were the way forward, he felt sure.

They went to the best tailor in the area and began mixing with men of business in Newcastle. Hallam hated it and did not care to get involved but Jay thought it was a good idea. Either they liked him or they admired how he was making money. He lived in a respectable house and was soon seen as a man who was on the way up.

Hallam jibed at him and stayed away from these gatherings. He didn't like people and most especially he didn't like rich men. He always spat when he said this, but it only made Jay smile and say nothing. In particular Jay admired the architect, Henry Charlton. He wished he had been this man's son. He wanted to be with him all the time, to be of his set, because he thought Henry Charlton was a genius.

He was building churches and large houses and a hospital. Jay discovered that Henry Charlton lived in a broken-down house by the river and he saw also that this man was so modest and caring that he kept nothing back for himself. He was astonished at this but also aghast when he saw Charlton's daughter at a distance;

the man's only child was beautiful. How could he keep her in such awful circumstances?

'Oh God,' Hallam said when Jay talked of her. 'You want to rescue her, don't you?'

There came an evening when Henry Charlton took him back to the house in the muddy lane by the river. There he introduced Jay to Madeline and Jay fell in love. He couldn't believe it. He thought the whole idea of love, especially falling in love, was nonsense, and so unguarded and costly that he would never have ventured there, but he did. He tried not to call it that, he would have named it dangerous and a thousand other things, but he would never have called it love before he met Madeline Charlton.

She was so beautiful that he thought he might have died happily just for having met her. She was all silver and black. Her hair was black and her eyes were silver-black and her skin was pale. Her clothes were grey-white and also silver somehow.

He knew it was an illusion, but he could not help it. He thought about her day and night. He conjured for himself a world in which she was his wife. She was the first real lady he had met, and he knew that he had to have her for keeps. He loved her voice and her smile and how kind she was and how she read and knew all manner of things that he didn't know.

He imagined them teaching one another because they had so much and so little in common, and yet everything. He was astonished that he could love a woman and yet glad; he felt like a bird soaring high. If he could have this woman, he could do anything with her by his side.

The next time he saw her was at a dance and he knew then that he did not want to be without her.

He did not know what to do to gain her. He had the feeling that if he spoke to Mr Charlton, he would never be in company with the man again because Henry Charlton knew who he was and where he had come from. Ought he just to creep away and hide his feelings and not acknowledge even to himself that he loved her? He had no right to love her – no chance of touching her ever in his whole life, he was sure – but since he had always tried to better everything, he went to her and told her how he felt.

He had never forgotten that day. It was winter in Newcastle and the snow was falling fast, despite the damned river which usually held it fairly well at bay. The tide with salt helped to turn the snow to sleet or even hail or rain.

He knew that he should not have gone and yet he did. She was by herself in the dark, cold house. He had hoped so, that her father would have gone to his club as he so often did in the middle of the evening. Jay knew because occasionally Henry Charlton took him along. It was the proudest evening of his life when Henry asked him to go there and introduced him to other influential men.

Henry went there to think things over with like-minded people, to mull over the day's doings, so he said, and occasionally he invited Jay to dine and drink among his friends. He discussed how things could be better on the morrow than they had been today.

So Jay went to the house and there she received him in the drawing room. He could have smiled at the idea. It was a ghastly little sitting room, cold and dark and damp and drear, and he wished he could have taken her out of it. As they entered, he thought he heard the scurry of mice, or was it rats? A lot of old buildings held vermin, but he had become unused to it. The curtains and furniture were shadowed and there were few books. The fire in the grate was tiny as though she did not stay in there for very long, and why would she, he thought. She looked very surprised to see him and he was worried about that because he was rather hoping that she liked him. It was the best he could ask at this point.

Draughts howled down the hallway and in the room, where they met the wind sweeping down the chimney until the whole room smoked. He had been very surprised when he first learned that they lived there, but was not now that he knew Henry better. But even so he ached to marry and take her to some lovely dwelling that he would build for her. He would buy her jewels and gorgeous dresses and take her to Europe and be proud of the fact that she was his. He would do anything to get her to accept him, but he didn't hold out much hope.

It was then that he saw this girl was almost always alone here. And though she was beautiful, her dress was shabby and old and had been mended several times by the look of it. There was no smell of a decent dinner. He wanted to ask whether her father was out every night and managed,

'I thought perhaps Mr Charlton would be here.'

'Oh no,' she said, 'he rarely comes home in the evenings.' She said it simply, without pity, but he longed even more after that to give her everything he could, to make her happy.

'Miss Charlton, I know we have only met twice and I'm sure this seems very forward, but I wondered whether you might let me see you sometimes.'

She looked mystified and then understood and the colour came up in her cheeks like a winter sunrise.

'Oh,' she said.

'If you dislike the idea completely, I will go away. I don't mean to intrude.'

'No, I – it's just that I don't know you very well.'

'Perhaps we might get to know one another a little better. Might you allow that?'

'I don't know. I'm not sure. I haven't really thought about it.'

'It's just that I have spent a lot of time thinking about you and I like you very much. Would you allow me to speak to your father so that I could come here from time to time? If you don't wish for this, please say so.'

She didn't. Her gaze turned from surprised to rather pleased.

'I did like you when we danced together,' she said.

'You did?' he said, hopeful. He remembered her then in a worn white frock, looking the nearest thing to an angel he might ever hope to meet. Ethereal and fragile, yet not.

'Yes, I – I have the feeling it had something to do with how tall you are. That's silly, I know, but I liked dancing with you.'

'You did?' he said again, unable to utter anything sensible. He couldn't help but smile and then felt stupid, having said the same thing twice. He had had a number of dancing lessons at a place in Pink Lane so that he would survive in society. Hallam had mocked him for it and then laughed at his enthusiasm. Jay thought he could go on looking at her for years.

'I felt safe there,' she said.

He wasn't sure that was the impression he wanted to make but it was certainly a start. He did want to look after her, he did want to shield her from hot sun and cold rain and poverty and loss and whatever else he could.

'Then if your father gives permission, I may visit you.'

She agreed and smiled and nodded and then he went off to her father's club very worried about what he would say and what Henry Charlton might think. But there was no other way; he could hardly address her without asking her father. So he braved the man.

Charlton had dined and had a few drinks, he could see, and he slapped Jay on the back and told him to sit down. He had ordered brandy and cigars for himself and several other men.

Jay thought of the girl alone at home, but for a maid, as far as he could judge. He had heard noise from the kitchen. In this club, men dined on the best food and wine, the most expensive brandy and cigars. That evening they had been drinking champagne. He tried not to think badly of Henry Charlton, but the picture of Madeline poorly dressed, and alone with a low fire which she was evidently letting go out – and only two candles to see by – came to his mind and he had to stop himself from becoming angry.

This club was of Georgian build and had every luxury. The long wide windows, the huge fires, the silk curtains which stretched from floor to ceiling, the smell of good food and wine, the men who wore evening dress and enjoyed what seemed to Jay the best of everything. He hated it.

He half thought he should tackle the man in the morning but when he said he had something to say, Charlton took him aside, insisting on giving him a cigar, though Jay loathed tobacco and had never been able to afford drink. He tried to explain that he had seen Miss Charlton, that he would like to get to know her. That was all he said, but Charlton's brow darkened.

'You went to my house?'

'I thought I should ask her whether I might approach her—'

'You didn't think to ask me?'

'That's what I'm doing now. But that would have been foolish if she had disliked me.'

'How could she possibly like you? She doesn't know you.'

'We've met twice and we've danced and I liked her the moment I saw her.'

'Well, of course you did. Half of Newcastle wishes to marry her. You think I'd let her go to an upstart like you?'

Jay told himself that he had no right to be offended by this, but he was.

'I can't help my background; I can't do anything about that. But if you would allow me to address her, I am doing very well and I do care for her.'

Henry Charlton laughed and that was when Jay saw him for what he was: a very clever man, but fat, red-faced, middle-aged. He drank too much, smoked too much and he was self-indulgent. Yet he wanted his daughter at home, waiting for him in that appalling, damp house by the river, as though she was some kind of plaything to be put down and taken up at his bidding. It was not much of a prospect for her if no one was allowed to court her.

'She is a prize you will never win.'

'Will any man ever win her?' Jay said, angered and affronted.

Henry Charlton frowned.

'She is all I have. No man is good enough for her.'

'Except you as her father. What about her future? What about when you aren't here anymore? What will happen when you die?'

Henry Charlton laughed.

'I will never die,' he said, 'and you will never address her.'

Overnight Jay tried to imagine Henry Charlton in the nasty throes of death. The trouble was that those you wanted dead lived forever and Charlton couldn't be more than fifty.

If you enjoyed the extract read on to find out more about

The Foundling
School *for* Girls

**She may be an orphan,
but she has hope for the future ...**

When Ruth's mother deserts her on Christmas Eve, her
father comes home drunk and commits an unthinkable act.
Without money or friends she has nowhere to go, but when
he hurts her a second time she has no choice but to leave ...

Rescued by Jay, a businessman who takes her to a convent,
she meets Sister Madeline. Along with the rest of the nuns,
Maddy provides food, shelter and education for orphans.

Ruth comes to look on her new friends as family and
things are finally looking up. But then a pit accident changes
everything, and they all stand to lose something –
or someone – they love ...

Available now in paperback, eBook and audio.

Quercus

The Quarryman's Wife

When hope is lost, can she rebuild her home?

After her daughter Arabella passes away, leaving a poor, motherless child in her wake, Nell Almond doesn't think her life can get any worse. But then tragedy strikes a second time and she finds herself widowed, with her husband's quarry to manage.

But it's baby Frederick, her grandson, who troubles her most. Being cared for by one of the local families, he lives in hand-me-down clothes in a cramped and unrefined home.

Nell desperately wants him to return to his rightful place, as heir to the quarry, but should she put all her hopes in one child?

Available now in paperback, eBook and audio.

Quercus

The Coal Miner's Wife

Torn between love and duty . . .

When Vinia walked down the aisle she knew it
was a marriage of practicality: as the owner of the
local pit, Joe could provide her with a life of status.
But her heart lies with another . . .

With gypsy blood in his veins and an intense passion in his
soul, Dryden has always held a torch for Vinia. And with
the death of his wife, he vows to make good on the lost
years when they were apart.

**Will Vinia find a new chance of happiness or be
forever destined to a loveless marriage?**

Available now in paperback, eBook and audio.

Quercus

Orphan Boy

He has no home to call his own.

Born to a mother who died in childbirth, and to a father who could never truly love him, Niall McAndrew grows up a solitary child. His only friend is Bridget, a young girl forced prematurely into womanhood. Niall has brains, spirit and ambition, as well as devastating good looks. He soon begins to make his own way in business, and becomes famous throughout the Newcastle area by befriending the wealthy and powerful mine-owner Aulay Redpath and his beautiful daughter Caitlin.

But Niall's loveless childhood has left its mark. Can he ever find the personal happiness he yearns for?

Available now in paperback, eBook and audio.

Quercus

The Runaway Children

BOOK TWO IN ELIZABETH GILL'S FOUNDLING SCHOOL FOR GIRLS TRILOGY

When little Ella's grandmother dies, she is turned from her home and forced into a life of cruel labour. Even her own mother won't help, too busy with her new husband. Seeking refuge at the Foundling School for Girls, Ella meets Julia, who has been torn apart from her twin, Ned. They must take matters into their own hands if they're to stay together despite their parents' wishes.

In a world of hardship and betrayal, three children begin a search for belonging. But years of strife have left their mark on Ella, Ned and Julia . . . Is it too late, or can they find the new start they need?

'Elizabeth Gill is a born storyteller'
Trisha Ashley

COMING SOON IN HARDBACK AND EBOOK
Available to pre-order now

Quercus